22/7/21

Please return/renew this item by the
last date shown to avoid a charge.
Books may also be renewed by phone
and Internet. May not be renewed if
required by another reader.

www.libraries.barnet.gov.uk

Abi Elphinstone, author of *Sky Song*

'Gripping, poignant and beautifully written ...

'A book of storms and heart and magical islands that sing your name through the rain and beckon you through layers of time ... A stunning story of courage and hope'
Cerrie Burnell, author of *Harper and the Scarlet Umbrella*

'Deep and lyrical ... Love and hope communicated is perhaps the greatest magic of all, and that's what Catherine achieved in this book'
Hilary McKay, author of The Casson Family series

'An incredibly special and magical book! I was spellbound'
Katherine Woodfine, author of
The Sinclair's Mysteries series

'*The Storm Keeper's Island* is unforgettable – the kind of story that will grab you by the heart and not let go'
Katie Tsang, co-author of *Sam Wu Is NOT Afraid of Ghosts*

'Funny, heartrending, terrifying ... I'm on tenterhooks for the next book'
Lauren James, author of *The Loneliest Girl in the Universe*

'A magical rush of an adventure story about family, bravery, and harnessing the storm within'
Anna James, author of *Pages & Co.*

Books by Catherine Doyle

The Storm Keeper's Island
The Lost Tide Warriors
The Storm Keepers' Battle

The STORM KEEPERS' BATTLE

CATHERINE DOYLE

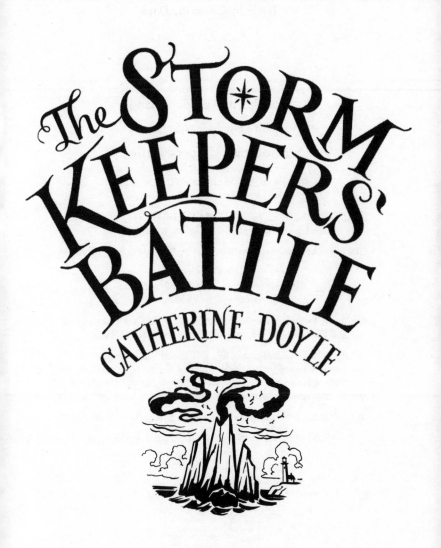

BLOOMSBURY
CHILDREN'S BOOKS
LONDON OXFORD NEW YORK NEW DELHI SYDNEY

BLOOMSBURY CHILDREN'S BOOKS
Bloomsbury Publishing Plc
50 Bedford Square, London WC1B 3DP, UK
29 Earlsfort Terrace, Dublin 2, Ireland

BLOOMSBURY, BLOOMSBURY CHILDREN'S BOOKS and the
Diana logo are trademarks of Bloomsbury Publishing Plc

First published in Great Britain in 2021 by Bloomsbury Publishing Plc

A catalogue record for this book is available from the British Library

ISBN: PB: 978-1-5266-0796-6; eBook: 978-1-5266-0795-9

2 4 6 8 10 9 7 5 3 1

Typeset by RefineCatch Limited, Bungay, Suffolk
Printed and bound in Great Britain by CPI Group (UK) Ltd, Croydon CR0 4YY

To find out more about our authors and books visit www.bloomsbury.com
and sign up for our newsletters

For Jack

Ten days have passed since Fionn faced Morrigan on the shores of Arranmore and said goodbye to his grandfather for good. Now Morrigan's brothers stalk the land in search of new souls, whilst the Merrows struggle to keep the growing forces of Black Point Rock at bay.

Chapter One

THE FLYING HORSE

Fionn Boyle was sure of two things:

One, he was full of an ancient, rippling magic that could explode from him at any moment.

Two, he had absolutely no idea how to control it.

Not for the first time, he had come to Cowan's Lake, hoping for a miracle. And right now, he was kneeling over its frosty waters while ravens glided overhead, cackling maniacally.

'I think they're laughing at me.'

'Attention-seekers,' muttered Shelby, who was glaring menacingly at the sky. 'They're only trying to put you off.'

Fionn flexed his fingers and tried to summon a flicker of magic. Beneath the skein of ice, a single rainbow fish

3

swished its coloured fin in greeting. There were no visions of past Storm Keepers to greet him today, just his own scowling reflection.

'Told you the lake was a bad idea,' said Sam, who was reclining against a nearby boulder. 'Not worth the frost-bite, if you ask me.'

'Cowan's Lake is full of magic. It might help.' Shelby crouched down beside Fionn. 'You just need to calm your mind. Think of something nice. Like puppies.' The shell around her neck glinted bone-white on the icy water. 'Or otters holding hands while they sleep. Or a bunny rabbit on a skateboard. Oh! Or an alpaca. Or –'

'An island made entirely of pizza,' said Sam dreamily. 'Where all the trees are pepperoni.'

Shelby rolled her eyes. 'Sa-aaam! Fionn *has* to find a way to make his magic work.'

Fionn sighed. He had rattled through a million different thoughts already; ones that made him happy, ones that made him sad, ones that made him laugh and others that made him want to tear his hair out. He was still trying to find the right emotion – the key that would unlock his magic again. Just like it had in Hughie Rua's Cove.

He stuck his hands in his pockets, his fingers brushing against Dagda's emerald. He had taken to carrying it every-where with him now, hoping it might bring him some sort of luck. Today, it was glowing faintly. 'Maybe one of you needs to be in mortal danger for my magic to wake up again.'

Sam glanced at Shelby. 'How do you feel about dangling upside down over a cliff?'

She cut her eyes at him. 'How do you feel about going swimming with the Merrows?'

'I'd rather eat my own shoelaces, thanks.'

'They wouldn't *really* hurt you,' she teased. 'They answer to me, remember?'

'*How* could I forget?' Sam returned drily. 'You have that *giant* shell hanging from your neck at all times which, quite frankly, is a crime against fashion.'

Fionn watched the lone rainbow fish sink to the bottom of the lake, and felt the same sinking feeling inside himself. It had been ten days since his grandfather had disappeared under the Northern Lights, never to return. Ten days since Morrigan had been resurrected from her tomb beneath the Sea Cave, and almost devoured Fionn's soul. Now they were trapped on the island, with little hope of rescue, expecting her to strike at any moment.

Winter haunted the island like a ghost. Christmas had come and gone with little ceremony, the new year slipping quietly through their fingers. On Fionn's grandfather's parting advice, the entire island had come together to try raise their own sorcerer – someone strong enough to destroy Morrigan – but so far the search for Dagda's grave site had turned up nothing.

Not to mention, they couldn't find Rose anywhere – the peculiar old woman who, according to Malachy Boyle, was the only person on the island who could help. No one had any idea where she lived, and she hadn't been down to the strand in over a week. She was proving to be just as elusive as Fionn's magic.

'... I am *not* jealous,' Sam was saying unconvincingly. 'I like my fish battered and with chips, thanks.'

'They are not *fish*. Stop making jokes about eating them!'

'What's Lír going to do? Come up through my plug-hole when I'm having a bath?'

Shelby folded her arms. 'Lír's the only thing keeping us all safe right now. I doubt she's got time to traumatise herself like that.'

Fionn was just about to turn from the lake when something white drifted across the surface, snagging his attention.

'*Guys!*' he gasped.

The reflection had *wings*. Their span was so wide, the shape looked like an aeroplane at first. But it was flying much too low, and the wings were *moving*. Then there

6

were the legs – four of them. And a mane too.

'It's Aonbharr!' shouted Shelby, right into Fionn's ear. She leapt into the air, as if she had caught fire. 'He's here! He's come to save us! I knew he'd come! I *knew* it!'

As if sprung from an impossible dream, Dagda's winged horse was soaring high above them. His coat was the silver white of a star at full brightness, his tail sparkling in the winter sun. He glided across the sky, his mighty wings disturbing greying gusts of cloud, so they could glimpse the blue behind them.

Aonbharr – for danger that cannot be outrun.

Fionn's magic erupted without warning, sending a familiar heat gushing through his bloodstream.

There you are.

The wind rose in a fierce gust. The ice in the lake shattered in a rippling *crrraaack*, the surface exploding into a riot of colour as the rainbow trout swam up to have a look.

Fionn hopped up on to the boulder and waved his arms above his head. 'Down here, Aonbharr!'

Sam and Shelby were jumping up and down, shouting at the top of their lungs.

The winged horse appeared not to hear their pleas. He climbed higher and higher, his mighty wings slashing through the churning clouds.

'He's leaving!' cried Sam.

Fionn leapt off the boulder. 'He's flying north. Let's follow him!'

They took off in a hurry, Fionn's magic gusting a trail through the grass as they bolted towards the forest. He flung his hand out and the trees bent backwards, their branches creaking as they twisted out of the way. Soon, all three of them were out the other side, panting but not stopping. They vaulted over a trickling stream and charged headlong through Tom Rowan's farm. Sheep bleated as they scattered, the wind nipping at their hooves. Fionn's magic snapped the fence in two and flung boulders out of the way as Fionn and his friends set a course for the silver-backed hills.

By the time they crested them, they were gasping for breath.

Aonbharr was getting further and further away. He was like a comet streaking through the clouds.

Fionn's exhilaration was fading. Frustration was rising in its place, and a slow-creeping fear chilled his bloodstream. The wind was dying. His magic was weakening.

'There! He's just passed over the cliffs!' heaved Shelby. 'Come on, guys. We're so *close*.'

They pelted down the hill at double-time, the northern plains of Arranmore unfurling before them in a patchwork of frosty grass.

Soon, Shelby's strides slowed, and Sam ran out of breath entirely. Fionn had a terrible stitch in his side. His blood was still warm – but the heat had changed. It was less the raging waterfall of ancient power, and more like the full-body burn of muscles that were not used to running.

Up ahead, the lighthouse was white and gleaming as it jutted from the earth. Just beyond it, a wedge of land called Eagle's Point curled into the sea like a crooked finger. Fionn and his friends climbed over its knuckle. Where only a little while ago flowers grew in long-stemmed meadows and white-tailed eagles came to nest, the earth was cracked and barren. It was like passing through a graveyard now, the only sound the icy whistle of an unforgiving wind.

Finally they stopped.

Sam scowled at the clouds. 'I trekked through all those mucky fields in my *good* shoes and risked an asthma attack for that horse and he just *flies away!*'

Shelby's shoulders slumped. 'I've been waiting my whole life to see him.'

'Maybe he didn't see us,' said Fionn, drifting towards the cliff-edge. 'Or maybe he was scared.'

From here, Fionn could see the smoking ruin that was once Black Point Rock. Over the past week and a half, the broken shards of the three sea stacks had bent towards each other, forming a volcano of shining black rock. It had become Morrigan's lair. Ravens circled the sky above it, their beady eyes trained on the island.

'The Black Mountain's growing,' said Fionn uneasily.

'And the sky above it is getting darker.' Shelby tugged him away. 'Come on. We shouldn't be here.'

'It belches too, you know. Sometimes at night, I can hear it hacking up stuff.' Sam pulled a face. 'Probably all that ash and smoke.'

They backed away from the cliff-edge. Fionn had the sudden, sickening sensation that Morrigan was watching them.

'I mean, *of course* an ancient undead sorceress would have *no* regard for the dangers of air pollution,' Sam went on.

Fionn wrapped his arms around himself. Out here, the sea air was colder, and without his magic to warm him, the chill was rattling through his bones. 'We should head back and tell the others about Aonbharr. It might mean something.'

'Of *course* it means something.' Shelby's braces glinted as she linked arms with them. 'It's a sign of *hope*.'

Her words were met with an emphatic snort.

'Aonbharr's return isn't a sign of hope,' came a croaky

voice from behind them. 'It's a sign of doom. Or don't you know your own island history?'

A hooded figure stood in the doorway to the lighthouse. It cocked its head, the lines of its face hidden in the folds of its shawl. But Fionn recognised the voice well enough. It was Rose. The woman who had helped his grandfather during the years he couldn't leave the cottage. The same woman he had been told to find.

'And the fourth gift, born of red skies and raging wind, was Dagda's own beloved Aonbharr, a horse of flight,' she went on, as though she was reciting the words from an ancient text. 'For danger that cannot be outrun.'

Shelby swallowed. 'I forgot about that part.'

'So, it's doom, then. Cool. Cool, cool.' Sam shifted from one foot to the other. 'How many of our four hundred or so islanders do you reckon will fit on his back?'

'The only one he deems worthy,' said the old woman flatly.

Fionn drifted towards her. 'Rose? We've been looking for you for over a week. What are you doing all the way up here?'

By way of answer, the old woman shuffled to one side. The door to the lighthouse swung open behind her. 'This is my home,' she said, as though it was the most obvious thing in the world. 'I think perhaps you three should come in.'

Fionn, Shelby and Sam exchanged a glance. And without saying a word, they stalked arm in arm into the lighthouse. The door slammed shut behind them, sealing them in.

Chapter Two

THE LIGHTHOUSE KEEPER

'Well, this is … rustic.' Sam's voice echoed around them as they took in the mismatched furniture and the exposed brick. 'I mean it's very …' He trailed off.

'Bleak.' Rose bolted the door. Twice. 'I'm aware.'

Fionn eyed the heavy lock-chain as she slid it into place. 'Are we safe in here?'

Rose's laugh was sudden and brash, like the call of a wild bird. 'We're not safe anywhere any more.' She shooed them into the middle of the room. 'But you may as well make yourselves at home. I'll put the kettle on.'

As Fionn's eyes adjusted to the dimness, he saw that the bottom floor of the lighthouse was like a museum and a library rolled into one. There were cases full of leather-bound books, and crooked shelves stacked to the brim with old newspapers. Most of the cement floor was covered by a sprawling, threadbare rug and the peeling walls were strung with fraying tapestries. A collection of Aran shawls hung on a coat-rack by the door, and beside them, old stone pots and bronze vases lay cluttered in a pile.

In the middle of it all was a kitchen – a stove and basin, wedged between two lopsided cupboards and a small wooden table marred by coffee stains. A tattered green armchair sat alone by a fireplace whose chimney seemed to lead to nowhere. But the room was strangely warm and there was fresh ash in the grate. The hairs on the back of his neck rose. There was magic in here. He could sense it drifting around them, like dust particles. He could taste it faintly on his tongue, sharp and zingy as a lemon.

Fionn scanned the clutter, looking for the source of it.

Rose was rummaging in a drawer. 'Milk and sugar?'

'Uh, sure,' said Fionn.

'Two spoonfuls for me, please,' said Shelby, who was studying a dark green tapestry of a battle scene.

'I'll have four, thanks. I need a pick-me-up.' Sam was examining a spiral staircase that wound up and out of sight. He crouched down beside a battered antique chest that had been wedged underneath it. 'Hey, what's in here?' he asked, jiggling the padlock.

'Don't touch that!' Rose raised her teaspoon in warning. 'It's not time.'

Sam splayed his hands and backed away from it. 'I was just *asking*.'

Fionn, who hadn't even noticed the strange-looking chest, realised it was exactly what he'd been searching for. He could sense the magic coming from it. 'Not time for what?'

Rose ignored him and busied herself with the tea.

'Right. Take a mug and follow me.' She disappeared up the spiral staircase, the floorboards creaking as the children scurried after her. The top floor of the lighthouse was much narrower than the bottom, the ceiling high and domed. Winter's glare poured in through windows that curved all the way around, showcasing both the Atlantic Ocean and the barren northern shelf of the island.

The air up here still tasted of magic, but all Fionn could see was a narrow bed and a chest of drawers. They were arranged around the focal point of the room, which was a mammoth lighthouse lens. It was a giant glass orb, rimmed in brass, and was certainly big enough to fit an entire human. Sam ducked under the brass casing and stuck his head inside. 'Hey, there's only one tiny lightbulb in here!' His voice sounded both faraway and distorted. 'Is that where the big massive beam comes from?'

'Yeah, it's called science,' said Shelby, making a face at him through the glass.

'Booooring. Who needs science when you have magic?'

'Well, we don't really have magic,' said Fionn awkwardly.

'Thanks for the reminder, Professor Doom.' Sam spilled some of his tea as he clambered back out. 'And I was just starting to relax.'

Rose was by the window now, looking out over the cliffs.

They joined her at the ledge. From up here, Fionn could see all the way across the Atlantic Ocean, to where the blue-grey water turned murky and dark at the horizon. Below them, Black Point Rock speared from the sea like an arrowhead.

'It looks even bigger from up here,' said Shelby uneasily.

Rose hmm'd. 'It's growing.'

'And the tide …' Fionn touched his forehead against the glass. There was barely a ribbon of sea between them and Morrigan's lair now. 'It's almost gone.'

'She's been draining it to get around the Merrows,' said Rose. 'The more her power grows, the closer she gets to our shores.'

Shelby paled. 'So Aonbharr really is a warning.'

'The least he could do is come down and say hello,' grumbled Sam.

'Yeah,' said Shelby. 'Say it to our faces.'

'Probably thinks he's too good for us.'

Fionn sighed. 'Guys, he's a *horse*.'

Rose snorted. 'Aonbharr has no sense of superiority. He began as an ordinary horse in an ordinary field. He only became a marvel years later. Much like our Storm Keeper here.'

Fionn frowned. 'Are you making fun of me?'

Rose went on, without answering. 'Aonbharr was Dagda's horse when he was a little boy. A proud white stallion with a quicksilver mane and a fiercely loyal temperament. They went everywhere together.'

Sam slurped his tea thoughtfully. 'Where'd he get those giant wings, then?'

Beneath the folds of her shawl, Rose's green eyes came to rest on Fionn.

'After both sorcerers collapsed during the battle for Arranmore, Morrigan's ravens carried her body to safety.' Her gaze darkened, the shadow of a secret moving inside it. 'Then they returned for Dagda. Aonbharr was so loyal, he leapt through a thousand of those wretched birds to rescue his master.'

She looked away, clearing her throat.

'Somehow, the sky turned red with the last of Dagda's magic and, beneath its full moon, the horse sprouted wings and carried him away to his final resting place.'

Fionn blinked. 'I don't think I know that story.'

'How did Dagda give Aonbharr wings if he was unconscious?' said Sam. 'It sounds a bit impossible.'

'If it sounds impossible, then it's probably true,' said Shelby sagely. 'That's how things work here.'

They sipped their tea, three pairs of hopeful eyes watching the faraway clouds, as though the flying horse might reappear at the sound of his name. Fionn wondered what he would even do if Aonbharr swooped down to meet them. He would never desert his own islanders. And besides, what could one lone horse and boy do against the likes of Morrigan?

No. Fionn was not going to flee. He was going to stay, and fight.

He turned back to Rose. 'Before my grandfather died, he told me to look for you. He said you might be able to help us raise our own sorcerer.' He frowned. 'Until today, I couldn't find you anywhere. I haven't seen you at any of the island meetings.'

'And you haven't joined any of our search parties either,' said Sam, somewhat pointedly.

'That's because they're a waste of time.' Rose took a noisy sip of tea. 'Malachy only half knew what he was talking about. A powerful sorcerer might well defeat Morrigan, but if you think finding Dagda's grave is the answer to your problems, then you're wrong.'

The silence expanded, Fionn and his friends exchanging worried glances as the lighthouse keeper deftly pricked a pin in their last hope.

When Rose spoke again, it was to Fionn. 'If you want my advice, you're better off finding your way to the Whispering Tree. It will have the answers you need.'

'I don't need answers,' said Fionn, with growing frustration. 'I need a sorcerer.'

'What you *need* is a battle plan that might actually work,' said Rose calmly. 'You can't just go around digging up old bogs and staring into frozen lakes hoping something will happen.'

'*Told* you that was a waste of time,' said Sam.

Shelby glared at him.

'You need a direction.' Rose took another sip, her eyes dancing over the rim of her mug. 'And I'm giving you one.'

'Can we have an easier one?' said Shelby politely. 'You know, since the Whispering Tree is a completely inaccessible all-knowing oak tree hidden in some impossible layer of Arranmore that none of us have ever seen before.'

'Well, I've seen it. With Bartley. Sort of,' Fionn reminded them, though he wasn't sure happening upon the Whispering Tree in someone else's memory really counted. 'But we had to burn a candle to get to it. And it was at the end of a really strange trail.'

Rose nodded. 'The Whispering Tree is the most magical place on Arranmore Island. If you seek its wisdom, you must first find a trail to take you to it.'

'I don't suppose we'd come across one of those on a nature walk?' said Shelby hopefully.

Rose released her brash laugh. 'You can go out looking for one all you like, but the trails decide when to appear. And to whom. They have a mind of their own.'

'Great,' said Fionn sarcastically. 'Just like everything else on Arranmore.'

Sam groaned. 'Why does our island have to be so *moody*?'

Rose gestured to the mountain in the sea. 'The island has grown wary. You can hardly blame it when that wretched hag is so near. Morrigan's followers might be empty, soulless vessels, but they wear human faces. The trails don't know who to trust any more.' She turned back to them. 'You'll need someone who's walked the trails before. Or, perhaps, something that once belonged to them.' Her gaze came to rest on Sam. 'There was a Storm Keeper who lived not long before you three. Her name was Maggie Patton …'

Sam beamed. 'She was my great-grandmother!'

'You remind me of her. It's that mischievous smile. It's what's given me the idea, in fact.' Rose's eyes glittered as she took another sip. 'Maggie visited the Whispering Tree more times than any other Keeper before her. When she played her flute, the island woke up. The flowers bloomed. The birds sang. Her music had a magic all of its own. Every so often, she came up here, to Eagle's Point. When she offered her music up to those white-capped waves, the Eagle's Trail always revealed itself to her. It was like clockwork. Like somehow they were old friends.'

Sam leaned forward without meaning to, drawn by the magic in Rose's story.

'There was one song in particular that she played,' she went on, tap-tapping her fingers along the mug. '*The Eagle's Call.*'

Fionn's cheeks began to prickle. There was magic in the air again – the citrusy tang gathering on his tongue. It felt familiar. It felt like hope. He caught the yellowed glint of the old woman's smile as she offered it to Sam.

'When Maggie died, she left her flute to her daughter, Maeve, who in turn left it to –'

'Me! Maggie's great-grandson!' Sam burst out. 'It's me!

I have the magical flute! I *knew* I was the most important one! I KNEW IT!' He waved his arms in victory, sloshing his tea everywhere. 'FINALLY! It's my turn!'

'Really mature, Sam,' said Shelby.

Sam was too busy victory-moonwalking to hear her.

Rose chuckled. 'If you return to the northern cliffs and play The Eagle's Call on Maggie's flute, you *might* be able to rouse the trail before Morrigan's dark magic chokes the memory of it from our island for good.' She shrugged, then added, 'Or you might not. I'm afraid it's only a bread-crumb.'

Fionn set his tea down. 'One breadcrumb is better than none.'

Shelby bolted for the stairs. 'Come on, Sam, let's go and get your flute.'

'Wait.' Sam paused mid-moonwalk. His face fell.

'What's the matter?'

'I don't know that song – The Eagle's Call. I've never even heard it before.'

'Your dad might know it,' said Shelby quickly. 'Or Donal. There are, like, a bajillion Pattons living on the island. One of them must know the island's favourite song.'

Sam's face brightened, but whatever he was about to say was drowned out by a thundering belch. The light-house trembled, the floorboards rattling against their feet.

Out to sea, the Black Mountain was hacking up a thick plume of smoke. Ash exploded in a mushroom cloud before raining down on the sea.

Shelby clapped her sleeve over her mouth. 'Ugh. It smells like rotten eggs.'

'That's dark magic,' said Rose, watching the sky turn black. 'And it's getting stronger.'

Fionn hurried for the stairs, pulling Sam with him. 'Come on. We need to find that song before it's too late.'

A minute later, the lighthouse door swung open to a rush of cold air, the Atlantic wind howling as if to hurry them along.

Chapter Three

THE RUBY EYE

After a morning spent searching the annals of the Arranmore library for a song that left no paper trail, Fionn and his friends broke for a much-needed lunch. They made camp at Sam's house, where his mum prepared a helping of delicious sandwiches, salt-and-vinegar crisps, and three giant slices of her famous banana bread.

When they had polished it all off, they moved to the sitting room for a brief stress-relieving session of Mario Kart. Shelby, the undefeated champion, claimed the beanbag as her throne, while Sam and Fionn sat shoulder to shoulder on the couch, scrabbling for second place.

Midway through the final lap of Bowser's Castle, the sudden siren of Fionn's ringtone filled the room.

'I'll get it,' offered Shelby, who had already finished the race.

Fionn tossed her the phone without taking his eyes off the TV. 'Thanks.'

'Hi, Tara. Yeah, he's here. We're playing Mario Kart. Oh.' Fionn could hear the squeal of his sister's rage from all the way across the room. He winced. 'Yeah, I'll tell him. OK. See you soon. Bye.'

'Whatever it is, she's not my boss,' said Fionn quickly.

Sam grimaced. 'Worse. She's your sister.'

'She wants us down at the beach,' said Shelby. 'Apparently it's urgent.'

'Yeah, but we're almost –'

'She also said she would hide all your socks and throw your pillow in the ocean if you're not down there in the next ten minutes.'

Fionn was on his feet in three seconds flat.

They bumped into Sam's older sister Una, and Juliana Aguero, in the porch, where the girls were shucking their coats and scarves.

'How come you three dossers missed this morning's search?' said Una, blocking their way like a bridge troll.

'We were up at the lighthouse having a secret meeting,' said Sam cryptically.

'Was it something to do with Aonbharr?' said Juliana

eagerly. 'Mia got a picture of him flying over our garden, but it's kind of blurry.'

'No time for chit-chat, I'm afraid.' Sam shooed his sister and her friend aside. 'There's something going on down at the beach and if we don't hurry, Fionn will lose all his socks.'

Una hastily re-zipped her parka. 'Well, we're coming too!'

Juliana jogged alongside Fionn as they left the garden. 'That secret meeting Sam mentioned just now. Is it anything I can help with?' Fionn could practically feel her fizzing with anticipation. 'I'd love to be more useful around here. Ever since school stopped, I feel like I'm not doing enough.'

'You're doing loads,' said Fionn. 'You're always at the search parties.'

Juliana harrumphed. 'I know I could do *more*. Where do you three keep sneaking off to? Is it something to do with your magic? Are you training? Do you think I could come alo—'

'Three is kind of our magic number,' interrupted Sam. 'Honestly, Shelby barely made it by the skin of her teeth.'

'Oi!' Shelby swatted him in the arm.

'We don't really need anyone else right now,' said Fionn. 'Sorry.'

'Is it because I'm not an original islander?' Juliana flushed beetroot red. 'Just because I'm not technically a descendant of Dagda doesn't mean I'm useless, you know.'

'It's got nothing to do with that, Juliana. I promise.'

She looked away. 'It's fine. Forget it.'

'Next time we need someone brave or loyal or clever to help us, you'll be the first person I ask,' said Fionn. 'Deal?'

Juliana shrugged, but a corner of her mouth lifted. 'All right, then.'

* * *

When Fionn reached the strand, a beachful of chaos was waiting for him. There was a crowd gathering down by the shore. The Merrows had surfaced, and were swimming rings around a small orange lifeboat. Lír was at the helm, tugging the bow by a rope between her teeth. Her yellow eyes were wide, her bone-and-coral crown glistening just above the waterline.

Niall Cannon was standing in the middle of the boat.

'He's back already.' Fionn tried to read the Lifeboat Captain's face at a distance. Niall had left for the north-west shore of Ireland yesterday morning, chaperoned across the slip of sea by a band of Merrows to warn the mainland of Morrigan's return. 'He looks stern.'

'He always looks stern,' Sam pointed out. 'That's his thing.'

Tara pounced on them halfway down the beach. 'Mario Kart?' she bellowed. 'Are you *serious* right now, Fionn?'

'Nice knowing you, mate,' said Sam, promptly scurrying away. 'See you in the next life!'

Shelby ran after him, flailing her arms. 'Wait for me, Sam!'

Fionn sighed. 'Thanks, guys.'

Tara folded her arms. Her silver parka was swollen with the last of their grandfather's candles, the pockets bulging at the seams. She looked as round as a barrel, but she wouldn't go anywhere without them. They were the last of the island's weapons and, as she seemed to be a natural at using them, she had become their keeper.

'You really need to sort out your priorities,' she snapped. 'We're on the verge of a war, you know.'

'Good afternoon to you too, Tara,' said Fionn sarcastically.

'If you're not going to bother with the searches, you could at least be trying to figure out your magic.'

'I *know*. We were –'

'Every minute is crucial right now,' she cut in. 'Who knows what Morrigan's up to in that big black mountain?'

'That's exactly why –'

'She's probably ten steps ahead of us, Fionn,' she interrupted, again. 'The last thing we need is you skiving off. You're supposed to be the Storm Keeper of this place.'

'Thanks for that, Tara. I'll be sure to subscribe to your podcast,' said Fionn, brushing past her. 'But right now, I'm busy.'

He stalked down to the water's edge to join his friends. The waves lapped at Shelby's sparkly trainers as she greeted Lír. Sam stood a few paces behind her, eyeing the creature warily. With little fanfare, the Merrows pushed the lifeboat up on to the sand, then peeled back, into the surf.

Niall stepped off the boat. At close range, Fionn could see the red wires in his eyes.

'Grave news, I'm afraid,' he announced. 'The mainland's in a bad way.'

'Did they believe you?' asked Fionn.

'They won't come after the Merrows, will they?' said Shelby, casting a worried glance at Lír.

Niall shook his head. 'I'm afraid I was too late. People have already gone missing.'

Fionn stiffened. 'What?'

Lír pushed herself up on to the sand, froth seeping through her teeth as she craned her neck to listen.

'There've been multiple sightings of two figures, more

monster than human,' Niall went on. 'One with arms and legs as thick as tree trunks and a bright ruby eye.'

'Bredon the Brutal,' said Fionn, giving the monster his name. The words were cold in his mouth, cold right down in his bones.

'And one whose mouth has been sewn closed.' Niall traced a finger over his frown, trying to mimic it. 'With thick black twine.'

Fionn shuddered. 'Aldric.'

Aldric the Silent.

Niall cleared the quiver from his throat, but the fear was still written all over his face. 'The locals say they walked straight out of the sea. They've been taking people. At least a hundred so far, but we can't know for sure.'

Fionn's knees began to buckle. It suddenly felt like the beach was shifting underneath him.

Niall kept talking, stacking up his findings. 'A group of teenagers went missing on Christmas night. The next morning, an elderly couple vanished further south. Then a local jogging group off the coast of Sligo, an amateur swimmer in Mayo, a bus full of tourists up north.' Niall shook his head, as though he couldn't quite believe his own words. 'Then a fishing boat turned up empty. Thirty-six fishermen disappeared without a trace. Conditions were calm, there was no distress call. I would have heard about it down at the station.

Not a peep. The coastguards reported a sighting of strange-looking dolphins.' He glanced meaningfully at Lír. 'The police don't know what to believe, but they're keeping people off the shore for now, and they've launched a national investigation.'

'They won't find anything,' said Fionn.

'No.' Niall sighed. 'But they didn't like my explanation much either.'

Fionn looked out towards the mainland. 'All this time, I've been worrying about protecting our island. I hadn't thought what might be happening on our doorstep.'

'What did you expect, Keeper?' hissed Lír. 'The Raven Queen is collecting new souls for her army. What she cannot get on Arranmore, she will take from somewhere else.'

The island trembled beneath a sudden, rumbling belch. Another cloud of ash was forming above the Black Mountain in the distance, its dark plumes spreading across the sky like tentacles. Even from here, it reeked.

They all looked up.

'*Oh*,' said Fionn, quietly.

Over the last ten days, the residents of Arranmore had grown used to the strange noises, the wretched wheeze of smoke that erupted at odd hours of the days and nights, but it was only in that awful moment, which seemed to stretch around them like a bubble, that they suddenly realised what exactly was causing it.

Souls.

Fresh souls.

'The proof has been under your nose.' Lír's frown was sharp and savage. 'But you have been idling.'

Shelby pressed a hand to her shell. 'What on *earth* have we missed?'

'A lot,' said Tara needlessly. 'All this time that mountain's been growing, so has Morrigan's army. Do you know what that means?'

Fionn swallowed. 'It means she's going to be even more unstoppable than we thought.'

Chapter Four

THE FLOATING SONG

Fionn, Sam and Shelby spent the rest of the afternoon asking every islander they could find if they knew *The Eagle's Call*. Meanwhile, the news from the mainland plagued Fionn's every thought, Morrigan's inky smoke taunting him as it stretched across the island.

She had an army.

And Fionn had a flute. Without a tune.

The evening slipped through their fingers, and when the moon was high and their eyelids heavy, Sam went to search his family home for the long-forgotten melody. Even a handful of notes might be enough.

Back in the little cottage on the headland, Fionn burrowed under the blankets of his grandfather's bed, breathing in his scent and the memory of his laughter.

When sleep found him, it was full of ravens. In darkness, their feathers beat against his face.

We meet, little Keeper, at the midnight hour,

Soon your soul will be mine to devour.

The birds parted to reveal Morrigan's shadow. It stretched all the way across the damp sand towards Arranmore, as though reaching out for Fionn. But there was no body to touch; she was in his head, showing him things he couldn't outrun.

The darkness shifted, and Fionn found himself inside the Black Mountain. Morrigan reclined on a throne of old bones. It glinted in the fractured moonlight, pale as the scythe of her cheekbones and the long column of her neck. Her cape of souls cascaded around her in an endless patchwork of suffering; the faces new and old.

I *watched you on the cliffs today,*

I *tasted your fear on the wind.*

She was on her feet now, striding towards him.

There is nowhere left to hide.

Nowhere left to run.

Fionn tried to back up, but he had no legs to carry him. He only had his thoughts now.

Morrigan's cackle echoed through his mind.

The darkness is almost upon you, Keeper.

Tell Arranmore I am coming.

Fionn could hear the clicking of her bones, the whistle of breath through the gaps in her teeth. She was too close to him now, too real. She reached out to touch him, and a shiver of ice rippled through his bloodstream.

Grandad, he told himself.

Think of Grandad.

The memory erupted like a spell. The nightmare dissolved into a cornflower blue sky. Fionn was standing in the back garden in a shaft of sunlight. The birds were chirping, yellow flowers swaying at his feet. His grandfather was sitting at his workbench, whistling a song Fionn had never heard before. Jaunty and light, it flittered about the garden like a butterfly, but every time Fionn really tried to listen to it, it floated just out of reach.

The scene grew fuzzy around the edges. Fionn slipped out of the dream, and into another. A different day, a different version of his grandfather, but the song followed him through each one, like a stone skimming on water.

When Fionn woke up, his chest was warm and his magic was crackling in his fingertips. A cool breeze had crept under the door and was tickling his ear lobes. Underneath his pillow, Dagda's emerald was a bright, blazing green. Fionn cupped it in his fist, until his magic slinked back into his bones and the gemstone grew cool to the touch. Then he lay with the blankets tucked up to his chin and traced the cracks in the ceiling, trying desperately to remember the song.

Chapter Five

THE STARLIGHT CANDLE

Fionn rose with the sun, showered and dressed in his warmest clothes, just in time to greet his friends at the door.

'It's even colder today than yesterday,' said Shelby, rubbing her gloved hands as she vaulted over the threshold. 'I should have worn a second scarf.'

'Sorry for the ungodly hour, mate. Did you get my texts? You know I only get up this early if it's really important.' Sam bustled inside, armed with a stack of old newspapers. He greeted Fionn by dumping them into his outstretched arms.

'Take these before my spine buckles.' He hurried past him into the warmth of the cottage, his flute case swinging from his shoulder. Fionn took this to be a good sign. 'I'm going to need a cup of tea *immediately*.'

'And probably a couple of ginger nuts,' added Shelby.

'Shall I feed you a few grapes too? Some caviar, perhaps?' Fionn shut the door and dumped the newspapers on the couch. He ducked into the kitchen and switched the kettle on. 'Did you find the song, then?'

'Not exactly,' said Sam. 'Dad said he recognised the name but he couldn't remember the melody. He did offer to read me one of his poems about the Whispering Tree, but it was full of nonsense words like *perspicacious* and *Arcadian*, so I didn't pay it much mind.'

'Well, at least he tried,' sighed Fionn.

Sam raised a triumphant finger. 'What I *did* find was a bunch of old newspapers up in our attic.'

'Yes, I can see that.' Fionn plated up some biscuits and carried two mugs into the sitting room.

Shelby was perched on the side of his grandfather's armchair. She took the tea gratefully and dipped a biscuit inside, before shoving the whole thing in her mouth, and grinning around it. '*Mmm. Sho goomph.*'

Fionn laughed, then did the same. '*Ghelishish.*'

They clapped their hands over their mouths to catch the crumbs exploding from their laughter.

'OK, toddler-brains, eyes on me,' said Sam impatiently.

'I've been up all night reading so you'd better listen.'

Fionn and Shelby exchanged a sheepish glance. 'Sorry.'

Sam continued. 'My great-grandmother composed *The Eagle's Call* when she was thirteen, and won a fancy ribbon for it at school. They even played it on the local radio.'

He handed Fionn a newspaper article that included a black-and-white photograph of Maggie as an old woman. 'The last mention of the song is in her obituary. Her daughter, aka my granny, Maeve, wrote it.' Sam traced his finger along the neat black lines, his voice dipping with reverence. 'See this part here. It says that when she died, Maggie was "so beloved even the stars wept for her". The night she passed away, there was the biggest meteor shower in Arranmore's history.'

Fionn scanned the old newspaper article, hope rising like a sun in his chest. He gulped the rest of his biscuit down in one go. '*A meteor shower.*'

'It says she was found by Cowan's Lake shortly after midnight, curled up underneath the Perseids.' Sam's voice quickened. 'And she had her flute with her.' Sam tapped the case, now on his lap. '*My* flute. A local farmer swore he heard Maggie playing *The Eagle's Call* just before they found her.'

Fionn was sitting poker-straight now. 'Did you just say the *Perseids*?'

Shelby was on her feet too, waving her second ginger nut around in excitement.

Sam was grinning like a Cheshire cat. 'The second I read that part I remembered –'

'There's a candle!' Fionn shouted, without meaning to. 'A memory about the *Perseids*!'

'Well, yeah,' said Sam, with a sigh. 'That's where I was going. Thanks for stealing my thunder.'

Fionn was already sliding across the room in his socks. 'I'll be right back!'

He hurried into his grandfather's bedroom and made a beeline for the shelf beneath the window sill, where the last of Malachy Boyle's private collection of candles stood side by side. Fionn had burned four of them already. *Record Low Tide 1959* had seen him almost splattered on the cliff steps during the summer; *Cormac* had sent Fionn's father to rescue him in his lifeboat inside the doldrums of Morrigan's cave; *Record High Tide 1982* had given Fionn a precious glimpse of his grandmother, Winnie; and *Aurora Borealis* had swallowed up his grandfather and taken a chunk of his heart with it.

Now, he was down to two.

Blood Moon, which was perfectly round, and red as a cherry.

And beside it, *Perseid Meteor Shower*, black and sparkling as the night sky.

Fionn plucked the candle from the shelf. The stars winked as he rotated it, the scent of smoky air wafting from its wick. And there, just underneath it – a sweet, rosy smell.

Flowers and stardust. The last moments of Maggie Patton.

And within it, if luck was on their side, *The Eagle's Call*.

Chapter Six

THE WEEPING SKY

They decided that Sam would travel with Fionn into the memory, while Shelby stayed behind to watch over the island and raise the alarm if anything went wrong.

She stood on the threshold to the cottage now, patting the black flute case under her arm. 'You never know, I might discover my inner flautist while you're gone.'

'Do not play my flute,' said Sam, a finger raised in warning. 'You are absolutely not allowed to play my flute while I'm away.'

'Maybe I'll do some baton twirling with it instead, then,' needled Shelby. 'I wonder how high I could throw it without dropping it.'

Sam pinched the bridge of his nose. 'Fionn, please tell Shelby to stop messing with my emotions.'

Fionn unearthed a lighter from his pocket. 'If Shelby plays your flute then you get to wear her shell necklace for the day. That's the deal.'

Sam smirked. 'I'm giving it a makeover, then. A fresh coat of paint to spruce things up.'

Shelby gasped. 'That's vandalism!'

Fionn handed the candle to Sam. 'Do you want to drive?'

Sam's grin pressed a dimple into his right cheek. 'Yes, please.'

They joined hands as Fionn flicked the lighter open.

Shelby offered up a queenly goodbye. 'Godspeed.'

Sam held up *Perseid Meteor Shower*. 'To Maggie.'

Fionn touched the flame to the wick. 'To Maggie.'

The candle lit up in a crackling blaze, and the world slipped out from underneath them.

The gate swung open and the wind kicked them into the past. They bounded out on to the headland, laughter hiccoughing from them as they broke into a run. Fionn could forget, sometimes, how casually he had come to exist on wonder. It seized him by the shoulders now, and made him giddy.

The grass shed its frost as the years slipped by, the

earth greening beneath their feet. They were prodded north, the land climbing through once barren fields made plush with flowers. Birds pinwheeled through the sky, the sun's rays bouncing off their wings as they threaded the layers together seamlessly.

'I never thought I'd be this glad to see a seagull again!' said Fionn delightedly. 'That squawk is like music to my ears!'

'I wish we could run away from all our problems like this!' Sam shouted.

The trees waved at them as they went by, white-washed cottages sprang up from the earth, their chimneys piping pale smoke into the sky.

They left winter behind them, racing through springs and summers, dandelion seeds clinging to their coat-sleeves as buds dappling bare branches grew to leaves the size of hands and feet, turning green and then orange before crumbling into brown.

They followed the breeze through the wilderness, until the Arranmore hills tumbled out before them like crests in a wave. Up ahead, the dying sun painted Cowan's Lake a soft, shimmering gold.

There were no rainbow trout to greet them – just a lone owl soaring over their heads.

The sky blinked and night fell. The owl *hoo-hoo*ed into

the darkness, and on the other side of the lake, an old woman appeared.

'Look,' said Sam very quietly.

Maggie Patton was peering over the water. Her once long hair was short now, the curling strands like a crown of silver on her head. Beneath a long blue dress that grazed her ankles, her bare feet were sinking into the grassy silt.

The boys hovered on the other side of the water, waiting for something to happen. 'I can't see the flute,' said Sam, rising to his tiptoes. 'Maybe she won't play it, after all.'

Fionn frowned at the starry sky. Each one was still fixed in place. The wax was trickling steadily over Sam's fingers, leaving silver tracks on his skin.

Fionn held his hand out. 'Pass me the candle, please.'

Sam inhaled through his teeth. 'I really hope this works.'

Fionn's fingers closed around the wax, and the wind punched him in the gut.

'Oof.' He doubled over, Sam's hand tightening around his, as Fionn was pulled, wholly, into the layer around them. This unexplainable gift – the ability to live and breathe and move in every layer of the past, to see and be *seen* – belonged solely to Fionn. He was still trying to decide if it was a blessing or a curse.

When he righted himself again, his magic was playing his spine like a xylophone.

Maggie Patton snapped her head up. A rogue breeze blew the hair from her face, revealing the fine lines around her mouth, a map of wrinkles along her forehead. Her silver eyes were just as Fionn remembered – quick and molten, and alight with magic.

'Ah, *there* you are,' she said, as though a twelve-year-old boy burning a candle beside Cowan's Lake in the dead of night was an entirely usual occurrence. 'I was wondering when you'd get here.'

Sam's grip tightened. 'Dagda's *beard*,' he breathed. 'She's been *expecting* you.'

'I – *oh*.' Fionn tried to wipe the shock from his face. His magic was restless inside him. It felt like it was looking through the bars of his ribcage. 'Sorry I'm late. To tell you the truth, I didn't know I was coming.'

Maggie waved a hand, her bracelets tinkling like wind chimes. 'Time is funny here,' she said, drifting towards him. 'I'm not sure there's such a thing as late – or early, really.'

'She sounds just like my dad,' said Sam, who was still whispering, despite his invisibility. 'He says that to his editor every time he misses a deadline.'

Maggie was a full head shorter than Fionn; she tipped her chin to look up at him. 'You look so much like Malachy.

I thought for a second it was him skulking around the lake, but he'd have been much stealthier. And besides that, you're much too young.' She frowned. 'You walk differently too. All hunched and narrowed, like you're trying to take up as little space in the world as possible.'

Fionn made a conscious effort to straighten his spine.

'And your eyes are haunted.' Maggie curled her arms around her body, like she was frightened of what she glimpsed inside them.

Fionn swallowed the fist in his throat. Somewhere behind him, beyond the rolling hills of Arranmore, his grandfather was beginning his time as Storm Keeper. And here was Maggie Patton, looking at him – a boy plucked from an unknowable layer in the future – without an ounce of confusion. 'How did you know I was coming?'

Maggie smiled at him – it pressed a dimple into her right cheek.

'*Oh,*' said Sam.

'I saw you in the Whispering Tree,' she said, with the casualness of someone who had lived an entire life steeped in impossibility. 'Or perhaps the Tree saw you in me. I think it's seen you in a lot of Storm Keepers. We've been waiting, all of us, for a very long time, you know.'

'For me?' said Fionn.

'For *her.*' Maggie spun from Fionn with the grace

of a dancer, and settled her gaze on the lake. 'We've seen Morrigan's darkness in the Tree, heard tales of the boy who would have to face her. A McCauley Keeper. Or a Boyle.' She smiled. 'Depends who you ask.'

'I'm both,' said Fionn. 'Not that it's helped me much so far. My magic is a bit … unruly.'

If Maggie was surprised by this revelation, she didn't show it. Instead, she gestured at the lake. 'What do you see?'

'A boy,' said Fionn, staring at his pale reflection.

'I don't see anything,' said Sam glumly. 'I feel so *ignored*.'

'I see a Storm Keeper with more magic inside him than any who have come before him,' said Maggie, her eyes shining in the still water. 'Enough to raze a wicked world to the ground. Enough to build a new one from its ashes.'

'Then you must see someone I don't.'

'Maybe I do,' said Maggie thoughtfully.

'Fionn, the *candle*,' said Sam.

A glob of wax dribbled over Fionn's thumb, reminding him of time spent. The memory was half gone already, and still the stars had yet to fall. It felt as if the island was holding its breath.

Maggie was watching the candle too. 'You'd like to know what else I saw in the Tree, wouldn't you? I'd spoil the ending but I'm afraid I don't know it. There were too many futures to chase,' she said ruefully. 'I saw Malachy long before I saw you, as an old man waiting in a white cottage. I saw another boy in his heart, but he was much younger than Malachy and much older than you. Eyes full of the ocean. I saw the storm come to claim him.'

Fionn's cheeks prickled. 'That's my dad, Cormac. He gave his life for mine in Morrigan's Sea Cave. He rescued me from her.'

Maggie frowned, her eyes darting as she searched her own memory. 'I saw Merrows riding on the ninth wave. Rocky spires split down the middle, spilling awful things into the world.' She shuddered. '*Cruel* things.'

'Yes,' said Fionn grimly. 'It's already happened.'

Maggie's words quickened with the terror of her visions. 'I saw an undead army marching across the sea, and an ancient oak tree burnt to ash. The earth around it splitting in two. And in the middle of it all, like a flame fighting its way through the darkness, there was *you*.' She raised her finger, and Fionn felt the pinprick of it on his forehead. 'A boy with haunted eyes waiting on the edge of this lake. For *me*.'

Her shoulders slumped then, and a strange kind of relief washed over her. 'I've come here every single night for the past three years, nine months and thirteen days, to find you. To warn you of a future you have already seen.'

The candle was starting to collapse.

'And to help me,' said Fionn quickly.

'I can't see a way to help you with your power.' Maggie laid her fingers flat against his chest. Fionn's magic leapt at her touch. The wind gusted around them, dusting the air with the scent of lavender. 'It doesn't move the way mine did. You're like no Storm Keeper I've seen in the wrinkles of this place, and they're all there inside the Tree, playing out their parts.'

Maggie pulled her hand back and curled it to her chest, and the wind splintered through the wild grass, retreating into the trees.

'I'm not here about my magic,' said Fionn. 'I'm actually here about your music.'

Maggie's brows lifted in surprise.

'I need to get to the Whispering Tree, but all the trails are gone. I have to wake them up again, to show the island that it can trust me. And to do that, I need to play your song. That's why I'm here tonight. To ask you to play *The Eagle's Call* for me.'

Maggie inhaled sharply, then turned and marched back to the place where she had first appeared and plucked a tartan blanket from the long grass. She unwrapped it like a package, the folds falling away to reveal a silver flute.

'I've walked this path in hail, rain, storm and snow.

I've spent hours standing in this very spot, like a lunatic, waiting for the boy I saw in the Tree to come and find me. And tonight ...' She shook her head in disbelief. 'And tonight, on a whim, I decided to bring my flute with me for company. I thought perhaps the nightingales might like a song. And here you are.'

'Here we both are,' said Fionn in mirrored disbelief. 'Exactly where we're supposed to be.'

The candle was still melting and the stars had yet to fall, but he could see their paths converging beneath them. Two Storm Keepers dwelling in one fleeting moment before they would diverge for evermore, towards different destinies.

And the crossroads was a song.

Relief smoothed the frown-lines from Maggie's forehead as she raised the flute to her lips. 'Will you remember this when I'm gone?'

'Yes,' said Sam, without hesitation. 'Every note.'

'Every note,' said Fionn, smiling sidelong at his friend. The candle was at his thumb, ribbons of onyx wax dripping down the column of his wrist.

Maggie hesitated. Her gaze travelled from the melting candle to Fionn's other hand. 'Do you have someone with you?'

Sam pushed up against Fionn's shoulder.

Fionn smiled. 'His name is Sam.'

Maggie was staring intently at the space beside Fionn, as though to trace Sam's shape in the breeze. 'Does he belong to me?'

Fionn nodded. 'He plays your flute. And he has your smile.'

'Ah,' she said, her eyes misting. 'What a wonderful thing.'

'Tell her I'm the greatest musician of my generation,' said Sam.

'He's very shy though. A real wallflower.'

'Is he kind?' said Maggie, smiling at Sam's chin.

'He's kind,' said Fionn, glancing at his friend. Sam's eyes were bright and his cheeks were flushing. 'And he's loyal too.'

'Sam.' Maggie savoured the word. 'This is for my Sam.'

A strangled noise seeped out of Sam. Fionn squeezed his friend's hand, as Maggie Patton brought the mouthpiece to her lips and began to play *The Eagle's Call*.

It began in a burst of sure-footed staccato. The melody was jaunty and light and, as it floated about them, sprightly as summer birds at play, an invisible weight shifted from Fionn's shoulders. He felt suddenly aware of the beauty of the world, the evergreens swaying all around them, the hills peering over their shoulders, keeping watch on an island that had endured for millennia, craggy and uncowed, the darkness in its belly no more than a passing cloud.

The song burrowed its way into the earth too. The lake rippled and the grass swayed; as though dancing in time with the music. The nightingales fell out of their songs and the flowers pricked their heads up to listen. Beside Fionn, Sam's shoulders shook, tears flowing silently down his face, and as Fionn lifted a finger to his damp cheek, he realised he was crying too.

For the first time in his life, there was no sadness in his tears. Only joy. *Hope.*

Sam began to hum, replicating the tune note by note, in perfect time with his ancestor.

Maggie's eyes were shut, her soul tangled in the ribbons of her song, as she poured it into the world. It seemed to age her – the shadows beneath her cheeks darkened, the crevices in her skin deepening. Her hair turned white before their eyes, her body swaying, until it seemed like she might keel over.

Sam lunged to steady her, but Fionn pulled him back. 'You can't.'

'But she's –'

'I know,' said Fionn quietly. 'But you can't.'

The Eagle's Call was Maggie Patton's final offering to

the island, and she surrendered it with every last drop of magic in her blood.

Fionn's own magic soared in answer, lifting into the sky like the first stirring of a bird in flight. It danced along the waters of Cowan's Lake, painting faces in the ripples. Across the glassy surface, past Storm Keepers rose to meet them. Beasleys and Boyles, Cannons and McCauleys, and Pattons smiled up at their sister Keeper. They had come to welcome her home.

Maggie's fingers slowed on the keys. The melody lilted, and the last of its notes floated up into the star-laden night. Fionn tipped his head back, as if to watch them go.

The sky blinked one final time and from the blue-black of endless night, the stars rained down like silver tears. They lit up the water in a mirrored blaze, until it looked like Cowan's Lake was weeping too. The remnants of the candle trickled over Fionn's fingers as Maggie Patton sank on to the grass. She laid her flute down and smiled up at the sky.

The Perseids had come to see her off.

'Magic,' whispered Sam.

Maggie turned to smile at him, the stars dancing in her silver eyes. 'The Tree said the sky would weep, but I think perhaps it's dancing. Don't you?'

Fionn opened his palm in farewell, the flame floating like a golden bead. 'See you on the other side, Maggie.'

The candle went out, and before Fionn could draw another breath, the wind carried them away. They left the lake behind, the stars shooting through the fabric of the island, where they turned to faraway seagulls swooping over white-capped waves. The earth spun until their heads swam and their stomachs rolled, and then they were home again, nestled in the heart of a cruel winter that pressed its palm against the same lake and turned it to ice.

Fionn and Sam released hands and wiped the tears from their cheeks. 'Do you remember it?' Fionn asked anxiously. 'Do you think you can play it?'

'Yes,' said Sam, with the stirring confidence of someone who was about to save the world. 'Every single note.'

Chapter Seven

THE WHISPERING TRAIL

For the second time in as many days, Fionn had returned to the craggy grasslands of Eagle's Point. The clouds were thick and heaving, the tide below still trickling out. Morrigan's lair was inching ever closer, and Aonbharr, wherever he had disappeared to, was long gone.

Fionn didn't know if that was a good thing or a bad thing.

'That mountain is literally my worst nightmare,' said Sam, who was peering over the edge of the cliff. 'I hate the dark, I have no respect for birds and I'm extremely claustrophobic. Even the *tide* looks scared of it. If I ended up in there, I would one hundred per cent wee myself.'

'If we don't get to this tree today, I probably *will* end

up there,' said Fionn, watching the ravens swooping overhead. 'And then I'll have to live out my days as a patch in Morrigan's creepy cape.'

'Don't even joke.' Shelby's eyes flashed with warning. 'Sam and I would *never* let that happen to you.'

'Well, depends on the circumstances, really.' Sam set his case down on a rock and began assembling his flute. 'I'd do my *best* …'

Shelby scowled at him. 'If anything happened to either of you, I'd storm that awful mountain and rip Morrigan apart with my bare hands,' she said confidently. 'I might be small but I'm extremely scrappy.'

Sam rolled his shoulders back, his flute at the ready. 'Well, here we all are, eh? The Storm Keeper, the Tide Summoner, and the Fantastic Flautist of Arranmore.'

'Was that really the best you could come up with?' said Fionn.

Shelby rolled her eyes. 'You can't just *appoint yourself* a nickname, Sam.'

'Just did.' Sam adjusted his fingers. 'Now shush. This is my big moment.'

The lighthouse stood sentry over their shoulders, looking out towards the wild Atlantic way. Fionn swore he saw Rose's face at one of the faraway windows, but when he blinked, there was only the sinking sun reflected back at him. He stuck a hand in his pocket, where Dagda's emerald sat snugly. If ever there was a time for luck – it was now.

Please let this work. Please.

Sam cast *The Eagle's Call* over the headland like a finely woven spell. It only took five notes before the air began to shimmer. Magic rose from the earth like dandelion seeds, kissing their cheeks.

Yes, the island seemed to say. I *remember.*

I *remember you.*

'Fionn, *look,*' whispered Shelby, as she tipped her head back. She was smiling with all her braces.

There was an eagle soaring overhead. Its sprawling wings shone golden in the dying light and its tail feathers were a bright, brilliant white. It circled the hilltop, swooping lower and lower.

Sam cracked an eye open. His curls were bouncing along his forehead and the collar of his jacket was flapping against his chin, but he held the rhythm, his fingers moving expertly along the keys.

The earth hiccoughed.

The grass peeled back on itself and, underneath, a stone pathway emerged, like a silver ribbon.

The eagle swooped over their heads, leading them onwards.

Fionn stuck his hands out, and Shelby and Sam took one each, all three of them holding on for dear life as the wind shoved them along the path. The rolling grasslands of Arranmore quickly lost their familiarity as the trail wound seamlessly into another layer. The world whipped past in blurs of blue and green and white, until it felt to Fionn like they were being threaded through the eye of the island. The sky soon shed its sickly pallor in favour of a bright, cerulean blue, and a new sun cast its eye over the earth. The eagle released a final cry, before soaring into it, its feathers disappearing in a blaze of amber.

The trail ended in a maze of tall-stalked lavender that brushed along their cheeks. The air was heady and sweet, the smell reminding Fionn of Maggie Patton. He wondered if all those visits to the Whispering Tree had become so much a part of her that she had begun to smell like its meadow.

Perhaps that's why his grandfather smelled like sea-salt and adventure.

The maze tightened, curling them into its bosom until they found themselves standing around a hole in the earth.

'Well, this looks familiar.' Fionn peered into the infinite blackness. The last time he had jumped in here, he had been inside a memory with Bartley Beasley. They had clung to each other so tightly, Fionn's fingers nearly snapped off. He could still remember the sound of their screams, ringing out in perfect, terrified harmony.

'I get motion sickness,' said Sam, making sure his flute was secure in his waistband. 'I can't guarantee this won't trigger it.'

Shelby stepped up. 'Well, don't vomit on me, whatever you do.'

'Just keep your hair out of my face.'

'I can't do that. It's Pantene perfect. It naturally fans out.'

They held hands, and took their last breath above ground.

'One,' said Fionn.

'Two,' said Shelby.

'Three,' groaned Sam.

They jumped into the earth, screaming at the top of their lungs.

Chapter Eight

THE BURNING TREE

Fionn barely had time to catch his breath before the wind grabbed him by the ankles, yanked him out of the earth and flung him up into a bright blue sky.

He landed with a mighty thud. Sam soared up over him, his arms flailing as the wind caught him by the coat-tails and dragged him to an unceremonious halt in the dirt. 'Well,' he said, sweeping the curls from his eyes. 'That was embarrassing.'

Fionn, who was untangling a crushed dandelion from his hair, smiled sympathetically. 'Happens to the best of us.'

Shelby came down last, landing in a perfect crouch, like Catwoman. She grinned at them, her braces sparkling in the sunlight, as she sprung easily to her feet. 'As I suspected,' she said, dusting her hands. 'I am fantastic at earth-diving.'

Sam and Fionn exchanged a haggard look as they rolled unsteadily to their feet.

'This place is *nice*, isn't it?' said Sam.

'*Nice* is not the word,' said Shelby, twirling on the heel of her shoe. 'This is *paradise*.'

'It's warm. It's quiet. It's *safe*,' agreed Sam. 'No Morrigan. No Soulstalkers.'

'No *sisters*,' added Fionn dreamily.

The meadow stretched out in every direction. It was lavished with wild flowers. Daisies and violets danced in the summer breeze, while butterflies and honey bees flitted between them, dusting the air with sweetness. Overhead, the sky was full of birds, and the birds were full of song. Fionn couldn't see a single raven.

Paradise indeed.

In the middle of the meadow, beneath a marshmallow cloud, the Whispering Tree climbed into the sky. Its branches reached up like the arms of a mighty warrior, while its roots plunged deep into the earth as though it was searching for something in the soil. Its trunk was impossibly large, so gnarled and twisted with age it looked as though a hundred faces were peering out from it.

Fionn drifted towards it, drawn by an invisible

magnet in his chest. Sam and Shelby moved with him. 'It's so *big*,' said Sam. 'Like, *skyscraper* big. Imagine *climbing* that thing?'

'Imagine putting a *tree house* in it,' said Shelby.

Sam dropped his voice. 'I feel like it's *watching* us.'

'It's definitely watching us,' said Fionn. 'Just like everything else in Arranmore.'

'And all the apps on our phones,' added Shelby serenely.

When they reached the base of the Tree, Fionn was seized by a sudden, roiling nausea. He had seen his grandfather stand in this exact place once. The Tree had climbed inside his head with such force, Malachy Boyle had fallen to his knees, twisting and thrashing as his spine was wrung out like a dishrag.

Now, it was Fionn's turn. 'I can't feel my face.'

'Relax.' Sam clapped him on the arm. 'There's only about a fifty per cent chance you'll die.'

'*Sam*,' hissed Shelby.

'I'm *joking*,' said Sam quickly. 'Worst-case scenario, you'll need a bout of therapy or two.'

'Don't listen to him, Fionn.' Shelby peered up through the branches of the mighty oak, her sandy blonde hair sweeping down her back in a curtain. 'Just take a deep breath. It'll be over in a minute.'

The tree *harrumphed*, startling them from their conversation. Fionn swore he glimpsed a frowning face in the bark, but then the trunk twisted and the grooves reformed. A single leaf floated from a faraway branch, and landed on his shoulder.

Fionn imagined his grandfather standing behind him, a steadying hand braced in that very same spot.

Go on, lad. You can do it.

Fionn placed his palm against the trunk. 'Here goes nothing.'

At first, there *was* nothing. Just the sound of his friends' nervous breaths. Then the tree shook itself awake. Its branches twisted and stretched as if it was yawning. The wind died. The birds fell out of their song as the island took a shuddering breath.

Then the sky erupted.

The lone cloud swelled, churning from milk-bottle white to a deep, violent purple. It bled across the sky like a bruise, swallowing the birds and the bees and every bit of blue. Thunder chased after it, growling through the meadow like an angry beast. There was an almighty *crack!* as a bolt of lightning darted from the clouds and skewered the trunk right down the middle. Shelby and Sam leapt backwards as the tree burst into a blazing inferno, the flames devouring the leaves until everything burned amber and gold.

'Fionn! Get away!'

Fionn kept his hand on the trunk. His grandfather had survived the same hungry blaze once. He believed he would survive too, even as his brow beaded with sweat.

The Tree began to whisper, the hiss and crackle of flames slowly turning into words.

Fionn Boyle.

Sssspeak or be ssspoken to.

Fionn's magic took a running leap at his ribcage. It was wide awake now, and it was everything he could do to keep from slamming face first into the bark.

'I am the S-Storm K-Keeper of Arranmore,' he began tremulously. 'With me are Shelby Beasley and Sam Patton.'

'I'm the Tide Summoner!' yelled Shelby. 'Just so you know.'

'And I'm the Fantastic Flautist!' added Sam.

'Sam!'

Yessssss, hissed the Tree. *Thissss I know.*

'Then you must also know that Morrigan has risen from her tomb under the Sea Cave.' Fionn tried to swallow the dryness in his throat, but his voice was croaky with fear. He had rehearsed this speech a hundred and more times, but the words marbled in his mouth now. 'We need Dagda back to help us fight her. We need you to help us find him.' He glanced behind him; Shelby had her chin squared to the fire, while Sam's was glued to his collarbone. 'We've come to ask you where Dagda is buried, so we can raise our own sorcerer too.'

The tree rumbled, as if deep in thought. The bark moved, and in its grooves, another face came and went. An eternity seemed to pass, all three children hypnotised by the flames that danced around Fionn's fingertips.

The Tree inhaled then, its branches sending a shower of leaves floating to the ground. They made a perfect semicircle around Fionn – a burning barrier through which his friends were not to pass.

They didn't dare.

FIONN BOYLE, boomed the Tree.

Fionn stiffened.

Your request is one that brings about an ending.

The air crackled.

Hear me as I crumble, heed me as I fall,

And in my ashes you will find your answer.

Fionn's heart was hammering in his chest. 'Wh-what does that mean?'

Shelby was leaning as far over the fire as she could afford without burning herself. 'What ending?'

'Maggie warned us,' said Sam urgently. 'She said she saw an ancient oak tree burnt to ash. That was an ending. I think you're about to kill the bloody Whispering Tree!'

Fionn yanked his hand from the trunk and stumbled backwards. 'No no no,' he told the Tree frantically. 'I don't want to bring about an ending. I just want to know how to raise Dagda.'

The flames devoured the last of the trunk. All the leaves had fallen, and now the branches were blackening. With a thundering *crack!* one broke off and hurtled to the earth. The branch landed with a thud, sending plumes of ash up Fionn's nose. He was seized by a sudden coughing fit.

Shelby screamed. 'Something's wrong! Get away from it, Fionn!'

'I can't! I'm trapped!'

The Tree's command rumbled through the earth again.

Hear me as I crumble, heed me as I fall,

And in my ashes you will find your answer.

Fionn opened his mouth to yell, but the world went black. The Tree climbed inside his head, and he fell to the ground, twisting and writhing as it wrapped itself around his mind.

Chapter Nine

THE LAST PROPHECY

A thousand images exploded inside Fionn's head, all jostling for attention. Storm Keepers and islanders trembled before the ancient oak as it told them their futures. Fionn saw them all from somewhere far above the perimeter of his mind – not as islanders, but as links in a chain that had gone unbroken for over a thousand years. They were the building blocks for a future in which he now sat, looking through the keyhole of an ageless tree.

He heard every question ever asked, and for a time he knew those answers too. But they left him just as quickly.

Let them pass, said the Tree, and so he did.

A new vision descended in a sheen of red. It was an

old battle on an ancient beach, where a flock of ravens shrieked above the shore. The sky was the colour of blood and, in the distance, Fionn spied two familiar white wings, beating through plumes of ash and smoke.

The Tree began to whisper.

The rise of the sorcerer is marked by blood-red skies,
A new dawn begins when the winged stallion flies.

Fionn squinted, trying to make out Dagda's body on the horse's back, but the vision shifted and he found himself standing now on the edge of a headland. Shelby was beside him, the sandy sweep of her hair blowing in his periphery. The tide was climbing up the cliffs, bringing the Merrows with it.

In the crush of waves, Fionn heard the Tree's whisper again.

Your loyalty will be tested when you find yourself alone,
Choose light or darkness when you stand against your own.

Without warning, Shelby stepped off the cliff and plummeted into the sea.

Fionn's scream was soundless, his hands grasping at thin air as the world shifted around him.

He was alone then, standing in the heart of Eagle's Point. The tide had drained away again, the seabed covered in dead fish and rotting seaweed. A soulless army marched over it, towards the island. Towards him.

A thunderstorm prowled across the sky, its under-belly crackling with whips of lightning.

In the growl of its thunder, Fionn heard the Tree's voice.

Gift fire, earth, wind and water
To every island son and daughter,
Those who fight for Arranmore
Will find their power on its shore.

Darkness then.

Fionn waited.

And waited.

He was more confused than ever.

He was frightened too. The visions hadn't put his mind at ease, they had filled him with a new, slow-curling dread.

'Is that the end?' he asked.

His own voice echoed back at him.

'Hello?'

'Are you still there?'

Dimly he could smell burning; he could hear his friends shouting his name.

'You said you'd tell me how to raise our own sorcerer,' said Fionn desperately. 'That's why we came here! I have to find Dagda!'

Then something unusual happened.

The tree chuckled.

With whose voice do you think I speak, Fionn?

The silence yawned, Fionn pondering the strange question in the tunnels of his own mind. He had never wondered who or what the tree was. But now that he really thought about it – the deep rumble of its whisper, the authority in its bodiless voice – he found himself picturing something else entirely. *Someone* else …

'Dagda?'

The darkness melted away. In the clarity of his mind's eye, Fionn saw a sorcerer standing before him.

Ancient and yet, somehow, ever living.

The sorcerer was smiling.

You have come to find me, Fionn.

Just as I have come to find you.

Dagda was impossibly tall. His tumbling hair was the colour of thunderclouds, and his mighty beard trailed past his knees. He wore a long brown tunic, roped at the middle, and thick brown sandals made of leather. His eyes were the deep blue of the ocean, and they were both wise and haunted.

Finding himself suddenly in the light of their gaze, Fionn felt like his heart might burst open. 'Please come back to us, Dagda. We can't defeat Morrigan without your power.'

Dagda looked at Fionn for a long moment, his beard twitching with the beginnings of a smile. *You already have my power, Fionn. It lives in you.*

Fionn started. 'What?'

The sorcerer turned from him. Fionn reached out to pull him back but the vision was already changing. An ancient battle unfolded before Fionn, the clash and clamour of weapons echoing in his ears. He looked down upon a deserted cove and saw Dagda on his knees. Morrigan was unspooling his soul from his body and devouring it gleefully.

In the gusting wind, Fionn heard the Tree's whisper.

Long ago, I was about to lose a great battle. I braced myself for oblivion. Not just my own, but the world's too. Humanity was ending, and in that ending there came a flash of impossibility. Like a firefly flitting through the darkness, something edged into the clearing.

The clearing shimmered below, and Fionn saw himself step out of thin air. He was younger, but not by much. His shoulders were hunched and his eyes were wide and darting. He was holding a burning candle in his fist.

Do you remember? whispered the Tree.

Fionn watched the ends of *Fadó Fadó* trembling in his hand. He recalled the moment he had first set eyes on

Morrigan with such vividness he still had nightmares about it.

'Yes,' he said. 'I remember.'

Fionn watched as his younger self slammed his hand against Dagda's back, his voice ringing out across the clearing. 'DO SOMETHING!'

He watched himself stiffen as a golden spark travelled up his arm like an electric current. A sunburst spread across his chest, then disappeared – gone as quickly as it came. Looking down on himself, Fionn saw now what he had not seen the first time around – the sudden sapphire blaze in his eyes, the pearly sheen of his skin.

He was glowing with magic. It was surely no coincidence that this was the exact moment the memory changed, and he had become flesh and bone before Morrigan.

At the same time, Fionn saw Dagda's soul return to his body in a spool of silver light. The sorcerer leapt to his feet and brandished his staff at Morrigan. She faltered, looking between them. Dagda seized the moment, and shot a bolt of lightning from his staff, while Fionn fell to his knees and disappeared.

The Tree whispered as the vision faded. *You gave me a spark of your strength at a time when I had none of my own. In return, I gave you a spark of my power.*

Darkness, again. The vision turned to stone, cold and

hard before Fionn, then came the stench of musty earth as it folded over him, again and again and again and again. Time passed in endless stretches, the only constant a thread of magic shining in the darkness of his mind. Fionn followed it through the blackness of a hundred ages, using it like an anchor to pull himself home. To the tree and the sorcerer, to the boy and the truth.

And so we became bound, you and I, by one magic, whispered the Tree. *When you returned to Arranmore last year, the island woke up. In you, it recognised me. My power was slumbering in your bones.*

The vision rippled, revealing a violent sea in storm. Fionn watched himself escape from Morrigan's Sea Cave, gasping and sodden as he was heaved up from the waves by his own father. He saw himself thrown from the vessel, flying through the air like a bird, while his father's boat went down, down, down, and Cormac was lost again, to time and destiny.

That night the island sent its storm for you, said the Tree. *You were chosen as its Keeper.*

Fionn remembered how he had been woken by the strange fizzing in his bloodstream. How the island had taken the Storm Keeper magic from his grandfather and given it to him.

That drop of magic was enough to wake the ocean already

inside you. The power that I gave to you long, long ago.

'No,' said Fionn, refusing to believe it. 'I would know if I had your power. I would feel it.'

He was alone again now, standing in a sunlit field of wild flowers. A phantom breeze swept over him, and the scent of the sea tickled his nostrils.

You have felt it already, said the Tree. *In every breath of wind that works in tandem with you. Every bird that chirps when you are near. Every flower that blooms in your presence. Every breeze that whispers to you in the night, each slant of sunlight that finds you in this endless winter.*

The island knows what's inside you.

The island has always known.

'No. No! If I was full of all that magic, I would be able to use it whenever I wanted,' argued Fionn. 'But it doesn't listen to me! It always feels like there's something in the way.'

The air shimmered, and suddenly Dagda was before him again. They stood apart from each other and the sorcerer smiled.

You are in your own way, Fionn.

The simplicity of Dagda's answer stunned Fionn into silence.

A sorcerer's magic is rooted in the soul, Dagda went on. *It responds to your strongest emotions.*

The sorcerer laid his hand on Fionn's shoulder. Fionn

75

gasped at the warmth and weight of it. He was surprised by how real this moment seemed inside his head. He could make out every coil in the sorcerer's beard and see the lines etched around his eyes. He watched them deepen.

You must master your fear to master your power. Only then can you be the leader your island needs you to be.

Dagda removed his hand and stepped backwards, into the gathering wind. The moment of peace was fading and the world was changing again. Fionn couldn't shake the sudden panic rising inside him, the sense that something else was coming. Something he could not bear to hear.

I am not coming back, Fionn.

The wind was howling now, and Fionn could hear his own heartbeat thundering in his ears. When he tried to reach out to Dagda and pull him back, he found he couldn't move. The sorcerer was getting further and further away.

He was leaving him.

A *sorcerer's power can have only one living master. Mine has taken root in you, Fionn. The choice has already been made.* Darkness was falling again, and with it, the distant hiss and crackle of flame. *All my prophecies have led to this moment, to you and me inside this Tree, on the brink of eternal darkness. And now, there is nothing more to say. The future is yours, Fionn Boyle. I will leave it to you.*

'No! Wait!' Fionn cried out. 'I can't do it! Please! I'm just a Storm Keeper! And a bad one at that!'

Fionn searched the darkness for the sorcerer's face, but found only his own staring back at him. A mirror hidden in the shadows of his own mind. The Tree's final words, when they came, were faint as a hummingbird's call.

No, Fionn Boyle. You are the new sorcerer of Arranmore.

Chapter Ten

THE STAFF IN THE ASHES

Fionn woke up with a jolt. The world was amber and gold, and the air was hazy with ash. Branches from the Whispering Tree littered the meadow like charred limbs.

'Sam, he's awake!' Shelby was leaning over Fionn, her grey eyes less than six inches from his nose. 'Oh, thank *God*! I thought you'd died there for a minute. And neither of us know CPR!'

She sat back on her haunches, revealing a sky full of charcoal smoke. It made a perfect halo above Sam's worried face. 'We thought your *spine* was broken, Fionn. Honestly. I've never seen a human being twist themselves up like that, and I've been to Cirque du Soleil twice. It was like you were possessed!'

'Can you move your legs?' asked Shelby. 'Or even speak?'

Remarkably, Fionn could do both. Apart from a dull ache in the base of his skull and a slight twinge in his back, he had returned to his body in full working order. He told them as much as he sat up.

'Dagda's not coming back,' he added, shaking his head in disbelief. The sorcerer's words were flooding back to him, and he was beginning to feel cold inside. Right down to his bones. 'It all happened so fast.'

Sam and Shelby exchanged a look. 'Fionn, you've been unconscious for hours.'

'That sky might look all plasticky and blue, but it's late in the real world,' said Sam.

While the last of the Whispering Tree gave itself over to the flames, Fionn filled his friends in on what it had shown him, and with whose voice it spoke.

They listened with wide eyes and slack jaws, their faces growing bleaker by the second.

'It was Dagda all along?' reeled Shelby.

'And now he's gone,' said Fionn quietly.

'What are we supposed to do without a sorcerer?' said Sam, stricken.

'He said we already have one.' Fionn turned his hands over, traced the blue veins stark against his skin. His magic slumbered somewhere deep inside him, unreachable. 'Apparently it's me.'

Sam's mouth fell open.

Shelby grimaced. 'Oh.'

'I know,' sighed Fionn. 'How can I be a sorcerer when I can't even control my magic?'

They were interrupted by a keening groan. They looked up just in time to see the burning trunk of the Whispering Tree teetering back and forth. A crack ripped through the bark, the charred column snapping in two and careening towards them like a flaming guillotine.

'MOVE!' Fionn shoved Shelby and grabbed Sam by the scruff of the neck, rolling as fast as he could. The tree thundered to earth with a deafening roar, sending up a shower of charcoal and bark.

Fionn rolled on to his back, stunned. Sam was half crushed underneath him. The trunk had shaved a button off his coat, and missed his ankle by barely an inch. On the other side of it, Shelby sounded like she was hacking up a lung.

'That's it, then,' she said, staggering to her feet. 'We're on our own.'

In the blink of a cosmic eye, the rest of the Whispering Tree turned to a mound of white, crumbling ash. The wind whipped up in a sudden gust and carried it away, leaving nothing but a piece of wood sticking out of the earth. It was shaped like a claw, brown and polished and cool to touch. They clustered around it.

'This doesn't look like it belongs here,' muttered Sam.

'*Hear me as I crumble, heed me as I fall, And in my ashes you will find your answer,*' said Shelby, recalling the Whispering Tree's words. 'I think it's supposed to help us.'

Sam wrapped his fingers around the base of the wooden claw and tried to pull it up, out of the earth. '*Nnngh!*' he groaned. 'It won't budge.'

'Here, let me try.' Shelby nudged him out of the way. 'I'm really strong.' She squatted low, wrapping both hands around the claw and heaved.

And heaved.

And *heaved*.

'Wow, ease up there, Hercules,' said Sam sarcastically.

When Shelby's face had turned bright red, she released the stubborn piece of wood. 'I swear it wiggled.'

'Uh-huh,' said Sam.

Fionn was still staring at the strange wooden claw. The most peculiar feeling was prickling in his cheeks. His magic was stirring, as if it recognised it.

Shelby pressed her hand against his back. 'Go on then, sorcerer.'

Fionn hunkered down, and wrapped his fingers

around the wooden claw. 'I'll give it a go, but I really don't –'

Crack! It came free with a sharp tug. He pulled it up out of the earth, surprised to find it was much taller than he expected. At full height, it appeared to be a staff – tall and heavy, and made of gnarled brown wood. The claw sat along the very top of it, like a twisted crown. With one final heave, Fionn wrapped his fingers around the middle and yanked the end of it from the earth.

He stumbled backwards, his magic rising like a tidal wave inside him. It lapped at the bones of his ribcage, streamed through the lining of his heart, before pooling in the pit of his stomach. '*Whoa.*'

'Are you OK?' said Shelby.

'*Yeah*,' said Fionn, a little breathless. 'That was … weird.'

'Tell me about it,' muttered Sam. 'I can't believe you're stronger than me.'

'I think it's more than that, Sam,' said Shelby in a low voice.

Fionn turned the staff in his hands. He recognised the intricate lines, the curving claw on top. He'd seen it before in the folds of *Fadó Fadó*. It had belonged to Dagda. This was his parting gift. A conduit for the magic he had left behind in Fionn.

Only it was missing something.

Fionn stuck his hand into his pocket to find the emerald glowing like an ember. Without even thinking, he slotted it into the claw at the top of the staff. The wood curled around it and snapped into place. 'Cool,' he said, planting the staff like a flag.

He felt taller, somehow. Braver.

He felt, a little bit, like Dagda.

Shelby grinned. 'Suits you.'

'Eh, guys? I think it's talking to us.' Sam pointed to the staff, where ancient words were appearing along the wood in neat, looping cursive. They shimmered faintly in the emerald's light.

Fionn tilted his head to read them.

When Solas glows above the ground,
Your leader is already found.

The wood flared white-hot against Fionn's fingers.

'Solas,' said Shelby, watching the words disappear. 'That must be its name.'

Sam's frown was sharp and sudden. 'Hey, do you feel that?'

The ground was trembling. They backed away from the hole in the earth, the dirt rattling violently against their soles.

'Earthquake!' shouted Shelby.

'The island's throwing us out!' Fionn whipped his head around, but there was nothing to grab on to and nowhere to shelter. There was nowhere to go. 'HOLD OOOOOOOOOOOOON!'

The meadow dissolved with remarkable quickness; the grass melting into a gaping black hole that swallowed everything in sight. Fionn, Shelby and Sam huddled together as the ground disappeared beneath their feet, and the bottom dropped out of their world.

Chapter Eleven

THE ACCIDENTAL HAIRCUT

They plummeted through the earth at such speed they left even their screams behind them. Fionn was flipped upside down and right side up, ripped from his friends by a whip of wind so strong it snatched the air from his lungs. The blackness swallowed him whole, the only light the faint twinkle of Dagda's emerald as it chartered them headlong through the ancient layers of Arranmore.

Approximately twelve seconds later, Fionn was thrown up from the earth. He flailed blindly in the dark, before landing with a resounding thud. He rolled on to his back and spat a blade of grass from his mouth. Time had moved quickly in their absence. The night sky was starless, and the ground was dense with frost. 'N*nnngh.*'

There was an answering groan from somewhere nearby. 'Am I dead?' wheezed Sam.

'Where are we?' Shelby was sitting up between them, the shell around her neck glinting silver in the fractured moonlight. Fionn could hear the distant rush of the ocean, tasted the tang of seaweed on the wind. The night flickered, then lit up in a bright golden blaze. The lighthouse cast its beam over their shoulders. 'Oh.'

The island had returned them to Eagle's Point.

Sam shielded his eyes against the blinding light. 'Oi! Can you turn that down a bit, Rose?'

Fionn rolled to his feet. Solas had landed just a foot from the cliff-edge. The emerald was glowing softly against the grass. They drifted over to it.

Below them, the tide was barely a trickle of greyish blue. Soon the Merrows would have to crawl on their bellies to protect them. After that, there would be nothing between Arranmore and Morrigan.

Nothing but Fionn.

'Hey! Idiots! If you three are just going to stand there in plain view you might as well jump off and swim over to Morrigan!'

'Fionn, I told you to be smart!'

Bartley and Tara were stalking across the headland. They were bundled into their winter jackets and scarves,

Bartley's blond hair glowing like a pearl in the moonlight. Even from a distance, Fionn could make out a candle in his sister's hand, a lighter at the ready in her other.

'What are you doing here?' he said, before gesturing at it. 'And you can put that away. We're all right.'

'We've been waiting all evening for you to get back,' said Tara impatiently. 'Rose said you'd probably end up here, but it's been ages and we were getting worried.'

'Did you find the Tree?' said Bartley, looking between them. 'Did it tell you where Dagda's buried?'

'Sort of.' Fionn's eyes flicked involuntarily to the staff.

'Where did you get that thing?' Bartley pointed accusingly at it. 'That definitely doesn't belong to you.'

'Actually, I think you'll find it does,' said Shelby primly.

'What do you mean?' Bartley narrowed his eyes at Fionn.

'Dagda gave it to me.'

Tara perked up instantly. 'Is he here?'

Fionn shifted uncomfortably. 'Er, no.'

'He's not coming back,' said Shelby.

'Ever,' added Sam.

Though Fionn knew this already, hearing the truth so plainly, and out loud, filled him with a fresh rush of dread.

'The Tree said we already have our sorcerer.' Shelby

smiled encouragingly at Fionn, but it flickered at the edges. She was just as scared as he was. 'And as it turns out, he has all the magic he needs.'

Tara and Bartley turned their horrified expressions on Fionn.

Fionn cleared his throat awkwardly. 'Err.'

'*You.*' Bartley stumbled backwards, as if he had been punched. 'You're telling us that *you're* our best hope?'

'I don't know,' said Fionn defensively. His chest was warming uncomfortably, and he was getting antsy. He didn't want to be here right now, teeth chattering on the edge of Eagle's Point, holding a stupid giant staff and answering to a venomous Bartley Beasley, before he had time to get used to any of this.

'Oh, Fionn,' muttered Tara. 'This isn't good.'

'Well, it's not *great*,' reasoned Sam.

'But at least now we know …' said Shelby.

'It's a *disaster* is what it is. If Fionn's our sorcerer then we've already lost.' Bartley raked his hands through his hair. 'He'll send us all to our deaths. Or worse, to a soulless existence inside that bloody thing.' He gestured at the faraway Black Mountain. 'We're all –'

'Shut up!' Fionn burst out. 'I didn't ask for this to happen, so just be quiet. Give me a minute to *think*.'

The staff buzzed in his fingers.

Bartley scoffed. 'There's nothing to figure out, Boyle. If you're our leader, we're as good as dead. You're the worst Storm Keeper this island has ever seen. You used *all* your magic against Ivan, and by some stroke of luck it actually showed up, and even then it wasn't enough to keep Morrigan in her grave.' He came a step closer, the gummy scent of his hair gel prickling in Fionn's nose. 'It wasn't even enough to save your own grandfather.'

'Bartley, *stop!*' snapped Tara.

Fionn brandished the staff at Bartley. 'I said *shut up.*'

The emerald flickered.

'You're no leader, Boyle,' Bartley carried on. 'You're just a fraud. You can't hide behind your grandfather any more. You should be glad he's dead, so he doesn't have to witness another one of your epic failures.'

Tara shoved Bartley. 'That's *enough.*'

'Take that back,' said Fionn through his teeth. He felt full up all of a sudden, like he could open his mouth and breathe fire into the world.

Shelby gasped. 'Fionn, your eyes. They're glowing like sapphires!'

'What's happening to you?' said Bartley, taking a wary step back. 'You look like a mutant.'

Fionn exhaled through his nose. He could feel lightning crackling in his bloodstream.

'I'm not scared of you,' said Bartley unconvincingly. 'No one is scared of you. You're just a stupid –'

'STOP!' Tara shouted, but it was too late.

A bolt of magic leapt from the emerald staff, and came at Bartley like a bullet.

Everyone screamed.

There was a flash of smoke.

Bartley fell to his knees, wailing, as his carefully curated hairdo sizzled away.

'Fionn!' shrieked Shelby. 'Oh my God! What have you done?' She dropped to her knees beside Bartley. 'Are you all right, Bartley? Let me see your face. Are you hurt? Should I call Mum?'

'Don't look at me,' cried Bartley through his fingers.

They were *all* looking at him. Despite the impromptu haircut, he appeared to be completely unharmed.

Sam clapped a hand over his mouth to keep from laughing.

Tara glared at him. 'It's *not* funny!'

'Tara, it's *hilarious*.'

Fionn lowered his staff. 'Oops.'

'FIONN BOYLE, I WILL FLAY YOU ALIVE!' Rose's anger reached him on a violent gust of wind. She was marching across the headland with the speed of a much younger woman. 'STOW THAT THING AWAY

BEFORE YOU GET US ALL KILLED.'

When she reached their huddle, she yanked the staff from Fionn, spun it around and batted the end of it against his legs. 'You foolish boy!' she scolded. 'If you're going to put on a magic show for Morrigan, you'd better have some kind of plan up your sleeve.'

Fionn startled. 'I wasn't. I mean, it was an accident. I was just –'

'I *was just*,' mimicked Rose. 'Save your excuses. I have eyes.' She used the wooden end of the staff as a pointer stick, brandishing it at the others. 'The rest of you, keep your bloody voices down. Everything carries on the wind up here.'

Bartley staggered to his feet. 'He tried to kill me!'

'No, I didn't!' said Fionn.

'You shot a lightning bolt at my head!'

'Well, you deserved it!'

Shelby leapt between them. 'Hey! That's my brother!'

'Yeah, well, maybe you'd be better off without him,' hissed Fionn.

Sam winced. 'Oof.'

Shelby's eyes flashed. 'What on earth has got into you, Fionn?' She gestured to the staff in Rose's hand. 'Maybe you should hold on to that thing until he calms down. He's acting like –'

'A sorcerer?' said Fionn.

'No,' said Shelby flatly. 'A maniac.'

Fionn folded his arms. 'It's not my fault. He pushed me too far.'

'So, you shot a lightning bolt at his head.' Shelby narrowed her eyes. 'I'll have to be careful not to get on your bad side.'

Fionn frowned. 'Don't be ridiculous. I would never –'

'Just leave it, Fionn.' Tara turned on Bartley. 'Are you all right now?'

Bartley shook his head. 'I don't think I'll ever be the same again.'

Fionn rolled his eyes.

'Oh for goodness sake, hair grows back,' said Rose impatiently. 'You five *won't* if Morrigan gets her hands on you. Come away from those cliffs.' She led them back across the headland, all five of them trailing after her like lost puppies. They huddled inside the lighthouse, far from the glare of Black Point Rock. The fire flickered in its hearth, casting their shadows across the walls.

Rose shut the door behind them. 'So, the Whispering Tree is gone,' she said, turning the staff in her hands. Beneath the folds of her shawl, her eyes were as green as Dagda's emerald. There was a strange sort of sadness in them. 'And the staff is yours.'

Fionn startled. 'Uh, yeah. That's ... exactly what just happened.'

'You're Dagda's heir.' It was not a question but a fact, and what's more, it didn't seem to surprise the old woman.

Fionn shifted under an invisible weight. 'Seems that way ...'

'So it's true then?' whispered Tara. 'Fionn *is* a sorcerer?'

'Yes,' said Rose simply. '*When Solas glows above the ground, Your leader is already found.*'

Sam and Shelby gasped.

Fionn scanned the staff, but the words had disappeared; the wood was smooth and polished. He noticed Rose's hands were trembling. 'How do you know those words?'

With little ceremony, Rose removed her shawl.

There was a shock of silence, all five of them staring at her as though they had never seen her before.

Perhaps they hadn't.

The old woman was no longer old. She was young. And she was *ravishing*. Her jet-black hair fell in waves to her waist, her eyes so green and bright they seemed to shine out of her face. Her skin was smooth and alabaster pale in the moonlight, her rosebud lips quirked into a smile.

'Do you know who I am?' she asked them, and now that Fionn could see her properly, he heard the difference in her voice. The croakiness was gone.

'Róisín,' said Shelby, edging closer to be sure. 'You're Róisín, First and Fearless.'

'Oh my God,' breathed Tara. 'You're *alive*.'

Not only was Róisín a fearless warrior, she was also the first Storm Keeper of Arranmore. She had been there, at the beginning of everything. She had fought side by side with Dagda during the first battle for Arranmore, and now she was here too. At the end.

The young woman flashed her teeth. 'Call me Rose. I've got used to it.'

'Where did you even *come* from?' said Sam, who was now looking around the lighthouse with great suspicion.

Rose shrugged. 'I've always been here. Since the beginning.'

'But *how*?' reeled Tara. 'I thought the only way for a human to live forever is to surrender their soul to a sorcerer.' A thought occurred to her. She took a step backwards, and the others did the same. 'Wait. Are you a Soulstalker?'

Rose snorted. 'Do I look like a Soulstalker?'

'Maybe there are loads of different types,' reasoned Shelby. 'Like butterflies?'

'Maybe there are.' Rose's smile was wry. 'Before the Battle of Arranmore, Dagda decided to preserve a secret weapon. Someone who would watch over the island, silent and unseen, should things not go as we hoped. I was to become a guardian, a Keeper of the Keepers, until the day he returned again to face the rising dark.' Rose raised the staff before them, drawing their attention to the glowing green gemstone. 'My soul is safe inside the emerald. When Dagda's magic flows through it, it comes alive. And I return to the warrior I once was.'

Fionn's brows drew close. 'But Dagda's not coming back.'

'His power has though,' said Sam. 'It's in you, mate.'

'I thought it would be you, Fionn.' Rose arched a slender brow, and Fionn was struck by the sudden suspicion that somehow she had seen him all those years ago, in the folds of Fadó Fadó. 'You're *different* to the other Storm Keepers. Full of magic – so much it practically shimmers in the air around you – and yet it never flowed from you the way it did from me, or from your grandfather.' She planted the staff, the claw reaching a foot above her head. 'That's why I sent you to the Tree. To see if you could retrieve Solas. It's the only thing on Arranmore that would truly recognise his magic.'

Fionn frowned. 'Well, now I feel kind of manipulated.'

'You and me both,' muttered Sam.

Tara shushed them.

'Now we know the truth about your power,' said Rose unapologetically. 'You're not a Storm Keeper, Fionn. You're a sorcerer.'

She drew her arm back suddenly and fired the staff across the room. Without thinking, Fionn flung his hand out and it came flying back to him. The others gasped as he caught it, the force of it knocking him backwards into Bartley. He shoved Fionn off.

Fionn's fingers curled around the wood. 'Whoa!'

Rose smirked. 'Good instincts.'

'So, what's the difference between a Storm Keeper and a sorcerer?' asked Tara, who was now regarding the staff like a snake about to strike.

'There are four.' Rose raised the corresponding fingers. 'The first difference is *place*. A Storm Keeper is bound to one area, to a well of magic that does not belong to them. In the case of the island, Arranmore chooses its Keepers and so it binds their magic here.' She spread her arms wide. 'A sorcerer, on the other hand, is boundless. Their magic comes from within. They can take it anywhere. Just as Dagda did.'

'And Morrigan,' said Sam uneasily.

'What's number two?' said Tara.

'Power.'

Fionn stood a little straighter.

'A Storm Keeper lives with a droplet of power inside them. A sorcerer contains an entire ocean,' said Rose.

Fionn's grandfather's words floated through his mind. *What you did back there to Ivan … that force that came out of you. You weren't controlling the weather, Fionn. You were creating it.*

'Oh,' he said, very quietly. He hadn't pulled the lightning bolt from the sky. He had pulled it from his soul. He glanced at Bartley's newly shorn hair, then at the staff in his hand. 'Solas makes it easier somehow. My magic comes quicker. It actually listens.'

Rose nodded. 'Magic is much simpler with a conduit. Especially if it's one that already recognises your power. One that's grown used to it.'

Fionn tried to take heart in that fact. 'A silver lining, then.' He smiled weakly. 'I won't be *completely* useless.'

'Unless you end up accidentally killing your own islanders,' muttered Shelby.

Sam glared at her. 'He won't.'

'He might,' said Bartley. 'He almost killed me.'

And Tara, standing between them, said nothing.

'What's the third difference?' asked Fionn.

'A sorcerer's power is immortal,' said Rose. 'At the end of your life, you can give it to the world, you can pass it on to another or you can keep it for yourself.'

'And become a creepy, raven-obsessed, all-powerful, cape-wearing, evil, ever-living skeleton woman,' supplied Sam.

'More or less,' said Rose, bemused. 'The last difference I will tell you tomorrow. It is, in this case, the most important difference.' She folded her arms, and that searing emerald gaze flickered from Fionn to Bartley. 'And right now, you're not ready to hear it.'

'How could I not be –' began Fionn.

'Aw, come on –' said Sam at the same time.

Rose swung the door open and a gust swept in. 'Go home and sleep off your anger. The end of the world is almost upon us, and we don't have time for infighting.' She shooed them outside. 'Off you go.'

'Goodnight to you too, Rose,' said Sam sarcastically as they traipsed past her.

She slammed the door behind them, and Fionn heard the locks clicking as they slid into place.

'I like her,' said Sam decisively.

'I'm scared of her,' admitted Fionn.

Sam nodded. 'Yeah, but in a good way.'

Shelby and Bartley didn't say anything. They simply turned from the huddle and started for home, walking arm in arm across the headland.

Fionn watched them go. 'She's really mad at me.'

'Well, you did almost kill her brother right in front of her, and then told her he deserved it,' Sam reminded him. 'How does that old saying go? "You don't make friends with lightning bolts".'

'Come on,' said Tara as she grabbed Fionn's arm. 'Before you do something else stupid.'

Chapter Twelve

THE FIRST RECRUIT

A short while later, Fionn and Tara slipped into the cottage on the headland. She paced across the sitting room.

'It's not the end of the world,' she said, more to herself than to Fionn. 'Not yet anyway. You'll have to practise. Lots. And we'll have to be really careful about how we tell everyone else. The sooner the better, I think.' She snapped her chin up. 'Maybe you should start practising now, just to be safe.'

Fionn threw the staff on the couch and massaged his temples. 'Tara, give it a rest.'

His heart was a drumbeat in his chest. There had been a seismic shift in his future tonight, and he had completely lost his footing. A magical staff was one thing, but being a sorcerer – in place of Dagda – was quite another. He needed a minute to get used to it all.

Tara grabbed the staff from the couch. 'There's no *time* to rest, Fionny.'

'That's mine.'

'Then start acting like it,' she said, waving it around. 'You need to focus now.'

'Put it down, Tara.'

'Make me.'

'DROP IT!'

'NO!'

'DROP YOUR MEGAPHONES!' The hall door swung open and their mother came marching in, in her dressing gown. Her hair was piled on top of her head and her eyes were bloodshot with exhaustion. 'What on earth is going on in here?'

'Tara won't leave me alone.'

Tara brandished the staff at him. 'I'm only trying to help you.'

'I don't need your help!' said Fionn viciously. 'All you ever do is whine and nag!'

Tara dropped the staff like it was on fire. 'Fine. Forget it.'

Their mother looked between them, then at the staff on the ground. The emerald was glowing faintly in the dimness. 'Where did you get that?' she said suspiciously.

Fionn swallowed thickly. 'Dagda's not coming back, Mam. He's given his power to me.'

Their mother blinked. 'What?'

'It's true,' said Tara sourly. 'We're doomed.'

Their mother was silent for twenty very long seconds. Fionn could almost see this new information slotting into place behind her eyes. She swayed a little on her feet, then cleared her throat, smoothing the stray wisps of hair from her face. It was much paler now. 'Right. Kitchen. Both of you. Now.'

Tara and Fionn traipsed into the kitchen. They sat, arms folded, at opposite ends of the table.

'Go through it all again,' said their mother, leaning against the counter to steady herself. 'Slowly, and from the beginning.'

So Fionn did.

'And now Tara keeps bossing me around,' he finished angrily.

Tara's lips twisted. 'That's because you aren't taking this seriously enough.'

'How would you know?'

'You almost killed Bartley,' she reminded him icily. 'You should never have taken that staff. Arranmore needs a *real* sorcerer.' Her dark eyes flashed. 'Now Morrigan's going to eat you for breakfast. And then she'll come for the rest of us, and we'll die screaming inside that awful black mountain.'

'Tara!' said their mother.

'It's true, Mam. We all know it.'

Fionn rounded on his sister. 'What do you expect me to do? Magic an army out of thin air? Line up four hundred frightened islanders and march them across the tide to fight her?' When Tara only glared at him, he went on. 'Newsflash: I don't know the first thing about magical battles!' Fionn's chair screeched as he pushed it back. 'I didn't choose the bloody staff. I didn't choose any of this!' He glanced at the empty mantelpiece, his heart clenching. 'And the worst part is, now I'm all alone. No one is here to help me, Tara. No *one*.'

Tara flung a tea towel at him. 'What about me, dummy? I'*m* here!'

'And so am I,' added their mother.

'I want Grandad.' Fionn pressed his fists against his eyes. 'I want someone who believes in me.'

Tara looked away sharply, tears pooling in her eyes.

The silence was a siren.

Their mother lowered herself into the chair between them. 'I can see my children sitting in front of me but I hardly recognise them.' She shook her head in disappointment. 'Where is the Tara who used to read bedtime stories to her little brother every night until he fell asleep? The

Tara who tracked down Fionn's bully in the school playground and held him by the scruff of his neck until he promised to leave her little brother alone for good?'

Tara cleared her throat. 'Yeah, so?'

Their mother turned on Fionn. 'And where is the Fionn who used to wake me up at six a.m. every year on Tara's birthday so he could make her special pancakes that were so full of syrup and chocolate, our stomachs ached for the rest of the week? The Fionn who learned how to do a French plait on YouTube so his sister could wear it to a sleepover and impress her friends?'

Fionn looked at the ground. 'That was ages ago.'

'Well, what about the children who travelled all the way across the country together to come here last year, and ended up escaping an evil sorceress together – *twice*?' Her eyes were glassy now. 'The children whose bravery and loyalty and *love* made it OK for me to finally face my fears and come home to a place I never thought I'd see again. The children who walked hand in hand with their grandad under the Northern Lights – even though it hurt – so he wouldn't be afraid to leave them.'

The silence stretched. Neither Fionn nor Tara were willing to break it.

'You know, when your father and I first started seeing each other, he was jealous of me and my brothers,' their mother went on. 'Cormac was an only child, but Enda, Sean and I were a team, even when we fought like cats and dogs. Even when we chased each other down Aphort Beach, lashing seaweed at each other in the pouring rain.' She smiled at the memory. 'Even when we made each other cry.'

She waited for them to look up. 'You two might think you know everything, but I have lived a lot longer than both of you, and one thing I know for certain is that your greatest ally is each other. You have shared every big moment in your lives – both the happy and the sad. There's no one who knows you better, no one who will fight harder for you when the darkness comes, and no one who will love you as much as you love each other in the end.' She cleared the wobble from her throat. 'Your grandfather's death has left an empty space between you. Now you have to figure out what to do with it. You can either fill it with fear or you can fill it with love.'

'The second one,' said Fionn quietly.

'Obviously,' added Tara. This time when she looked at Fionn, the fight had seeped out of her. 'Just so you know, I'm always going to be here, no matter what happens. It might be your job to protect the island, but it's my job to protect *you*. And there's no one as brave or as fearless as a big sister.'

Fionn's smile was watery. 'I don't suppose you have

another three hundred Taras stashed away somewhere? I could really do with an army of them.'

Tara tossed her ponytail. 'I'm afraid I'm one of a kind.'

'Well, it looks like you have your first official recruit, Fionn.' Their mother pressed a warm hand on each of their shoulders as she rose to her feet. 'As for the rest, I've already made a few phone calls. Let's see what the next few days bring. Whatever lies ahead of us, we'll face it together.'

Fionn felt a little better then. He might not have an army as great as Morrigan's, but he had two warriors right here at home, willing to fight alongside him, no matter what happened. And that, at least, was a start.

Still, he was relieved to return to the sanctuary of his grandfather's bedroom. He changed into his pyjamas and closed the curtains, noting *Blood Moon* standing alone on its perch underneath the window sill. He propped Dagda's staff carefully against the wall before crawling into bed and burying himself under the duvet.

'I wish you were here, Grandad,' he whispered into the darkness.

There was only the soft hum of the radiator to answer him and, somewhere in the distance, the chirping of a nightingale. It sang Fionn to sleep, the realisation drifting after him like a lullaby.

The birds had returned to Arranmore.

Chapter Thirteen

THE HURRICANE IN
THE RUINS

Fionn stood in the ruins of the old McCauley farmhouse and watched the dawn light bleed across the sky. He had risen early, dressed in his favourite hoodie and jeans, devoured two bowls of cereal, and then slipped out of the slumbering cottage in search of a secluded spot to practise.

He'd found it in the rubble of his ancestor's home. The old farmhouse was little more than a mass of weather-beaten stone. There was a broken chimney lost to brambles, and a garden gate still swinging on its hinges. The rest of the farmhouse was covered in moss and lichen. Still, it was one of the few spots on Arranmore Island where you couldn't see the sea. Or better yet, where the sea couldn't see you.

Fionn turned the staff in his hands.

'Sorcerer.' He rolled the word along his tongue, trying to get used to it. His magic warmed in his chest. 'Let's see about that.'

He stirred a gust in the air. It rippled through the long grass, dancing and twisting until he could feel it catching in his cheeks. Fionn grinned as it lifted the hair from his head and flapped in the ends of his coat. With Solas, it was as simple as breathing, as easy as thinking.

The next gust was fierce and howling. It raced around him in a circle.

Seized by the giddiness of his magic at play, Fionn spun on his heel, casting another gust, and then another.

The old walls shook, the broken gate groaning as it swung back and forth.

Fionn decided to unearth the chimney from the undergrowth. He turned his wrist, making the next gust short and quick as a cannonball. It ripped through the brambles and flung the chimney across the garden, where it shattered against the old shed door.

Fionn flinched. 'Oops.'

There was a sort of skill to it. Not just in casting the wind, but in choosing the right *kind* of gust, in weaving it seamlessly with what was already out there. He had to find the balance between nature and magic, to work hand in hand with the island instead of upheaving it.

Fionn decided to practise on himself. He twirled the staff backwards and tucked it underneath his arm, the emerald blinking over his shoulder. He summoned a gust of wind, then started to sprint, the force propelling him forward like a jet-pack. For six seconds, Fionn ran as fast as a superhero, the world blurring all around him, then he lost his footing and went flying head first into a hawthorn bush.

He plucked the twigs from his hair as he clambered back out. 'I really wish someone had filmed that.'

That gave him an idea. Fionn slipped his phone from his pocket and set it up on a nearby rock. He clicked the 'record' button, backed up ten paces, then grinned at the camera.

'Here goes nothing.' He turned his staff upside down and pointed the emerald at the space between his feet. 'FLY!' he yelled, releasing a blast of wind. The force sent him skyward, his arms and legs flailing as he shot up like a rocket. 'Too high! Too high!'

Fionn screamed as he came careening back down to earth. He swung the staff, blindly, casting another gust to cushion his fall. The wind caught him like a hammock, then rolled him on to the grass. Fionn spun on to his back, and laughed giddily at the sky. 'Whoa!'

The birds were laughing too.

He clambered back to his feet and hurried over to his camera, only to find that the moment he took off like a rocket, the entire video had gone out of frame. Fionn wilted. 'There's no way I'm doing that again.'

Instead, he cast another gust in the air. This one was lively; it chased the robins around the trees, and sent a flock of starlings into a glorious murmuration. He was getting better at it already. The power inside him was simply an ocean that needed taming. And the staff was making that possible.

So Fionn practised. And practised. And practised, until his bones ached and his throat burned. Until the sun climbed over the horizon and the seagulls swept in from the sea to watch him too.

By then, all of Fionn's gusts had banded together to become a full-blown hurricane. The forest bent backwards with a thundering groan. Mossy stones skipped along the earth and then took flight. The garden gate flew off its hinges to join them, strips of yellow ivy racing after it, until the sky was streaked with colour and peril.

Fionn stood in the eye of it all, laughing like a maniac. The foundations of the old farmhouse orbited around him like planets, the green eye of Solas glowing in the centre like the sun. His arms were shaking and his forehead was marred with sweat, but he had seized control of every gust. He was a conductor, and the howling wind was his orchestra.

Finally, his magic was working.

And more than that, it was *fun*.

A blur moved in his periphery. Fionn spun around, startled. A boulder fell from the sky and pounded out a divot in the grass.

'FIONN!' Shelby was crouched halfway across the field, covering her head with her hands. 'CAN YOU TURN THAT THING OFF FOR A SECOND?'

With a final *whoosh* Fionn sent the wind splintering through the trees. The birds chased after it, as the rest of the ruins tumbled from the sky in a steady stream of *thunks*. They made a perfect circle around him. He stood inside his own miniature Stonehenge as his hair settled on his head like a mop. 'Sorry,' he said, blowing it from his eyes. 'I didn't see you.'

Shelby rolled to her feet. 'Well, that explains why you weren't answering your phone. If it wasn't for that *insane* hurricane you were brewing, I might not have found you at all.'

Fionn laid the staff down. 'I'm glad you did.'

'Yeah, well, I actually came down here to make peace,' said Shelby. 'And by "make peace", I mean "let you apologise" for last night.'

'Right. Yeah.' Fionn smiled, sheepishly. 'I was going to call you about that this morning, but –'

'You had to brew a giant hurricane first?'

Fionn cleared his throat awkwardly. 'Time got away from me.'

Shelby surveyed the mess around them. 'So did a lot of things, by the looks of it.'

'I really am sorry about last night, Shelby.'

'Which part?'

'I didn't mean to ruin Bartley's hair like that,' said Fionn truthfully. 'I didn't mean to hurt him at all, honestly. I just got angry and it sort of happened. I'm sorry it frightened you.'

Shelby narrowed her eyes as she weighed up his apology.

'I would never actually kill your brother. I know how important Bartley is to you, even if he's … mildly satanic.' Fionn gestured around them, at the chaos. 'Anyway, that's why I came down here early this morning. I need to practise. I don't want something like that to ever happen again.'

Shelby joined him in his stone circle. 'I know Bartley said some really horrible things to you, Fionn. I yelled at him about that too. A *lot*.' She sighed. 'He's just so scared and worried and *jealous* of you. It brings out his worst side.'

Fionn feigned surprise. 'Oh, does he have another side?'

Shelby swatted him in the arm. 'I know he's far from perfect.'

'He's on an entirely different continent.'

'Yeah.' Shelby's shoulders slumped. 'But he's –'

'He's your Tara,' said Fionn. 'I get it.'

Shelby nodded. 'Just please don't fire any more lightning bolts at his head?'

'You have my word.' Fionn extended his hand. 'Friends?'

Shelby shook it vigorously.

Fionn deflated with relief. 'I really hate fighting with you.'

'Were you afraid I'd set my gran on you?' teased Shelby.

Fionn snorted. 'Only a little.'

'Nice henge,' she said, surveying the fallen boulders. 'How long have you been out here?'

Fionn blew out a breath. 'Hours?'

'We should get going. The meeting is starting soon.'

Fionn swallowed, hard. 'I hope the islanders don't react to the news the same way your brother did.' His confidence was starting to fritter away at the thought of all those shocked faces. 'They already think I'm a useless Storm Keeper.'

Shelby picked up the staff. 'There are things that

matter just as much as magic, Fionn. Things like loyalty. And bravery. You can't teach that or inherit it. You can't dig it up after a thousand years. It just *is*. And a bunch of frightened islanders like my brother – who you are absolutely *not* allowed to incinerate – can't take that away from you.' She handed him the staff. 'We'll have to figure out the rest as we go along.'

The staff buzzed against Fionn's fingers, warm and sure. 'You're right.'

'I'm always right,' said Shelby. 'Are you coming?'

Fionn turned back to the scattered remains of the farmhouse. 'You go ahead. I'm going to clean up some of this mess.'

'All right, but don't be late.'

Shelby took off, the pine trees stilling as she weaved through them.

Fionn cast the stone slabs into the air, one by one, and shattered them with bursts of lightning. The farmhouse exploded in fireworks of rock and shale and, as Fionn watched them fall to earth, he decided that perhaps he could do this after all.

He could be the sorcerer Arranmore needed.

Chapter Fourteen

THE TURNING TIDE

By the time Fionn set off for the island meeting, he was feeling confident. Down by the pier, the sea was calm. Seagulls coasted on a frigid wind, chattering and cawing with reassuring obnoxiousness. The ground here was still frostbitten, the road glittering beneath a slick of ice. Fionn pointed his staff at it, relaxing into the familiar rush of heat in his bloodstream. The ice melted in a warm swell, and the ground grew steady and sure beneath him. The primroses raised their heads, and unfurled their petals in thanks.

It was at this precise moment, of peace and possibility, that a terrible howl rang out.

Bartley Beasley, shorn-haired and pale-faced, was sprinting down the road towards him. 'BOYYYYYYYLE!'

Something about Bartley's frightened expression made Fionn feel suddenly very afraid.

'Shelby's gone!' he said, rounding on Fionn and shaking him by the shoulders. 'I was waiting for her by the bridge, but she never showed up.'

Fionn felt the colour drain from his face. The bridge was less than a ten-minute walk from the old McCauley farmhouse. She should have made it twice over by now.

'I found this.' Bartley's eyes flashed as he held up her phone. The screen was smashed. 'I think she's been taken.'

All the air rushed out of Fionn, his gaze tunnelling towards the shattered glass. 'Come on!'

Fionn ran with Solas tucked under his arm, sprinting faster than he ever had in his life. Bartley matched him stride for stride, both boys racing past the school and across the climbing headland until they reached the lighthouse.

Beyond it, the Merrows were shrieking.

No, no, no, no, no.

Bartley flung his arm out. 'There!'

At the edge of the headland, where the ancient cliff steps crumbled down to the retreating sea, was a single sparkly shoe.

They reached the cliff-edge with their hearts in their mouths. Bredon was already at the bottom of the steps,

Shelby flung like a sack of potatoes over his shoulder. She was pounding her fists against his back, wriggling and squirming and shouting, but he seemed not to notice.

'SHELBY!' Both boys screamed at once.

She snapped her head up, still struggling. 'I can't get free! Help me!'

The sea was too shallow for the Merrows to get to her. They were clustered further out in the waves, shrieking in fear for their Tide Summoner.

'I'm coming!' Fionn slid over the cliff-edge and landed on the broken steps. He pulled the staff down after him.

'Hurry!' cried Shelby, who was halfway across the strand already. 'I can't go in the mountain! Please, don't let me! I c-can't!'

Bartley swung his legs over the cliff-side, but Fionn prodded him back. 'Get help! You need to raise the alarm!'

But Bartley stayed frozen on the grassy edge, screaming Shelby's name over and over like a terrible siren.

Shelby was screaming back, but her voice was getting fainter and fainter.

Fionn kept his eyes on his feet as he half climbed, half tumbled down to the shore. One foot, and then another. Don't look up. Don't look down. Panic rushed through him, joining the current of his magic. When he reached the bottom, Bredon was already sloshing through what was left of the tide. Fionn brandished his staff in a panic, sending a sharp gust to knock him off course. The wind howled as it barrelled into the Soulstalker. He wobbled a little, and Shelby leapt from his arms, like a fish. He caught her in mid-air, and yanked her back.

'No!' Fionn climbed over the rubbled sea cave, shooting gusts at the sea around Bredon. It was no use. By the time Fionn made it into the water, Bredon had already reached Black Point Rock.

Shelby was still fighting him, screaming herself hoarse. 'NO! Please! NO!'

'I'm coming, Shelby!' Fionn sent a sweeping wind out, blasting the waves back as he charged through them.

Across the tide, Bredon carried Shelby through a crevice in Black Point Rock and completely disappeared. Her screams faded to silence.

'SHELBY!' Fionn sloshed onwards, dreading the worst.

'Run! Run! Run!' hissed the Merrows. 'Swim! Swim! Swim!'

The Black Mountain began to wheeze.

The sky was filling with smoke.

'SHELBY!'

Somewhere over Fionn's shoulder, Bartley was still screaming.

Lír was gnashing her teeth in the water. 'Quick, boy! Or she's gone for good!'

Fionn ripped the slip of sea up like a blanket and cast it aside, flinging Lír with it. The waves rushed back at him in a fury, but he was almost at the Black Mountain now. Just a few more feet and then he would –

There was a terrible eruption of ash. It filled the air like a cloud, putrid and rotting and thick with dark magic. Somewhere far behind Fionn, Bartley howled. The staff went slack at his side. The sea surrounded him again, the water lapping at his hips as he stood, frozen in horror, before the Black Mountain.

Like a spectre crafted from the deepest shadows of the world, Morrigan stepped through a crevice in the rock. Her cape billowed around her like the wings of an avenging angel. She was holding Shelby by the wrist. Her sandy hair was a mess, and she was only wearing one shoe. The Tide Summoner still hung from her neck.

'Shelby!' cried Fionn.

But Shelby didn't answer.

'Hello, Fionn,' Morrigan crooned, as though they were old friends, meeting by chance. Her keen eyes came to rest on Solas. 'Now *where* did you find that?'

'It belongs to me.' Fionn tightened his grip. 'Give. Her. Back.'

'It seems I have a new sorcerer to play with.' Morrigan's smile was a scythe. 'How kind of Dagda to send you to me, though I would have preferred more of a challenge.'

Fionn pointed Solas at her head. 'I said, let her go.'

A stray soul curled around Morrigan's waist. 'How good is your aim, little sorcerer?'

'*Exceptional*,' lied Fionn.

'Very well, then.' Morrigan tugged Shelby sharply, positioning her like a shield. 'Take your best shot.'

Fionn lowered his staff. 'Shelby, talk to me.'

Shelby didn't answer.

Morrigan prodded her in the back, and she stumbled forward. 'Talk to your little friend before he starts to blubber.'

The Merrows hissed at Fionn in warning.

'You're too late. You have failed her,' seethed Lír. 'You have failed *us*.'

Fionn inched towards his friend. '*Shelby?*'

Shelby didn't blink. She didn't know him. She didn't even know herself. And in that awful moment, it felt to Fionn as though a sliver of his own soul had been taken too.

Lír's eyes flashed in warning. 'Don't be a fool, boy. *Run*.'

But Fionn couldn't turn back now, even if he'd wanted to.

'Shelby, please look at me,' Fionn begged. '*Please*.'

Morrigan's laugh was a twisted, choking thing.

Fionn bared his teeth at her. 'You're a monster.'

Morrigan bared her teeth right back. 'Thank you.' She gestured lazily at Shelby. 'If you found that impressive, then I think you're *really* going to enjoy this.'

As if programmed by a hidden remote, Shelby stumbled into the water.

And brought her hands to the shell around her neck. She held it to her heart and began to whisper.

One by one, the Merrows crawled towards their Tide Summoner. They weren't looking at her with fear or distrust. Their eyes were shining with loyalty, their bond to her unbreakable, no matter the darkness behind her eyes. No matter what side of the war she stood on.

Fionn had a sudden, bone-chilling realisation.

Shelby might be a Soulstalker, but she wasn't alone. She had an army around her.

Fionn was the one by himself. Standing behind enemy lines. In the middle of a hostile tide.

It was a trap.

And he had fallen for it.

Lír's crown glinted in his periphery. 'I warned you, boy.'

Morrigan drifted to Shelby's side, her fingers curling over her narrow shoulders. 'Are you brave enough to kill her?' she taunted. 'Or will you lose all your precious Tide Warriors too?'

Solas warmed in Fionn's grip, as though it knew what he should do. Fionn's breath was too loud in his ears. If he left Shelby alive, Morrigan would have a new army.

But if he killed her ...

No.

No.

In the chaos of his thoughts, an ancient voice whispered to him.

Your loyalty will be tested when you find yourself alone,

Choose light or darkness when you stand against your own.

Fionn backed away from Shelby. Into the icy sea.

Morrigan clucked her tongue. 'What kind of sorcerer are you?'

'The kind that will never be like you,' said Fionn fiercely.

The water was deepening with each step. It lapped at his hips, and then his middle, rising like a vice around his chest. Morrigan had released her leash on the tide.

'Then you will die,' she sneered. 'The Merrows will devour you whole, and I will bask in the music of your *honourable* screams.' She flicked her gaze to Shelby, an unspoken command passing between them. 'I expected you to put up more of a fight. But if you wish to die in a puddle instead of a battle, I am happy to oblige.'

Shelby raised the Tide Summoner to her lips.

'No!' cried Fionn. 'Please don't, Shelby.'

Morrigan cackled.

'Fight it,' pleaded Fionn. He was moving quicker now. His feet slid over rock and silt as he tried to navigate his way back to the strand. He kept the staff raised above the waterline, but he refused to point it at his friend. 'I *know* you can fight it, Shelby.'

The Merrows circled him like sharks, waiting for the signal to attack.

And then something unexpected happened.

Shelby froze. The shell hovered just below her chin. She made a strange whimpering noise, like she was trying to speak but couldn't quite remember how.

Their eyes met, and although Shelby's were dark and fathomless, Fionn sensed in them the barest flicker of loyalty.

It was enough.

Fionn sent a bolt of magic straight for Morrigan. She shrieked as she dodged it, the blast tearing a chunk out of the mountain and buying Fionn a few more precious seconds.

He turned on his heel and charged towards the shore.

The Tide Summoner rang out. Clear and haunting as a funeral knell.

Fionn didn't dare turn around. The Merrows shot

after him, releasing their battle cry before disappearing underneath the water. Every ripple felt like a webbed hand grasping at his legs, every frothy crest a merrow's teeth gnashing at his throat.

The cliffs sloped down to meet him. The waves pushed him up, up, up. Fionn reached for a crumbling step, his fingers losing purchase on the slick rock. A merrow swiped at his ankles. Fionn kicked her away. Another came for his staff.

Fionn screamed as he jerked his arm free. He threw the staff; it landed five steps up, the emerald looking over the edge like a bright green eye. A mouthful of seawater slipped down his throat. He spat it out, lunging for safety. This time, he caught a tuft of grass sprouting from a rock. He tried to drag himself up, but a merrow grabbed his foot and yanked him back. They were all around him now, gnashing their teeth.

Clink! Clink! Clink!

Then there were footsteps, rushing down to meet him, a familiar voice calling his name. Rocks slid past him and tumbled into the sea. Fionn flung his arm out, and this time, someone caught it.

He kicked with all his might, and slowly, painfully, he was lifted out of the water. A merrow leapt after him, but she was beaten back in a flash of silver.

'Get back or I'll skewer you!' yelled the voice.

Fionn scrabbled on to the steps on his hands and knees,

seawater pouring out of him in great, heaving retches. When he looked up, it was into the face of a warrior. Róisín, First and Fearless, was standing before him like a shield.

Her spear streaked through the air like lightning as she beat the Merrows back, back, back. 'Move!' she shouted at Fionn. 'Get up those steps!'

Fionn grabbed Solas and did as he was told. Rose backed up the cliffs after him as the Merrows retreated into the waves, unable to chase her on land.

Out of the immediate jaws of danger, Fionn's adrenalin began to wear off. In its place came fierce and pulsing pain. His throat burned from the seawater. The back of his leg was on fire. He found a merrow tooth the size of a two-euro coin lodged in his calf. He winced as he pulled it free, then dragged himself on to the grass and began to cry. Awful, sucking sobs racked his shoulders. He didn't want to lift his head and see the smoking sky, nor the ravens circling overhead.

He didn't want to see his friend being dragged back inside that prison.

'GET UP, BOYLE!' Bartley grabbed him by the hood and hauled him to his feet. 'YOU LOST HER! YOU LOST MY SISTER!'

'I'm s-s-sorry!' cried Fionn, trying to find his balance. 'I couldn't help her. I –'

Bartley shoved him. 'YOU LET MORRIGAN TAKE

HER!' His eyes were red and wild. There was snot running from his nose and tears rushing down his cheeks.

Fionn was crying too. 'I t-t-tried. I'm s-s-sorry.'

Fionn was so sorry he couldn't see straight. He felt like he was drowning. Like no matter how hard he gasped, he couldn't take in enough air. Like he would never be able to breathe properly again.

Bartley shoved him. Fionn tripped over his feet and landed on the grass. Bartley tried to kick him, but Fionn swiped his leg out and Bartley came crashing down on top of him. He grabbed Fionn by the throat and raised his fist. 'It's all your fault, Boyle!'

Fionn squeezed his eyes shut and braced for impact.

'ENOUGH!' Then Rose was between them, wrestling Bartley off Fionn. 'FOR DAGDA'S SAKE, PULL YOUR-SELVES TOGETHER!'

Fionn sat up, panting.

Bartley was panting too.

'We are at war!' heaved Rose, looking between them.

'I know!' spat Bartley. 'He betrayed us!'

Rose glared at him. 'Not with Fionn, you imbecile. With Morrigan. And you two decide to fight *each other* instead. Tell me, where's the sense in that?'

Bartley scrubbed his cheeks with his sleeve. 'He abandoned my sister.'

'He did not. He did what he could,' Rose shot back. 'Or weren't you watching? Do you think this is what she would want to happen right now? Her best friend and her brother trying to kill each other in full view of Morrigan?'

Fionn rolled to his feet. His knees were trembling, and so was his voice. 'He's right though. I did fail her.'

Rose turned on him, steel-eyed. 'Enough self-pity. Walk it off. I'll come for you later.'

Fionn plucked Solas from the grass and tucked it into the crook of his arm. It felt heavy as a sledgehammer. The faint buzz of his magic brought him no comfort. It was no use to him now. As he trudged away from the cliffs, his tears came fast and freely. He was conscious of Bartley's burning stare on the back of his head, every step of the way.

The seagulls flew after him, chattering and cawing, but Fionn didn't notice.

He had lost his best friend *and* the Merrows to Morrigan.

And the war hadn't even begun.

* * *

When Fionn got home, Tara was in the kitchen boiling the kettle. 'There you are! You missed your own meeting.'

Fionn hurried past her, flinging the emerald staff on

to the couch, before locking himself inside the bathroom, where he curled around the toilet bowl and vomited.

When he finally stopped retching, he sat back against the door and hung his head between his knees. He tried to tune the rest of the world out, but the wind was rattling the bathroom window.

There was a knock at the door.

'Fionn?' Tara's voice was muffled on the other side. 'Are you OK?'

'No.' Fionn pressed the heels of his palms against his eyes. 'I want to be alone.'

'Bartley called me. What happened to Shelby wasn't your fault, Fionn. You can't blame yourself.'

A tear slipped down Fionn's cheek. 'It *is* my fault. Like Bartley said, I couldn't save her.'

'He's just upset, Fionn. He's mad at himself too. Can you come out, please?'

'Just leave me alone.'

She slipped a piece of paper underneath the door. 'Read this, at least. It just came for you.' Her footsteps faded, and Fionn was alone again. He picked up the note.

If you want to save your friend and protect the island, then meet me at the old promontory fort. NOW.

R.

'What the hell?' muttered Fionn.

When he returned to the sitting room, Tara was waiting for him.

'I've spoken to Mum. She's gone over to the Beasleys,' she said. 'Juliana and Una are making sure everyone knows what happened. Telling them to keep off the shores. Just in case Lír attacks.'

'Right,' said Fionn, picking up the staff. 'I'm going down to the old fort. Rose wants to see me.'

'Yeah, I read that,' said Tara mildly. 'Will you be back for dinner?'

'You shouldn't open my letters.'

'Least of our problems right now, Fionny. I can make lasagne.'

Fionn didn't argue. 'Thanks, but I'm not hungry.'

He slammed the front door behind him, and marched down the headland with grim purpose.

Chapter Fifteen

THE MYSTERIOUS CHEST

The old stone fort on Arranmore Island had been around as long as Róisín, First and Fearless. It stood on the edge of a low-lying headland just beyond the school, and was now little more than a stone wall that curved protectively around the cliff-side before throwing its arms wide open to the Atlantic Ocean.

When Fionn arrived, Rose was standing in the middle of it, waiting for him. Her hair was long and loose, and her eyes were bright. At her feet, Fionn noticed the old antique trunk from the lighthouse. Why had she tugged it out and hauled it all the way down here?

'Feeling better?' she said, by way of greeting.

'Tell me how to get Shelby back,' said Fionn.

Rose blinked.

'In your note, you said I could save her. Is that really possible?' asked Fionn. 'To turn a Soulstalker back into a human? Has it ever happened before?'

Rose hesitated. 'No.'

'So you lied.' Fionn turned to go.

'But there have always been rumours,' she called after him. 'About Morrigan's cape.'

Fionn looked over his shoulder. 'What kind of rumours?'

'No one's ever got close enough to know for sure – not even Dagda.'

'Tell me what you think you know, then,' pleaded Fionn. 'I need something. *Anything.*'

'I know that the last difference between a sorcerer and a Storm Keeper is the most important one,' said Rose. 'It's *sharing.*'

Fionn frowned. Of all the things he expected her to say, this was not one of them. 'What?'

Rose went on. 'When Morrigan created the cape of souls, it was so she could be all-powerful. With dark magic, she managed to make an army of Soulstalkers, cursed with unnatural life, who would follow her to the ends of the earth. But the cape is her greatest weakness too. If they are separated, she loses her army and her power.'

'What happens to the souls?'

Rose looked at him. 'I believe the souls will go free.'

'So I can get Shelby back?' said Fionn, hope burning in his chest.

'No one knows,' Rose conceded. 'But as long as Shelby's body is still whole, there's a chance her soul will return to her.'

Fionn tightened his grip on the staff. 'So all I have to do is march into that mountain and rip the cape from Morrigan's neck?'

Rose arched a brow. 'Is that your grand plan, then?'

If anything happened to either of you, I'd storm that awful mountain and rip Morrigan's cape apart with my bare hands.

'Shelby would do it for me.'

Rose waved a hand in dismissal. 'You're too impetuous,' she scolded. 'You could have died today going after her like that. With only the barest grasp of your own power, and no one with you. You're not just facing Morrigan, Fionn. You're facing her entire army. Her ravens. Her *brothers*.' She shuddered. 'Those two are a horror unto themselves.'

'I don't care,' said Fionn resolutely.

'And as of today, you're facing your own people too,' Rose reminded him. 'Sparing Shelby might have been noble, but it wasn't clever. An islander lost to Morrigan is an enemy made to fight against you. To *weaken* your resolve, and then take advantage of it.'

'Are you saying I should have killed her?' said Fionn angrily.

'It is almost an impossible thing to stand against your own people. I know that better than anyone.' Rose held his gaze as she came towards him. Her eyes darkened, and so, too, did her voice. 'During the first Battle of Arranmore, Morrigan turned my sister Bronagh into a Soulstalker. Aldric used her against me. It was sport for him, this sick kind of revelry. I was stronger than Bronagh. Faster too. But I couldn't kill my own sister.' Rose flinched as an old pain etched itself across her face. 'That moment of weakness almost cost me my life. I almost doomed the entire island …'

'What do you mean?' asked Fionn.

Rose looked away, shame and regret warring in her face. 'I mean it is a mistake we cannot afford to make again. If you want to lead, you need to make decisions with your *head*, even if your heart begs for mercy.'

Fionn squared his jaw. 'My heart is the only thing keeping me standing.'

'I know,' said Rose wearily. 'Sorcerer's soul, human heart. It can't be helped, I suppose.'

'Is that really such a bad thing?' Fionn challenged.

'Only in a war.'

'Well, I'm sorry that I don't know the first thing about being a sorcerer,' he said sourly. 'Dagda had his whole life to learn how to make merrows and flying horses and giant talking trees. Do you know what I know about? Pizza toppings. Superhero movies. Freddo bars. Mario Kart.'

'You don't need to know everything, Fionn. You just need to know *enough*. Enough to survive. Enough to *fight*.' Rose bent down and unlatched the chest at her feet. 'You won't win this fight on your own.' She heaved the lid open and a cloud of dust erupted from it. 'You will win it by using Morrigan's trick against her. By *power-sharing*.'

Fionn eyed the chest with mounting suspicion. 'You're not about to give me a cape, are you?'

Rose's smile curled. 'You will build your army a different way. Not with a cape, but with a storm.'

Fionn stared at Rose, wondering if she had, perhaps, gone mad. 'You've lost me.'

'You're going to brew a power-storm, Fionn.'

'A *power-storm*,' said Fionn, feeling the word out. 'Right … I have no idea what that is.'

'Yes, you do.' Rose's eyes glittered. 'You were there, weren't you? Your grandfather told me how you burned the end of *Fadó Fadó*. You walked amid the first Battle of Arranmore. You saw the thunderstorm rain down magic on us. You saw us reach up and take from it. That's how we fought, Fionn. Not just with our weapons, but with Dagda's magic. That's how we defended the island.'

Fionn was suddenly struck by the memory of what he'd seen *before* he came upon Dagda in the cove. Somehow the awful ending of that memory had eclipsed the beginning. But Rose was right. He had seen impossible things. *Magical* things.

'I *saw* you.' He remembered it now – Róisín, First and Fearless, reaching her spear up to the sky and wreathing herself in magic. With sudden, vivid clarity, he could picture the moment she used that spear to stir the ocean and drown a Soulstalker twice her size. 'You were glowing.'

'We were all glowing.'

Fionn recalled Dagda's mighty storm cloud, how it had puffed from Solas like smoke from a steam-train and prowled across the sky, full and dark and heaving. 'So *that's* how he did it.'

'A good sorcerer can make a Storm Keeper. But a great sorcerer can make an army of Storm Keepers,' said Rose. 'Dagda was a great sorcerer, Fionn. And if his magic has taken root inside you, that means you can be a great sorcerer too.'

'You make it sound so simple,' said Fionn, unconvinced.

'Perhaps it is,' said Rose, with a shrug. 'There's only one way to find out.' She turned back to the chest. 'You'll need Clan Leaders, of course. Islanders you can trust to follow you into the unknown. Dagda couldn't do it alone, and neither can you.'

'Well, we can agree on that at least,' muttered Fionn.

'You'll need every person on Arranmore to fight against Morrigan. They'll be able to wield the power-storm's magic with their bare hands, but it's tricky, like mixing cake batter without a wooden spoon. It can take months to master it, and we don't have time, I'm afraid. It's much easier with a conduit.' She gestured at the staff. 'Just as Solas helps the flow of your power, weapons will help direct the flow of theirs.' Rose began rummaging around in the chest. 'In a battle, they make the best conductors.'

'Right. So if my magical power-storm fails, you can just use your spear to stab someone,' said Fionn darkly.

Rose's chuckle echoed in the din of the chest. Then she jerked backwards and flung a giant axe in his direction.

Fionn jumped backwards. 'Hey!'

It clattered at his feet. Fionn picked it up, the weapon hefty in his hand. The handle was made from dark wood, and the blade was pristine pewter, engraved with intricate Celtic swirls.

'That is the axe of Sorcha Patton,' announced Rose.

'During the ancient Battle of Arranmore, she fought tire-lessly until sundown on the third day. Choose its wielder wisely. It's not for the faint of heart.'

'Clearly.' Fionn set the axe down with a dull thud. 'What's so special about it?'

Rose rolled back on her heels. 'The weapons in this chest belonged to the original Clan Leaders of Arranmore. They have used power-storms before, so they will recog-nise yours. The magic will be easier to control. It may even be more powerful. After all, they contain the memory of their wielders.'

'And there's magic in memory,' said Fionn quietly. 'My grandfather used to say that.'

'Your grandfather was right.'

'What else do you have in there? And please don't throw it at –'

Rose flung a whip over her shoulder. This time, Fionn caught it in mid-air. It was roped and knotted with dark leather, its handle carved from shiny red wood. 'The bull-whip of Angus McCauley,' said Rose, with simmering admiration. 'He took Aldric the Silent down by his ankles and died for it.'

Fionn whistled under his breath, then reverently set it down by the Patton axe.

Rose was already holding the next weapon. She slid

it from its scabbard to reveal a gleaming short-sword, its handle inlaid with cherry-coloured jewels. 'Please don't throw that at me,' said Fionn quickly.

'I do have some sense,' said Rose drily. 'How do you think I've lived this long?'

'Well … magic.'

Rose smirked. 'Magic and intelligence.'

Fionn took the sword from her, marvelling at how shiny it still was after all these years. How *sharp*. '*Ouch*.'

'Do I really need to tell you not to touch the blade?'

'Not any more,' grumbled Fionn as he stowed it back in its scabbard.

'That's the sword of Rian Boyle,' said Rose. 'She crept up on Bredon the Brutal and took his eyeball right out of its socket.'

It was then that Fionn noticed the empty setting at the very bottom of the hilt. There was a ruby missing. He knew exactly where it had ended up. 'As leader of the Boyle Clan, I would have suggested you take this weapon for yourself.' She gestured at the staff. 'But you already have one.'

'I'm sure I'll find a use for it.' Fionn laid it with the others. 'No sense in letting a perfectly good sword go to waste.'

Rose lugged the next weapon out. 'The shield of

Orla Beasley. She stood against a warship of three hundred Soulstalkers and gave her life in protection of her clan.'

Fionn eyed the bronze shield but didn't move to take it. He was thinking of Shelby, and how much he would have liked to give it to her.

Rose, sensing his hesitation, laid it with the others.

When Fionn looked inside the chest, there was nothing left. 'So *you're* the Cannon leader,' he said, with dawning realisation.

Rose removed her spear from the inside of her cloak and twirled it once in her hand. 'First and Fearless.'

Fionn frowned. 'I thought you were a Beasley.'

'You also thought I was dead.'

'Good point.' Fionn gestured at the spear. 'What cool thing have you done with that then? I'm guessing there's a story too.'

Rose smiled, but there was a touch of sadness in it. 'My story is not yet over. I hope to add to it before it ends.'

Fionn shifted uncomfortably. 'Still plenty of time to make a name for yourself, I suppose.'

'Aye.' Rose's eyes glazed with some distant thought. 'Go and pick your leaders, Fionn. The island meets tomorrow morning. I suggest you spend the rest of the day working out how to make a power-storm.'

Fionn rubbed the back of his neck. 'Yeah ... And how do I do that, exactly?'

'I'm afraid I have absolutely no idea.' Rose smiled blandly. 'You'll have to figure that out on your own, *sorcerer*.'

'Right.' Fionn gathered up the weapons. They were warm in his arms, glowing faintly with the remnants of old magic – with memory. Strangely, they were a comfort to him. 'I'd better find good homes for these.'

Chapter Sixteen

THE CLAN LEADERS OF ARRANMORE

The Patton Clan Leader

'So let me get this straight,' said Sam, eyeing the axe of Sorcha Patton with great trepidation. 'You're going to brew a storm so powerful that magic literally bursts from the clouds and falls down, like rain.'

'Yep,' said Fionn.

'Uh-huh.' Sam's eyes narrowed. 'And when that rain falls down, we can just take the magic and *use* it …'

Again, Fionn nodded. They were sitting in the kitchen at the back of Sam's house, the axe squatting like a centrepiece between them. 'You become a Storm Keeper for as long as the storm lasts.'

Sam arched a brow. 'Then do we all turn into pumpkins?'

'I'm so glad you're taking this seriously, Sam.'

Sam leaned back in his chair. 'So, basically, we get to be our own versions of Maggie Patton and Hughie Rua and Róisín ... the stuff of legends.'

If *it works*, thought Fionn.

'The stuff of legends,' he concurred. From the corner of his eye, he could see the blurry shapes of Sam's parents pressed up against the glass door to the conservatory, listening in.

'That part, I like,' said Sam. 'As you know, untold fame and adoration have always appealed to me.'

'So, will you be my Patton Clan Leader?' Fionn slid the axe towards him. 'I'm going to need all the help I can get.'

Sam took the axe with both hands, and sagged under the weight. '*Oof.*'

'It'll take some getting used to,' said Fionn awkwardly.

Sam settled the axe in his lap, tracing the spirals with his finger.

For a moment they were silent.

'I wish I didn't have to ask you,' said Fionn quietly. 'I wish I didn't have to ask anyone, to be honest. But I don't think I can do this on my own.'

Sam shook his head. 'It's not that, mate. I'd be

142

honoured to go down in history with you. Even if it means spraining my hands on this unwieldy thing. I have a flautist's wrists, you know. They're delicate things.' His smile faded, and he looked away. 'It's just … I'm not brave. Not like Shelby. It's not my thing.'

'It's not my thing either,' admitted Fionn.

'I wish Morrigan had taken me,' whispered Sam, so his eavesdropping parents couldn't hear him. 'Then you'd have her. And she'd be so much better at all this battle stuff. She'd know the right things to say too.'

'We *will* have her,' said Fionn. 'We're going to get her back.' He swallowed thickly. 'Once I figure out how to get that cape off.'

Sam took a deep breath. 'I'll do my best, then. For both of you.' He glanced sidelong at the frosted doorway. 'For all of us.'

'Thank you,' said Fionn earnestly.

'My sister won't take orders from me though.'

'Probably not.'

'But it'll be a nice change.' Sam brightened, a little. 'Getting to boss her around.'

The Beasley Clan Leader

'What do *you* want?' Elizabeth Beasley glowered at Fionn through the crack in her front door. The lock-chain was still in place. 'If you've come to apologise about Shelby, you can save it. We don't forgive you and you're not welcome in this house.'

Fionn exhaled through his nose.

Be *nice*.

Be *nice*.

Be *nice*.

'Is Bartley in? I need to talk to him.'

'My poor Bartley can barely stand to look at you after what you did to his sister.'

'Gran. It's fine.' Bartley voice rang out behind her. 'I can handle this.'

Elizabeth threw Fionn one last withering look before stomping away. Bartley slid the lock-chain free and swung the front door open. He stood on the threshold in a grey tracksuit and stripy green socks. Without his trademark blond locks and his sneering confidence, he looked a little lost.

He folded his arms. 'What do you want, Boyle?'

Fionn set his schoolbag down with a thud. He unzipped the top and removed the bronze shield from inside it. Then he laid it on the doorstep between them. 'This belonged to your ancestor Orla Beasley. She fought with it during the battle of Arranmore.'

Bartley stared down at the shield, then back at Fionn. 'So?'

Fionn sighed. This was going to be harder than he thought. 'I need a Beasley Clan Leader.'

Bartley's eyes widened for a heartbeat before he masked his fleeting surprise. 'I'm sure my gran would kill for it.'

'I want it to be you.'

Bartley cocked his head. 'Why?' he said suspiciously.

Because I hate your grandmother with the fire of a thousand suns.

Fionn went for a different truth. 'Because I don't think there's anyone else on Arranmore who would fight harder for Shelby than you.'

Bartley looked at the shield again. An eternity passed. 'That's true,' he said quietly.

'I think we can save her.' Fionn picked up the shield, jaw clenching from the strain. 'I think we can save the island. But we have to work together.'

There was a heavy beat of silence.

And then Bartley stuck his hand out. 'Give it here, then.'

The shield passed between them.

It felt a little like a handshake.

Then Bartley slammed the door in Fionn's face.

The New Clan Leader

By the time Fionn left the Beasleys, the sun had set and he was *starving*. The bag on his back was much lighter now. He reached the next cottage in a matter of minutes, hurrying up the garden path and knocking sharply on the door.

His breath made clouds in the air.

A nightingale watched him from the chimney, head cocked in curiosity.

And then … the door swung open, to a brightly lit hallway and a burst of warm heat.

'Fionn? What's up? Is everything OK?' Juliana Aguero was wearing a dark blue dressing gown, and her face was covered in what appeared to be some kind of bright green slime.

'What happened to you?' said Fionn, with great alarm.

'Oh, God.' Juliana threw her hands up in embarrassment, shielding her face. 'I forgot about the face mask.'

'Oh. Right.' Fionn chuckled. 'Well, as long as it's not some kind of flesh-eating bacteria.'

Juliana dropped her hands. 'Can we please change the subject?'

'Gladly,' said Fionn, removing the short-sword from his bag. He held it out. 'I have a favour to ask.'

'Is that *a sword*?'

'Yeah, and it's really sharp.'

'OK …' said Juliana uncertainly.

'It belonged to my ancestor Rian Boyle,' Fionn went

on quickly. 'She fought with it in the Battle of Arranmore. Took Bredon the Brutal's eye out with it, in fact.'

'Gruesome,' said Juliana approvingly.

'We're going to have to fight Morrigan again.'

'Yeah, I figured.'

'And this time around, we already have a Boyle leader.' Fionn pointed, unnecessarily, at himself. 'And I already have a weapon. You'll see it tomorrow. But it occurred to me, we might need another Clan Leader,' he explained. 'Someone who can lead all the new families of Arranmore.' Fionn offered the sword, feeling nervous all of a sudden. 'I would really like that to be you, Juliana.'

Juliana plucked the stray wisps of hair from her face goo and tried to look as dignified as possible. 'It would be my honour.'

'Well, you don't know the plan yet.'

'It doesn't matter,' she said, taking the sword and holding it against her chest. 'Arranmore's my home. These are my people. The answer is yes.'

Fionn was struck by the sudden urge to hug her. He blinked, furiously, then cleared his throat. 'Thanks, Juliana.'

'And anyways,' said Juliana, flipping her dark hair. 'I'm a prefect. I tend to excel at things.'

Fionn rolled his eyes and slung the empty bag on to his back. 'Right, then. See you tomorrow.'

Juliana waved him off, and when she thought he was out of earshot, she swished the sword through the air and squealed.

Fionn smiled to himself as he slinked away into the darkness.

The McCauley Clan Leader

'So what is it, exactly?' asked Tara, in the garden of Tír na nÓg.

'It's the bullwhip of Angus McCauley,' explained Fionn. 'Rose says during the Battle for Arranmore, he used it to –'

CRACK!

Tara brought the whip down on the garden wall. A chunk of stone split clean in half, sending a shower of shale across the headland. 'Yeah, yeah, I got it,' she said, admiring the handle. 'This is *so* me.'

'Cool,' said Fionn, relieved. 'So will you be the McCauley Clan Leader?'

CRACK!

'Does that answer your question?' she said with a smirk.

Fionn backed away from her. 'Yeah, but if you could stop destroying our garden wall for dramatic effect, that'd be great.'

CRACK!

Fionn leapt out of the way. 'TARA!'

His sister's laughter soared. 'Oh, calm down. That was nowhere near you.' She wrapped the whip around her arm, admiring it in the sinking sunlight. Despite the years on it, the leather was pristine. 'I'm not giving up my candles though. I want a back-up. Just in case your power-storm thingy fails.'

'Thanks,' said Fionn sarcastically.

'Are you coming inside? The lasagne's almost done.'

Fionn's stomach grumbled. 'I'm *starving*.'

Tara gestured to the bullwhip. 'For *this*, you can have two helpings. And garlic bread.'

'I'll be right behind you.' Fionn lingered a moment in the garden. Overhead, the moon was hidden behind a thicket of grey clouds, the stars snuffed out by Morrigan's creeping smoke. He thought of Shelby holed up inside the Black Mountain, her soul screaming alongside thousands of others. It was almost too much to bear.

Without thinking, he closed his eyes and raised his staff. In one sweeping arc, he painted a moonbow all the way across the night sky. The colours shimmered atop the smoke, bright and bold for all to see. The clouds parted, and the moon came to rest on its arc like a pearl.

'I hope you see this and remember us.'

Fionn sent his wish up with a fresh gust of wind.

'We're coming for you, Shelby … I promise.'

Chapter Seventeen

THE RETURNING R✹SES

After dinner, when Fionn's family were getting ready for bed, he returned to the garden in his pyjamas and winter coat. With only the moonbow watching over him, and an owl *hoo-hoo*ing from a faraway tree, he stood in the middle of the empty garden and tipped his head back to the sky.

'Right,' he muttered. 'Power-storm.'

As Fionn recalled, Dagda's storm from *Fadó Fadó* had puffed effortlessly from his staff, making a canopy of clouds that hung low in the sky. He decided to try making one small cloud first, so he closed his eyes and pictured it in his mind's eye.

It took more concentration than Fionn was used to,

more sweat and heat and steadied breaths, but soon he could feel a strange stirring inside him. It was slower than wind and softer than lightning, but he could feel the beginnings of a storm taking root. He cracked an eye open, to find a wisp of cloud uncurling from his staff. It smelled citrusy – like lemons and grapefruit – and it had come from the very centre of his soul. He cast it off. It swelled as it floated up, up, up, before turning to a deep rumbling violet. The owl spread its tawny wings to follow it, and Fionn watched him go.

'*Cool*,' he whispered.

Right away, he set to work on another.

And then another.

And another.

Fionn practised his power-storm until his back ached and his eyelids drooped, until the owl got bored and flew away. He cast hundreds of clouds over the little cottage on the headland, until they swallowed up the sky and turned everything purple.

When the night was at its darkest, and Fionn could barely stand from exhaustion, he lowered his staff and retreated indoors. The power-storm lingered over the little cottage on the headland as he collapsed into bed, too tired to brush his teeth or even take his shoes off. Sleep washed over him, deep and dark and endless.

In the quiet of Fionn's mind, Morrigan was waiting for him.

Sleep while you can, little sorcerer.

Her face appeared in the darkness, too pale and too close.

Soon we will go to war, and your pathetic island will cower at my feet.

She was still skulking in her mountain, where figures flitted about in the shadows. Fionn could see the rock glistening with water droplets, and the faraway glimmer of Bredon's ruby eye.

CLACK!

CLACK!

CLACK!

Morrigan turned sharply. Her grip on Fionn's mind loosened, and the vision began to slip away. But in those split seconds between awareness and sleep, Fionn glimpsed a girl kneeling in the dark. She was wearing a single sparkly shoe, and was smashing a white conch shell against a spire of rock.

CLACK!

CLACK!

CLACK!

Morrigan shrieked as she swooped on Shelby. Her cape flew out behind her, and then everything went black.

Fionn snapped his eyes open. He blinked twice, then sat bolt upright in bed. If he hadn't seen it with his own eyes, he might not have believed it. Shelby was trying to destroy the shell. She was trying to break the bond between herself and the Merrows. And that meant there was hope, still.

For her, and for all of them.

Outside, dawn's golden fingers were already spreading across the sky. There were birds chirping on the roof, and a strange new warmth lingering in the air. Someone was awake inside the cottage; he could hear the pitter-patter of busy footsteps in the sitting room. Then the hallway. They stopped outside his bedroom door.

It burst open. 'FIONN!' Tara stood in the doorway in a bright green hoodie and tracksuit bottoms. Her hair was freshly washed and her cheeks were pink. 'COME OUTSIDE! QUICK!'

Fionn rubbed his eyes. 'What? Why?'

'Just come on!' She cracked the McCauley whip along the floorboards, denting a line in the wood.

'If you do that again I'm confiscating it!' snapped Fionn.

Tara was already skipping down the hallway.

Fionn got out of bed, shrugged his dressing gown on, and followed her. Tara had left the front door swinging on its hinges. Fionn stalked through it, then froze instantly.

The garden at Tír na nÓg had been completely trans-formed. Where yesterday a single, tattered rose bush wilted in the dirt, now there were twenty bushes, each one bright and full and beautiful. The roses had flowered in every colour – white and red and violet and yellow and pink. They lined the walls and peeked through the gate. They kissed the drainpipes and crept up old trellises. One had even made it to the chimney.

A robin watching from the window sill cheeped in delight, and from the dawning sky, more birds came down to gaze upon the garden in full bloom. Fionn leaned in to smell the roses. An unmistakeable tang tickled his nose.

'Magic.' He tipped his head back. The power-storm over Tír na nÓg was gone. The rain had fallen overnight, and it had left behind the most precious gift. 'It *worked*.'

'Was it you?' said Tara, twirling on the heel of her shoe. 'Did you really do all of this?'

Fionn could hardly believe it himself. 'Impressed?'

Tara chewed the edge of her smile. Then she threw her head back and shouted 'MAAAAAAAAAAM' at the top of her lungs.

Fionn winced.

There was a distant drumbeat of footsteps, and then their mum bounded out of the house in her pyjamas.

'What is it? What's –' She stopped in the middle of the garden, her eyes filling with tears. 'Oh, my goodness.'

Tara pointed at Fionn. 'He did it with his magic.'

Fionn's mother rubbed the sleep from her eyes. 'Oh, Fionn. It's like something out of a *fairytale*.' She slipped a petal between her finger, to check if it was real. 'If only your grandmother was here to see it.'

'Maybe she is.' Tara was standing by a fresh patch of purple flowers that had sprouted by the gate.

Forget-me-nots.

Fionn grinned. The world might have been gloomy and grey, but here was a patch of new brightness tucked away just for them.

And Fionn, the sorcerer, had made it.

A new dawn had arrived and hope on Arranmore was not yet lost.

Chapter Eighteen

THE UNWELCOME AUDIENCE

When Fionn and his family made their way down to the strand that morning, the beach was teeming with islanders. Many of them had come dressed in their Sunday finest, and, on their Clan Leaders' orders, were armed with a whole host of makeshift weapons, ranging from kitchen brooms and pitchforks to curtain poles and hurling sticks. Juliana's mum had even brought a crucifix. The islanders passed their objects back and forth, appraising each one, like they were on the *Antiques Roadshow*.

Sam jogged to meet them, the Patton axe making him lumber a little to one side. He was wearing a brown trench coat, patent leather shoes, and a burgundy scarf, and looked more like he was about to attend a fashion show than fight a battle. 'Pattons are all ready and assembled,' he announced proudly. 'Though I'll admit they took a bit of wrangling.'

'I'd better get the McCauleys sorted,' said Tara, pulling their mum away. 'Good luck, Fionny!'

Some islanders fell out of their conversations when they noticed Fionn's arrival. Word had spread of his visit to the Whispering Tree and the meaning of the staff in his hands. They watched it now with a mixture of curiosity and apprehension.

Elizabeth Beasley, meanwhile, was fuming. Fionn could tell by the way she charged towards him, hatred burning in her beady eyes. She was tucked up to her chin in her plush fur coat, and was wearing a peculiar headpiece that looked not unlike a desk-lamp.

'Fascinator,' said Sam.

'Fascinating indeed,' muttered Fionn.

'I don't know how you managed to rip that staff out of the Whispering Tree, but once again the island has made a mistake that will cost us all,' she said, by way of greeting. 'You should have left it where it was.'

'Good morning to you too, Betty,' said Fionn blandly. 'Do you think you could go and join your Clan Leader? We've got a lot to do.'

Elizabeth's face soured.

'He's just there,' said Sam, pointing unnecessarily at Bartley, who was standing less than three metres away and looking deeply uncomfortable. 'He's the one with the really short hair.'

Elizabeth turned on him. 'And where were *you* yesterday when my granddaughter was kidnapped? I suppose I shouldn't be surprised you deserted her too. Your cowardly lot never stick their necks out for anyone.' She gestured to the axe in his hand. 'You should give that to someone who deserves it.'

Sam flushed.

'He *does* deserve it,' said Fionn sharply. 'And we already have our enemy, Betty. She's living in that big black mountain in the sea. If you're just here to bicker, you might as well go home.' He pulled Sam away. 'Come on.'

It was at that moment that Rose arrived. She wasn't wearing her shawl any more, and her new appearance attracted a lot of attention. Everyone knew her true identity by now, but this was the first time the islanders were able to look upon Róisín, First and Fearless, in the flesh.

And *everyone* was staring at her.

'Ready?' She flashed her teeth at Fionn.

'I hope so,' he said, as he clambered up on to the beach wall. 'Uh, hello? Can you all hear me?'

A smattering of people looked up from their conversations.

Fionn raised Solas, and shot a bolt of silver lightning into the sky.

Crrrrack!

The islanders stood to attention.

Sam laughed.

'Sorry,' said Fionn, without a hint of remorse. 'But we're short on time.'

Even though he had practised for hours last night, Fionn found himself feeling nervous now. The islanders' expectations weighed heavy on his shoulders. Every time his gaze landed on a Beasley, he thought of Shelby, alone in that awful mountain, clutching dearly to the last shred of her humanity.

'Right then,' said Fionn, before his confidence could sputter out completely. 'Here's how we're going to kill Morrigan.'

With little ceremony, Fionn launched into everything Rose had said about the cape of souls. The islanders listened in nervous silence as he detailed a plan to destroy it that would involve every single person standing before him. And, possibly, a great deal of luck.

'And *how* exactly are we supposed to accomplish any of this without getting ourselves killed?' demanded Elizabeth, once Fionn had finished.

'With magic,' he said simply. Then he raised his staff to the sky.

The first cloud unfurled in a perfect grey plume. It broke off in a flourish, and floated down the beach on a rogue gust of wind. It was then that Fionn noticed the Merrows. Down by the shore, the sea was full of glowing yellow eyes. They were creeping through the waves, some even crawling through the shallows on their bellies to get a closer look.

Uneasy murmurs rippled through the crowds. Where once the Tide Warriors' presence had brought comfort to the people of Arranmore, now they brought fear.

Fionn glanced at Rose. 'We have an audience.'

She had already clocked them. 'Nosy cretins,' she said, taking off in a hurry. 'Leave them to me.'

She brandished her spear as she stalked towards the sea. The islanders parted to let her through. The Atlantic wind made streamers of her dark hair as she rooted herself on the shoreline, spinning her spear into a blur of silver.

Lír peeled backwards to welcome her. 'First and Fearless,' she crooned in her eerie oceanic lilt. 'The warrior returns.'

Though Rose's back was to the beach now, Fionn could hear the smile in her voice. 'She never left, Lír.'

With that, she raised her weapon to the lone storm cloud. Fionn's magic rushed down to meet the tip of the spear, and Rose lit up like a flare.

The islanders gasped. She angled the spear at the water, and with a flick of her wrist reversed the flow of the ocean. The waves backflipped, drowning the Merrows in an explosion of froth. Lír shrieked as she clawed her way back to shore, but Rose worked the spear like a conductor in an orchestra, rolling the ocean back on itself until the spying Merrows and their raging queen had been completely washed out to sea.

The last wisp of cloud dissolved as the islanders sent up a rousing cheer. Rose threw her head back and laughed; it was the sound of a caged bird that had finally been set free. And suddenly, without meaning to, Fionn was laughing too. After just one night's practice, he had managed to make a Storm Keeper. Not bad.

If everything went to plan, there would soon be hundreds more.

Chapter Nineteen

THE SHATTERED STORM

Rose stowed her spear and casually strolled back to the top of the beach, as though she hadn't just half-drowned a seaful of Merrows.

'You made that look easy,' said Fionn.

'It *is* easy,' said Rose.

'I can't *wait* to have a go,' said Tara enviously. 'Hurry up, Fionny. Make some more clouds!'

Fionn piped a new wisp into the sky. This one came even easier than the first. Rose's display had given him confidence, and with it, his power. It flowed from him like a sigh, each cloud unwinding from the staff in a perfect plume of grey. 'It's *working.*'

The islanders fell silent as they watched the storm

weave itself together. Soon thunder came snarling through the clouds, the grey turning to violet, the violet beginning to crackle. The smell of the air turned zingy and sharp.

Fionn's knees began to tremble. He felt the stretch of his power, like a rubber band going taut. 'How am I doing?' he asked, half breathless.

'Good,' said Rose, in a tone that implied he could do better. Bigger.

'We should test it,' said Fionn.

A hundred hands shot up.

'I think this privilege is mine!' came the sudden, high-pitched squall of Elizabeth Beasley. She barrelled through the crowd, swiping Tom Rowan's pitchfork as she passed, and without so much as a 'thank you' went charging towards the sea.

Elizabeth raised the pitchfork, and a wisp of cloud rushed down to meet it. It began to sparkle, turning the ruddy old farm tool to a mighty glittering trident.

A giddy laugh sprang from her. 'LOOK! I'M DOING IT!'

She was glowing like the North Star. Fionn knew the effect was from his magic, but there was glee there too – the spark of a destiny that had once slipped through her fingers now returned to her at the eleventh hour. She pointed the trident at the sea. Seafoam leapt from the water and danced around her. The wind pulled her hair across her face, the fascinator flying off her head and taking flight like a crow. 'I'M FINALLY A STORM KEEPER!'

Without waiting for instruction, Douglas Beasley sprinted into the sea to join his mother. He lit up in a blaze of glory, the stick in his hand twisting itself into a steel-tipped spear. He scooped up the sea without even touching it, and bellowed with delight as the water spun around him too.

'DOUG! GRAN!' yelled Bartley as he hurried across the beach after them. 'WAIT FOR THE REST OF US!'

Sam tutted under his breath. 'Bartley really needs to get his clan under control. I mean, can you believe they just –'

'Let's go, loser!' hollered Una, who was, at that moment, hauling a piece of driftwood across the sand. 'Last one down is a rotten egg!'

'Una!' shouted Sam. 'You're supposed to wait until Fionn –'

'I'm not letting the Beasleys have all the fun!' She hoisted the driftwood into the air, swinging wildly to keep it airborne. A wisp of cloud coiled around it, catching it before it fell on top of her. The wood shrank, its edges smoothed and whittled until it was a spear every bit as impressive as Rose's. Una pointed it at the sea, and the water leapt up in a torrent of froth. She whooped with delight, and a slew of younger Pattons raced down to join her.

Sam hopped from foot to foot. 'I'd better go down there and make sure everything's all right.'

'Go on, Sam,' said Fionn, grinning through the swell of another cloud. 'Embrace your inner Storm Keeper.'

'Thanks, mate!' Sam was already sprinting down to the shore. As he ran, he raised the axe above his head, and watched it turn a bright, brilliant silver. He tossed it in a circle and caught it easily with a *whoop!* The rest of the Pattons followed him in a rush of giddy excitement, waving their weapons above their heads.

Fionn lurched, as wisp after wisp broke away from the power-storm. All around him, islanders were reaching up to the sky and becoming Storm Keepers. It was a remarkable sight, but an uncomfortable feeling. He gritted his teeth, trying to weather the strange pulling sensation in his chest. It felt as though he was being unravelled in a hundred different directions, his magic fighting tirelessly to keep up with the demand.

'The better the sorcerer, the bigger the power-storm.' Rose was still beside him, her hand braced on the wall, like she was waiting to catch him. 'Hold your nerve, Fionn.'

A bead of sweat slipped down Fionn's forehead. 'I'm trying.'

He *would* be a good sorcerer. He *had* to be a good sorcerer.

Most of the islanders set their new-found magic to work on the ocean. One by one, whirlpools sprang up along the shoreline, seafoam leaping from one, only to wind itself into another. The longer they worked, the steadier their water-spouts became, the higher they climbed towards the sky.

Tara, meanwhile, had other ideas. She led the McCauley Clan across the middle of the beach, cracking the bullwhip with the expertise of a lion tamer. The sand responded in kind, whipping up in great grainy fistfuls. They hovered in the air like miniature golden planets. The McCauleys used the wind to toss them back and forth, whooping with excitement every time one exploded.

'They're fast learners,' said Rose approvingly. 'See how quickly they adapt.'

'Mmm.' Fionn winced as another swell rippled through him. It was beginning to feel like someone was scooping his insides out.

'HEY! WATCH THIS!' yelled Juliana, who had spotted the McCauleys' sand boulders and seemed determined to outdo them. She brought her sword down sharply, as if to stab the air, and out to sea, beyond the jutting pier, a cluster of rocks exploded.

The new islanders erupted in delight.

'How did you do that?' said her little sister, Mia.

Juliana tossed her hair. 'I just concentrated on those rocks and the magic did the rest,' she said primly.

Tara snorted. 'Yeah, well, look at *this* for concentration.'

The McCauley Clan had hoisted fifty giant sand boulders into the sky, and were now orbiting them slowly around the beach.

'Very creative,' muttered Rose.

Tara reached up to the clouds to add another.

Fionn wobbled on his feet. '*Nnngh*.'

The power-storm flickered.

'Hold your nerve,' said Rose, watching him from the corner of her eye. 'To brew the storm is one thing, but you have to *sustain* it.'

Fionn was too breathless to respond. His knees were shaking and his arms were like jelly. He forced himself to straighten his spine, pushing his magic up and out.

Up and out.

Up and out.

For Shelby.

A band of ambitious Pattons, prompted by Sam, were using the wind to stack the rocks out to sea. Boulders soon became legs, then torsos and arms to match, until they looked like two cumbersome giants splashing through the tide. The triumph of it only set the Beasleys to work harder. They honed their whirlpools, sending them skittering towards the rocky giants.

Fionn's eyes were streaming. 'I d-d-don't th-th-think I c-c-can ...' He trailed off as he stumbled to his knees.

Rose's hand shot out to steady him. 'Focus.'

'I'm. Trying.' As Fionn's magic weakened, so did his control. He kept thinking of Shelby, trapped in the Black Mountain. His grandfather, wandering alone under the Northern Lights. His father drowning in a thrashing sea.

How did you steal that old magic in your bones? whispered Morrigan's voice in his head. *I know you did not earn it. I know you do not deserve it.*

'Fionn.' The power-storm was flickering again. Rose moved in front of him, her green eyes flashing. 'What are you doing?'

Fionn was thinking of Dagda now, standing on this same beach long ago. He remembered how easily he had suspended the storm above the island and still managed to fight at the same time.

So why, then, was it so hard for Fionn to stand up?

Because you're no leader, boy. You don't have what it takes.

Now the Beasleys were crushing their whirlpools together. The ocean was climbing towards the sky, the horizon replaced by the tallest wave Fionn had ever seen. Whips of seaweed writhed like snakes inside it.

'Beautiful!' cried Elizabeth Beasley. 'It looks like a painting.'

'Oi! Careful with that thing!' yelled Niall. 'You'll drown us!'

'When the Pattons drop their creepy rock giants, we'll lower our wave!' said Bartley.

'Stop messing with the wind!' cried Juliana. 'Those sand boulders need to come down before someone gets hurt!'

'Higher!' Elizabeth shouted over her. 'Let's make a wave to drown Morrigan herself!'

'No …' The word died on Fionn's lips. He was gasping now, the magic inside him stretching and stretching and *stretching*. Just as another sliver of cloud broke off and rushed down to meet the point of Elizabeth's trident, Fionn's power *snapped*.

He let out a keening cry.

Then several things happened at exactly the same time.

The rock-creatures exploded into smithereens.

The wind dropped, bringing the sand down like golden fireworks.

And the Beasleys lost control of their wave.

The wave became a tsunami, with nowhere to go and

nothing to stop it. The water roared as it leapt over the shoreline. The islanders were swept away in its stampede, screaming at the top of their lungs.

With the tidal wave bearing down on him, Fionn fell face first into the sand and passed out.

Chapter Twenty

THE RUNAWAY SORCERER

Fionn was flipped upside down and downside up, spiralling into rock and sand and seaweed. Froth shot up his nose and stung his eyes. He forgot where he was. He forgot *who* he was. There were only the distant screams of drowning islanders, fading … fading.

Then there was laughter, cackling from the far reaches of his mind.

Failure, taunted a familiar voice. *You drowned your people like you drowned your own father. You cannot wield magic you don't deserve.*

Fionn let the words flow through him, swift and icy as a river. He didn't have the strength to bat them away.

Give up your war, little Boyle.

Come to the Black Mountain,

Come to me before I come for you.

The blackness shifted. The world was crowding in on Fionn again. He was rolled on to his side. A stream of water spurted out of him. He coughed himself awake, blinking through salt-laden lashes to find himself curled up in a mass of sopping seaweed.

Tara was kneeling beside him. Her hair was drenched and her teeth were chattering. 'W-what j-just h-happened?'

'The power-storm broke,' croaked Fionn. 'I lost control.'

He sat up. All across the beach, islanders were on their knees, coughing and spluttering. Rose was vomiting seawater nearby. Others were completely unconscious.

One was marching towards him, with fire in her eyes.

'What in Dagda's name are you playing at?' demanded Elizabeth Beasley. Her silver hair was plastered across her face, her fur coat draped over her like a dead animal. 'Are you trying to get us killed?' She pointed her ruddy pitchfork at the emerald staff, wedged in the sand. 'If you had any sense at all, you'd give that to someone who can actually use it.'

'That's not how it works,' said Tara, turning on her. 'Try it.'

Elizabeth threw her a withering look. 'I think we've seen enough magic today.'

Islanders were beginning to stagger to their feet. Fionn spied his mother across the beach helping Niall. She had a nasty cut on her forehead, and she was swaying from side to side. Mia was crying. Bartley was looking around frantically for his shield. Sam and Una were trying to rouse their dad, and Juliana was using her sword to cut Donal free from a tangle of washed-up fishing tackle.

'We don't stand a chance,' said Elizabeth, echoing his thoughts. 'You're no sorcerer.'

Fionn dropped his head. He still couldn't control his magic. Even with Solas, he wasn't enough.

He rolled to his feet, leaving the staff behind him.

'Where are you going?' Tara called after him, but Fionn was already sliding over the wall. The wind chased after him, howling like a wounded dog, but Fionn kept his eyes on his feet.

He needed a minute. He needed a *year*.

But more than anything, in that moment, he needed his grandad.

Chapter Twenty-One

BLOOD MOON

When Fionn got back to *Tír na nÓg*, he slammed the door and shut the wind out. Like a homing pigeon, he drifted towards his grandfather's bedroom. He paced the room, the floorboards creaking underneath him. He had nowhere to go. No one to confide in.

Only a memory.

'I'm lost, Grandad.' Fionn pressed his fists against his eyes to keep the tears from bursting free. 'I don't know what to do without you.'

The wind tapped at the window, but Fionn ignored it. He sank to the floor and laid his head against the end of his grandfather's duvet. The faint scent of sea-salt and adventure tickled his nose.

'I can't do this,' he sobbed. 'I'm not a leader, Grandad.' He hiccoughed. 'I'm just going to let everyone down.'

The birds flocked to the back garden. Fionn could hear them rustling in the bushes, walking on the roof slates, screeching down the drainpipe. The bedroom window was rattling awfully. Fionn stuck his head between his knees and tried to shut the world out.

But the world had other plans for him.

A stray breeze slipped under the door frame. It tickled his ankles, before flitting across the room and fluttering in the ends of the curtains. Then it curled like a finger around the last candle standing on his grandfather's special shelf.

Fionn raised his head just in time to see Blood Moon tumble to the ground. It rolled across the floorboards, coming to a stop by his baby toe. Fionn swallowed, waited. The window had stopped rattling. The birds had stopped squawking. The wind had snuffed itself out.

'Hello?' he asked the room, feeling a little scared.

The silence swelled.

Fionn plucked the candle from the floor. It sat plump as a tomato in the palm of his hand. It was curiously warm, but he couldn't tell whether it was the flare of his own magic, or the candle wax.

Perhaps it was both.

'You're the last one,' said Fionn quietly. The final piece of his grandfather – some unknowable, important memory that he had chosen to put aside for all these years. 'I was saving you.'

For what? said a tiny voice inside his head.

It occurred to Fionn that the end was already upon them. There was nothing left to wait for, no hope brewing beyond the horizon. He might not have tomorrow. He might not even have *tonight*. So he stuck his hand in his pocket and pulled out a lighter. With the island holding its breath somewhere beyond the windowpane, he brought the flame to the wick of Bl*ood Moon*.

It lit up in a *whoosh!*

Fionn gasped as the cottage tumbled down around him. First the walls, and then the rest, while the ceiling was whipped away by a sharp gust. He hurtled into a different layer, the wind roaring in his ears as it swept the rest of his world away.

'Hello?' Fionn looked around for his grandad, hope fluttering like a butterfly in his chest.

But the cottage had disappeared completely. Fionn drifted across the headland. The years were still racing by, the island slowly stretching its rocky limbs out into the ocean, as if caught mid-yawn.

And then, at last, the earth settled.

The headland was plush and green now, dappled with wild flowers and towering oak trees that climbed towards a tangerine sky. There were no pathways worn into the headland, no fields bricked off by uneven stone walls, not even a single sheep wandering about. There seemed to be no life here at all, save for the birds chirping in the trees.

The wind grew insistent, pushing and prodding Fionn across the headland. He trod a winding pathway by the coast, the ground gently sloping beneath him. Soon the grass grew worn and muddy, ancient footprints visible in the old pathways that led down towards the sea. Evening fell quickly, and the air grew thick with the scent of sulphur. Fionn knew that awful smell. It stuck to the insides of his nostrils and filled him with a slow-curling dread.

Then came a familiar sickening sound: the sky was shrieking. Fionn had left Morrigan's ravens behind, only to find them in another layer. He eyed the candle with mounting distrust. It wasn't the colour of any moon he'd ever seen. It was the colour of crimson skies; of ancient war and dreadful bloodshed.

By the time Fionn came upon the beach, the battle between Morrigan and Dagda was already over. He hadn't arrived at the beginning; he had arrived at the end.

Chapter Twenty-Two

THE ENCHANTED INFERN⊕

Fionn stalled at the top of the beach, fear like a fist in his throat. The shore was littered with fallen bodies. Groaning Soulstalkers lay face down in the sand, while ancient clansmen curled around spears and long-swords. Out to sea, Morrigan's fleet had been overturned, the black-sailed boats lying on their sides like beached whales.

It was a graveyard.

Amidst the falling darkness, the candle glowed redder in Fionn's fist. He thought about blowing it out and hurtling back home, but he knew the island wanted him to see this. The candle was on his grandfather's special shelf for a reason. He had saved it for all of these years, and if Fionn didn't find out why now, then he never would.

The wind tugged him by the coat-sleeves. Fionn stepped on to the beach, and gingerly made his way across the sand. He arced around a cluster of Soulstalkers missing clumps of hair and fistfuls of teeth. Most were unconscious, although one craned her neck all the way around to watch him go.

Fionn quickened his pace. 'Whatever you want to show me, please hurry up.'

The wind guided him all the way down to the shoreline. He tried not to linger over the shield of Orla Beasley when he passed it in the froth, averting his eyes from the warrior that still clung to it.

The ravens were gathering on the far side of the beach. Fionn recognised the little cove. He had been here long ago in a different candle. He knew what – or rather, *who* – was inside it.

Blood Moon was leading him to Dagda.

Fionn broke into a run. He vaulted through the surf with such speed he nearly tripped over a half-conscious warrior. Róisín, First and Fearless, groaned as she raised her head. Her eyes were bloodshot, and her lip was bleeding. She crawled through the lapping waves towards him, but when she tried to speak, she coughed up a stream of seawater. That's when Fionn noticed the spear sticking out of her side. Blood was bubbling around the fresh wound, turning the water pink.

'Rose!' He rushed to help her.

She batted him away. 'Go!' she hissed, seawater gushing through her teeth. 'Help him!'

The ravens had made a tornado of themselves at the end of the beach, and hundreds more were shrieking as they swooped down from the sky. Through a break in their feathers, Fionn spied Dagda lying alone on the sand.

'Hurry!' cried Rose.

Fionn left her, trusting in the wind as it thundered alongside him. He could feel the urgency of the memory as it closed in on him. The moon was rising. Candle wax was running through his fingers, blood-red and molten hot.

The sorcerer was lying unmoving on the sand. His silver hair spilled out around him, his skin ghostly pale in the moonlight. He looked peaceful. Fionn knew this part from Rose's story – Dagda was in a deep sleep. The battle was over, and the last of his magic had been spent. Morrigan's ravens surrounded him. They had carried their sleeping queen to safety and now they were back, pecking at Dagda's tunic, dragging him, inch by inch, towards the water.

'Oi! Get away from him!' Fionn sprinted towards them, using the candle flame to ward them off. It was hopeless. The birds swarmed him. 'Ow! Get off! Get off me!'

Fionn fought his way through to Dagda. He almost

tripped over Solas, half wedged in the sand. The ravens spotted the staff at the same time, but he dived on it like a rugby player, curving his body over the emerald as the birds jabbed at his spine and shrieked in his ear.

With *Blood Moon* in one fist and the staff in the other, Fionn inched his way along the sand on his elbows. He felt like a soldier on a recon mission, the enemy swooping down on him from every angle. When Fionn reached Dagda, he leaned over his body to protect his heart. Then he brandished the staff behind him and started swinging wildly, to keep the ravens away.

He knew what was supposed to happen next.

Aonbharr was so loyal and fearless, he leapt through a thousand of those wretched birds to rescue his master.

'Come on, Aonbharr,' muttered Fionn. He glanced anxiously at the candle. He had only minutes left. Then the sleeping sorcerer would be on his own again. 'Where the hell are you?'

He scanned the whirling feathers, searching for a break in the fray. It came in brief glimpses.

Darkness.

The sand shimmering in the moonlight.

Darkness.

The tide lapping at the shore.

Darkness.

A couple of Soulstalkers, dragging their broken bodies across the beach.

Darkness.

More Soulstalkers stumbling, searching. They were coming this way.

'AONBHARR!' yelled Fionn. 'AONBHARR! WHERE ARE YOU?'

Then he saw it – a flash of white moving in the distance. The horse was galloping towards them. His hooves sent froth spiralling through the air, the thunder of his gallop like a heartbeat in the sand. He had no wings in this layer and yet he seemed somehow just as enchanting. His mane glowed silver in the moonlight, and as he tossed his mighty head, his whinny reached Fionn on the wind.

The candle flame grew higher. The ravens closed ranks. Aonbharr disappeared from view.

'Get out of the way, you little creeps!' Fionn leapt to his feet and brandished Dagda's wooden staff. The candle licked his thumb, and he felt his magic flaring inside him.

'I SAID MOVE!' A bolt of crimson lightning leapt from the staff and went spiralling into the wall of ravens.

They erupted in a mighty inferno. The birds shrieked as the magic devoured them whole, their feathers exploding in plumes of fire and smoke. Fionn dropped the staff and dragged Dagda's body away from the flames. 'Oh no, oh no, oh no.' They were surrounded by a wall of fire.

Through a curtain of smoke, Fionn saw Aonbharr still thundering towards them. The wind came with him, casting fistfuls of sand in its wake. 'Stop!' Fionn tried to shout, but the horse didn't hear him over the roaring inferno. The sky had turned red and the air was zingy now, the taste of citrus suddenly heavy on Fionn's tongue. He couldn't uncast the spell, or return the flames to the staff. He could only watch in horror as Aonbharr tossed his head one final time, then leapt straight into the fire.

The island inhaled.

The moment stretched, fate and magic flickering in the flames between Fionn and Aonbharr. Then the horse sailed through the inferno with a determined whinny before landing with a rattling thud on the other side. Right in front of Fionn.

There was an almighty explosion, magic shooting out in every direction, like fireworks. Fionn was flung backwards, screaming. He skidded through the surf, froth shooting up his nose, as he struggled to keep the last of the candle aloft. There was only a puddle of it left now, but the flame was still fighting.

When Fionn sat up, the fire on the beach was gone. So, too, were the ravens. The air was clear of smoke and the wind was blowing the ash away.

The moon was a deep, crimson red.

Before him stood a majestic white horse, with great, shimmering wings. He blinked at Fionn.

Somehow, the sky turned red with the last of Dagda's magic, and beneath it, the horse sprouted wings and carried him away to his final resting place.

Fionn staggered to his feet. 'So that's how it happened.'

It was me.

Aonbharr huffed as he knelt down beside Dagda. Fionn rushed to help him, straining as he dragged the sleeping sorcerer on to the horse's back. He laid his free hand against Dagda's chest then, relieved to feel the steady thud of his heartbeat.

When Aonbharr stood up again, he was almost twice the height of Fionn. He fanned his mighty wings, preparing for flight.

'Wait!' Fionn grabbed the emerald staff from the sand and slipped it underneath Dagda's arm. 'This has to go too,' he told Aonbharr. 'So it can make the Tree.'

Aonbharr neighed softly, then dipped his head. Fionn could see the shadow of his reflection in the horse's brown eye. He raised his hand – gently, so as not to startle him. The horse pressed his muzzle against his palm, his warm breath snuffling through Fionn's fingers, as the candle flame in his other went out.

'See you again, Aonbharr.'

When Fionn took his hand away, the horse was gone. Somewhere in a different layer, Aonbharr was gliding under a blood moon, ferrying their sorcerer to safety. Fionn closed his eyes and tried to imagine it, as the wind wrapped its arms around him and brought him home.

Chapter Twenty-Three

THE FERRY ON
THE HORIZON

The beach changed quickly around Fionn. The sand was stripped of groaning bodies, their weapons sifted and discarded. The island twirled like a spinning top, entire centuries streaking past like shooting stars. The Whispering Tree's words echoed in the wind.

The rise of the sorcerer is marked by blood-red skies,

A new dawn begins when the winged stallion flies.

Fionn studied the red wax along his fingers in disbelief. Aonbharr had been *his* creation all along. The flying horse was proof that his destiny had been entwined with Arranmore's from the very beginning. The island hadn't made a mistake in choosing him – there was no denying it now.

'It's really me,' he muttered. 'I'm exactly where I'm supposed to be.'

The dried splodges of wax were proof that he belonged here, just as much as anyone; that he had earned the power inside him *and* the staff that wielded it. Fionn rolled his shoulders back.

There was work to do.

The last layer of Arranmore came upon him in a sudden, fierce gust. The shore was still packed with damp islanders. They turned to watch him walk out of thin air.

'You're back!' said Juliana. 'How did you *do* that?'

'Magic,' said Mia. '*Obviously.*'

'Where did you run off to, Boyle?' Bartley was hugging the shield to his chest, like it was a stuffed animal. 'Tara's gone looking for you.'

Fionn cleared his throat. 'Sorry, everyone. I just … I just needed a minute.'

'Right after you drowned us,' said Elizabeth snidely. 'How convenient.'

'Actually, it was *your* clan who made that giant wave in the first place,' said Sam pointedly. He was sitting up on the beach wall with his family, his hair frizzy from seawater. 'You can't really blame Fionn for that.'

'Well, we wouldn't have made the wave, if you hadn't made those ridiculous rock giants,' said Douglas Beasley.

'We were making *art*,' said Sam's dad defensively.

Una rolled her eyes. 'Here we go again.'

With remarkable speed, the islanders descended into bickering. Fionn left them to it and went in search of Rose. He found her down by the shoreline, holding his emerald staff.

He held up his wax-stained hand. 'I'm back.'

'*Blood Moon*,' she said, knowingly. 'I was wondering when you'd burn that.'

'I saw you in the sea. You were wounded.' Fionn gestured at her spear, tucked in the crook of her arm. 'With that.'

Rose pressed her free hand against the phantom wound in her side. 'It almost killed me.'

Fionn remembered then what she had told him about her sister. 'Was it Bronagh who did it?'

Rose turned her face to the sea. 'What was left of her,' she said darkly.

Fionn swallowed. 'So *that* was the first time we ever met?'

'I never knew your name. There was a time when I thought it had been Malachy. And then your father. You were all so alike. But they never remembered ... and then you came along.' She smiled. 'And the pieces fell into place.'

'You never mentioned it.'

'It's best you discover these things for yourself. That's how the island likes it. And ... well, it wasn't my finest hour.' Rose looked away, ashamed. 'I should have gone to Dagda. I should have been the one to save him.'

'To be fair, you seemed a bit ... skewered.'

Rose glared at him.

'Uh, anyway, never mind that now,' said Fionn quickly. 'I was thinking ... If I can make a real, live flying horse, then I can definitely make a proper power-storm.'

Rose handed him his staff. 'My thoughts exactly.'

'I don't know what happened to me before. It got hard, and I got scared that I wasn't good enough,' he admitted. 'I was afraid I was going to let everyone down. And then –'

'HE'S NOT AT THE COTTAGE!' Fionn was interrupted by the arrival of Tara, who came barrelling down the strand in a panic. 'I'VE LOOKED EVERYWHERE. I THINK SOMETHING BAD MIGHT HAVE –'

She fell out of her sentence when she spotted Fionn.

He waggled his fingers. 'Hello.'

Her face changed, her expression flickering from fear to relief to anger. She swung herself over the wall and chased after him. 'You are in *so* much trouble when I catch you! I thought you'd been kidnapped!'

Fionn yelped as he ran from her. 'Stop. Chasing. Me. I'm. The. Bloody. Sorcerer!'

'You will be bloody in a minute!' said Tara as she drew level with him. She kicked his ankle, tripping him up and sending him flying face first on to the sand. Fionn rolled over and spat the grains from his mouth. 'H*ey!*'

Tara stood over him. 'Don't *ever* scare me like that again.'

Fionn groaned as he sat up. He was conscious that everyone was watching him now. Most of the islanders were trying not to laugh, except Sam, who was bent double with amusement. 'Was that really necessary, Tara?'

'Yes,' she said crisply. 'You don't run. We don't run. No matter what happens. That's the deal.'

'All right, all right. I get it.'

'Good.' She offered him her hand. 'Now get up and get to work.'

Over her shoulder, there came the resounding blare of a ferry horn. It was long and keening, like a dying cow.

Tara froze. 'Who is that?'

Fionn shot to his feet. 'Someone's coming.'

The islanders swarmed the shoreline in a panic. There was a ship gliding over the horizon. It had a thick green body, a white wheelhouse and a blinking orange masthead.

The people on board were squished shoulder to shoulder along the deck.

'Soulstalkers,' said Bartley, who was standing on the wall. 'They're coming this way.'

'Doesn't Morrigan have *enough* soldiers already?' Tara patted the pockets of her coat, where the last of their candles were tucked between the seams. 'We need a plan. Fast.'

'What do we do, Fionn?' asked Juliana.

The islanders turned to him, their faces fearful.

'We're not ready.'

'We can't face them.'

'We don't know what to do.'

Dread pooled in Fionn's stomach. They had minutes at best. There wasn't time for another power-storm.

'Get back!' he said, shooing them away from the waterline. 'Get up by the wall. Quick! I'll deal with this.'

The islanders retreated up the beach, where they crouched on the other side of the stone wall. Poised to watch. Poised to flee. Rose scattered those who lingered, shooing them with her spear, until the shoreline was completely clear, except for Fionn.

And five others.

Rose, with her spear.

Sam, with his axe.

Tara, with her bullwhip.

Juliana, with her sword.

Bartley, with his shield.

'What are you doing?' said Fionn urgently. 'I told you to get back.'

Sam dangled a purple candle in front of him. 'We're your Clan Leaders, mate. We're not leaving you. And anyway, we've got our own miniature power-storms right here.'

Juliana and Bartley were holding candles too.

'You have a better chance with back-up,' added Bartley. 'So just shut up and take it. I'm not losing to a bunch of latecomers before I can save my sister.'

Tara handed a bright yellow candle to Rose, before stalking back to take her place beside Fionn. 'We may as well use what we've got left,' she said, before squaring her shoulders to the sea. 'Now, drown them or something before they breach the shore and we all die in horrible, screaming agony.'

'Charming,' muttered Sam.

The ferry's horn blared again. It was sluicing through the water at alarming speed, accompanied by the whoops and hollers of those onboard. They were flailing their arms, as though they were waving.

Strange.

Fionn pointed his staff at the ocean. The water stirred under an invisible gust, then rolled back on itself.

Tara's hand came to his arm. 'Wait.'

Out to sea, the Merrows had surfaced and were swimming rings around the ferry boat. They darted faster and faster, their metallic tails glinting like jewels in the surf.

'What are they doing?' said Fionn.

'They're attacking them,' said Sam, pointing to a merrow, who was clawing up the starboard side of the boat.

Fionn stalled, with his magic in his fingertips. 'Why would Morrigan attack her own reinforcements?'

'Why indeed.' Rose waded into the sea to get a better look.

There was a sudden, ragged shout from over his shoulder. Fionn turned to find his mum tearing down the strand towards them. She was waving her phone, the screen blinking as she shouted. 'THEY'RE OURS, FIONN! THEY'RE FOR ARRANMORE!'

When she reached him, she pushed his arm down, directing the staff at the sand. 'Don't drown them,' she heaved. 'Bring them in. *Quick.*'

'Who are they?' said Fionn, alarmed.

'*Descendants.*' She flashed her phone, and Fionn saw his Uncle Enda's name on the screen, could hear the pitch of his panic squealing down the line. 'I didn't think they'd make it in time. Especially not *that* many.'

'Oh my God,' said Tara, turning back to the sea. 'They're going to be killed.'

The passengers were screaming now. They were holding on to the railings for dear life as the Merrows rocked the boat from side to side. Fionn pointed the staff at the ferry. The emerald winked, his vision tunnelling until there was nothing between them any more – not the sea or the sky or even his own lingering doubts. There was only an intention.

Bring them home.

The ocean lurched, the ferry boat rising on the swell of an unexpected wave. The Merrows hissed as they fell away from the hull. More leapt from the sea and flung themselves at it, nails screeching against the metal. The ferry boat dipped to one side. The passengers screamed again.

Fionn kept his concentration.

The wave was storming towards the island, gathering height and speed, faster than even the Merrows could swim. Fionn felt the pull of his magic like a thread between them. He tilted the staff back, like a fishing rod. The wave jumped higher, taking the boat with it, as though the ocean itself was hooked on the end of Fionn's fishing line.

A cheer went up behind him.

The boat thundered towards the beach on the crest of Fionn's magical wave. He could see the passengers' faces now, arms curled tight around the white railings. He could hear the islanders whooping at his back, the patter of their footsteps as they raced down to the shoreline.

'Take it down.' Rose was at his side, her voice urgent in his ear. 'Before the boat comes in on top of us.'

Fionn started. At close range, the wave was much higher than he had thought. It thundered past the pier.

He sent out a fresh burst of magic.

Break.

The wave hiccoughed, and the boat dropped. The passengers yelped as their stomachs bottomed out.

Fionn frowned.

It was still careening towards them.

It was at this precise moment he realised he hadn't done anything about the *speed* of the wave. 'Uh-oh.'

The islanders scattered in panic, the passengers on the boat flinging their arms over their heads to protect themselves from the oncoming crash.

'Fionn! Run!' Tara grabbed Fionn's wrist. 'It's going to flatten us!'

Fionn shook her off.

He pointed the staff at the wave, just as it curled over the shoreline.

Freeze.

There was a blinding flash of silver and the wave froze, a school of mackerel caught open-mouthed inside it. The ferry stopped less than a metre from his forehead. Fionn took several steps backwards, looking up at the railings, where a hundred frightened faces stared back at him.

He flashed an awkward smile. 'Bend your knees.'

With a swish of Solas, Fionn shattered the wave into a million pieces. Ice exploded across the beach, blanketing the sand like diamonds. The ferry dropped on to the shore with a shuddering thud.

There was a beat of silence, passengers flinching as they peeked through their fingers to see if it was over. Then a deafening cheer rose up. The passengers spilled out of the ferry in their droves, Cannons and Pattons, Boyles and McCauleys and Beasleys returning from the far reaches of the globe to join in Arranmore's last stand. It was a sight to behold – all these long-lost cousins, brothers and sisters and aunts and uncles, old friends and new, reuniting along the glittering sand.

Fionn stood apart from it all, catching his breath. 'I can't believe they all came.'

'Arranmore is built on more than sand and stone,' said Rose, who had remained at his side. 'It's a spirit. A community. The island is never lost to us, no matter how far we travel from it.'

Fionn's cheeks prickled. 'Sounds like a different kind of magic altogether.'

Rose smiled. 'Why do you think we fought so hard for it in the first place?'

The crowds parted, and Fionn's uncles appeared, grinning from ear to ear. It had been several years since Enda and Sean had visited his mother in Dublin, but they greeted him now with such warmth, it felt like only days had passed.

Enda scooped him into his arms and swung him around, until Fionn's legs flew out behind him. 'All hail the boy wonder! He's one of ours!'

'Easy, Enda, that's our sorcerer you're manhandling. Put him down before he pukes.' Sean muscled his brother out of the way, and drew Fionn into an embrace. 'That was pretty cool what you did with the sea just now. Morrigan must be shaking in her cape.'

'Could have done without the Merrows though,' added Enda. 'I'm definitely having nightmares tonight.'

'Hopefully we'll be having roast chicken too,' said Sean longingly. 'I smuggled a few bits over on the ferry.'

'You'll have to earn your dinner first, lads.' Fionn's mother joined their huddle, looking brighter than she had in months. 'We've got a lot more practice to get through.'

Fionn chuckled. 'Come on, then,' he said, stalking up the beach, staff in hand. 'Let's get on with it.'

By the time the sun had melted along the horizon, Fionn was feeling more confident than ever. Not just in his Storm Keepers, but in himself too. When the moon was high, and their bellies grumbling, the islanders headed home for a precious meal with their loved ones, and a final sleep before a fateful dawn.

It had been decided: tomorrow morning, they would attack the Black Mountain.

Chapter Twenty-Four

THE LAST SUPPER

Dinner that night was a boisterous affair, the smell of roast chicken and gravy wafting pleasantly through the kitchen. Sean and Enda held court over the kitchen table, trying to outdo each other, first with how many jacket potatoes they could eat and then with stories of their lives overseas.

While they shared the same dark eyes and rounded cheeks as Fionn's mother, their time away from Arranmore had changed them. Sean, the youngest, had neat, dark hair and a thick Chicago accent that got stronger with each glass of wine. Enda, the eldest, had a shock of tawny blond hair and a golden tan, courtesy of his home in California, where he had left his wife and twin boys behind. 'We thought the boys might be a bit young for battle at two.' He grinned around a sprig of broccoli. 'What do you reckon, Fionn?'

'I'm afraid the cut-off age is actually four,' said Fionn solemnly. 'We had to turn a lot of toddlers away.'

Enda harrumphed. 'Between you and me, they're not very sturdy. A real pair of jelly-legs.'

'And what about the ferry boat, then?' asked their mother. 'Where did you rustle up one of those at such short notice?' She gestured at the apple pie sitting on the counter. 'Not to mention all these delicious supplies.'

'Marian Beasley has a fleet of boats down in Cork. She was a fierce banshee when we were kids but she turned out all right,' said Sean. 'Very rich. She has nine Pomeranians.'

'Marian is Elizabeth's sister,' said Fionn's mother. 'I thought they were estranged.'

Sean shrugged. 'Seems war has a nice little way of bringing people back together.'

'I wonder why were they estranged?' fished Tara.

'Have you *met* Elizabeth Beasley?' said Fionn, which made everyone chuckle.

'I'm not sure how she'll fare against Morrigan tomorrow,' said his mother.

'Probably quite well, since she doesn't appear to have

a soul,' said Sean. 'Unless things have changed since we last met?'

'Nope,' they chorused, before collapsing into laughter.

Dinner was followed by warm apple pie with extra helpings of ice cream. When dessert turned to nightcaps of whiskey, Tara pulled Fionn away from the kitchen table. 'Come with me. I want to show you something.'

'What is it?' said Fionn, following his sister into their grandad's bedroom.

Tara shut the door behind them, then flattened her back against it. Her eyes were wide, and there was the hint of a scheme inside them. 'I have an idea.'

'Why does that make me nervous … ?' said Fionn.

'I was counting the last of the candles before dinner,' she went on. She slipped her hand into the pocket of her hoodie. 'Anyway, I found this one among them.' When she uncurled her fist, there was a thin blue candle sitting on her palm. It had no scent – nothing at all to distinguish it from the others. 'April 30th,' she said. 'That's what the label said.'

It took a couple of seconds to dawn on Fionn. 'That's Dad's birthday.'

Tara's smile turned conspiratorial. 'I know we need all the help we can get tomorrow, and that the candles are still precious, but I just figured that this one is –'

'Special,' breathed Fionn. Outside in the garden, a nightingale was singing. Fionn's cheeks were prickling. There was magic in the air, and it had brought a last-minute sprinkling of possibility with it. 'I wonder what's inside it?'

'Or *who*,' whispered Tara. 'Do you want to find out?'

'Right now? It's almost midnight.'

'When else but now, Fionny?'

Fionn smiled. 'Go on, then. One last adventure. You can burn it.'

He stuck his hand out, and his sister wrapped her fingers around it. He grabbed a lighter from the bedside table and brought the flame to the little blue candle. Tara jabbed the wick into it, and the flame alighted with a gentle *whoosh*.

The room began to change around them. The curtains were drawn back, the bed remade with a yellow duvet covered in sunflowers. Eight throw pillows sprouted up out of nowhere, and a crocheted blanket draped itself along a rocking chair by the window. The wardrobe swelled to bursting, and the teetering pile of books beside it tidied themselves away into shelves, stacked between a pin-box full of sparkly hairclips and a wooden jewellery box. On the nightstand, a photo-frame of Fionn's grandparents on their wedding day appeared next to a vase of fresh pink roses.

Fionn inhaled deeply, breathing in their scent – the smell of this perfectly preserved moment.

The setting sun cast its rays through the window. Fionn spied his grandfather's workbench in the garden, adorned with fresh wax pebbles and candle moulds, the old wood marred with rainbow splodges. There were shirts and sundresses blowing on the clothes-line, and a short, dark-haired woman with a basket under her arm was unpegging them one by one.

Fionn could hear her singing to herself. 'That's Gran!'

They tried to open the window but an insistent gust tugged them back. The bedroom door blew open behind them, the wind whistling in their ears as if to say, *Get a move on!* They were shoved out into the hallway, and prodded through to the sitting room, where the front door was already swinging on its hinges.

'I smell birthday cake,' said Tara, as they were ushered past the kitchen, where two battered cake tins squatted in the oven.

The headland welcomed them with a warm breeze. Everything felt familiar, and yet there was a sense of calmness here – the gentle magic of springtime in full bloom – that made it feel a million miles away from their own Arranmore.

When they passed Donal's shop, they caught a

glimpse of the younger shopkeeper with a thicket of bright red hair. There were teenagers swinging their legs over the beach wall, children chasing each other along the strand. The sea was full of fishing boats, and the waves were absent of Merrows. The blue ferry was filling up with passengers, the old wooden pier stretched out like a finger pointing west, towards the setting sun.

When they came upon the lifeboat station, the wind began to settle. The candle flame flared, bright as a golden arrow, and a familiar laugh rang out.

Fionn's heart lurched in his chest. 'Grandad.'

Just beyond the station, where the land sloped down towards the sea, a man and a boy stood side by side, looking out at an orange lifeboat. Fionn's grandfather was much younger now, sporting waterproof overalls, black wellingtons and a mop of tangled brown hair. His arm was slung around Cormac's shoulders, who looked just a few years older than Fionn.

'Stop laughing, Dad,' Cormac was protesting. 'I'm *serious*.'

'Hi, Serious, I'm Malachy,' said Fionn's grandfather. 'Nice to meet you.'

Cormac folded his arms. 'You told me there was a birthday present waiting for me down here.'

'The present is my unparalleled wisdom.'

Cormac groaned. 'I was hoping for something a bit cooler.'

'Is that right?' Fionn's grandfather drifted down to the water, beckoning at his son to follow. Fionn and Tara went along too, creeping to one side to get a better look at their dad.

'He's got your ears, Fionny,' said Tara. 'See how they stick out, like little handles?'

Fionn threw her a withering glance. 'You have the same ears.'

Malachy flexed his fingers. 'All right, birthday boy, let me see what I can rustle up for you.' With a simple flick of his wrist, he raised a wave as tall as a house. It leapt over the orange lifeboat showering every inch of it in seawater. Fionn swallowed his scream, while Tara hugged the candle close to her chest. 'Be careful with that thing, Grandad!'

'Be careful with that thing, Dad!' yelped Cormac, at the very same time.

Malachy crooked his finger and called the wave to shore, as though it was a dog being brought to heel. It thundered towards them. 'Is this cool enough for you, lad?' he said, laughing wildly.

'Dad! Don't!' Cormac crouched down and covered his head. 'Mum will kill me if I wreck my new jumper!'

Fionn and Tara screamed as the wave leapt out of the

sea and crested over them. At the very last moment, it froze mid-arc. Fionn glanced at Tara, and they burst into delighted laughter.

Malachy jerked his head suddenly and, for a heartbeat, Fionn swore he looked right at them. Then his eyes glazed over, and he smiled. 'Do you hear that, lad? I think the wind is laughing.'

Cormac peeked through his fingers to find the ocean suspended above him. He stood up slowly, and frowned. 'You really have to stop doing that.'

'Says who?' Malachy twirled his hand and gently folded the wave back into the water. The sea rippled as it swelled, the last of the sun's rays melting away inside it.

'I never saw Grandad use his magic when he was alive,' said Tara quietly. 'He was good.'

'He was *great*,' said Fionn.

'*You* could be great, lad,' said Malachy, and for a heartbeat, Fionn thought he was talking to him. But Tara was holding the candle, which meant they were both invisible, and Malachy's hand was on Cormac's shoulder, not his. He wasn't laughing any more; he was being serious. And something about his tone made Fionn and Tara stand a little straighter, as though this version of their grandfather – full-haired and smooth-skinned and decades younger, belonged to them too.

'The day I turned sixteen, my father took me down to the lifeboats and opened this same door to me,' Malachy went on, inclining his head at the waves. 'The door to the sea – to all its peril and wonder. He invited me to join his crew. Of course, I said yes on the spot. Aside from marrying your mother, having *you*, and making that delicious shepherd's pie last week, it was the best decision I ever made.'

Cormac was silent now, contemplating.

'You could be a great lifeboatman, Cormac. You have a wonderful affinity with the sea. You would be a fearless sailor. Someone who could look any storm in the eye and meet it head on.'

'I'm not like you, Dad,' said Cormac uncertainly. Desire and fear warred across his face. It was hard for Fionn to believe this was the same person who would one day launch himself into a treacherous storm to rescue a son he had never known. 'I don't know if I have it in me.'

'Courage is not a state of being, lad,' said Malachy thoughtfully. 'Even the bravest people have moments of cowardice, and cowardly people have extraordinary moments of bravery. Storm Keepers, even ones as handsome and clever as me, are no different.'

Cormac chewed the inside of his cheek. 'Seems to me that the Storm Keepers of Arranmore were all perfect,' he said, a little ruefully. 'At least that's how the stories make it seem.'

'That's what stories are supposed to do,' said Malachy. 'They round the sharp edges off history. You'd never find anything about Marigold the Unpredictable's famous bursts of anger. Bridget Beasley accidentally set her mother's house on fire when she was seventeen, and everyone knows how reckless Hughie Rua could be. Stone mad half the time, but the island loved him for it. Patrick Cannon was famously broody, kept all the library's first editions locked away in his office for himself.' He pressed a hand to his chest. 'The *scandal* of it.'

Cormac snorted. 'That's not so bad. I don't let anyone near my comic book collection.'

'Yes, well, young Ferdia McCauley was only supposed to swim *with* dolphins, not surf them,' Malachy went on, undeterred. 'As wonderful as our Storm Keepers were, history would have us believe they were gods. But the truth is, Cormac …' He lowered his voice, his expression suddenly grave.

Cormac inhaled.

Fionn and Tara leaned in.

'I've hung my fair share of storm clouds over the Beasley house.' He tapped the side of his nose. 'Between you and me, Betty's had wetter winters than most.'

'Dad!' said Cormac, jostling him in the shoulder. 'That's so sneaky!'

Malachy chuckled as he turned back to the sea. Fionn watched a familiar shadow move in his grandfather's eyes. 'We're all human, Cormac. None of us really know what we're made of until the world decides to test us.'

Fionn felt very sorry for his dad then, knowing what the world would soon throw at him. Without meaning to, he drifted a little closer, until their shoulders were almost touching.

'Fionn, the candle's almost gone,' whispered Tara.

'Let it run out,' said Fionn, as he stood side by side with his father, both boys looking out at the Atlantic Ocean and wondering what it might have in store for them.

'All right, then,' announced Cormac, his face brightening a little. 'I'll join the lifeboat crew. I just wanted to make *sure*.'

Malachy turned to beam at him. 'That's my boy.' His smile faltered, and for the briefest moment, his gaze flickered over Fionn. Then Tara. He narrowed his eyes, as if to trace them in the breeze. But the candle flame was dying, and the wind was already repainting the world.

Malachy turned his face to the sky as he faded away. 'You know, lad, for all the magical things we know about this place, there's a million things we don't,' he said, his voice getting fainter and fainter. 'I think the real wonder of Arranmore lies in the unknown.'

Then the island exhaled, and they were gone.

Fionn and Tara stared at the space where they had been standing, both of them lost in their own thoughts.

'You know,' said Tara, after a while. 'That speech kind of felt like it was meant for us too.'

'Yeah,' said Fionn, quietly. 'It did.'

They turned for home, and although the island was solid beneath their feet and the memory had long splintered into the wind, they held hands, tightly, all the way up the headland and into the rose garden at Tír na nÓg.

They tiptoed through the sitting room, where their uncles were now soundly sleeping. Their snores followed them down the little hallway where they whispered good-night outside their grandfather's bedroom.

Fionn was just drifting off to sleep when he heard a familiar voice.

Sweet dreams, Fionn. See you in the morning.

Fionn smiled. In the haze of his exhaustion, he thought it was his mother whispering through the door, but as the darkness enfolded him, he realised the voice was too sweet, like poison laced with syrup.

Long before his alarm went off, Fionn woke to a blood-red dawn and a shrieking sky.

Chapter Twenty-Five

THE SORCERER'S SPEECH

Fionn Boyle stood in the shadow of the lighthouse, and took a long, steadying breath. Above him, the sky was full of ravens, swooping and shrieking between plumes of smoke. Below him, where the jagged cliffs sluiced a restless sea, the Merrows were circling the Black Mountain. Hissing, waiting.

And before Fionn, assembled along the rolling plains of Arranmore, with chins raised and weapons readied, stood the islanders.

His army.

Gift fire, earth, wind and water
To every island son and daughter,
Those who fight for Arranmore

Will find their power on its shore.

Fionn spied the top of Sam's curly hair bobbing through the masses as he jostled his way to the front. Tara, whose coat for the first time in weeks was not swollen with candles, hovered nearby with their mother, the McCauley bullwhip curled around her forearm. Beside her, Bartley shouldered his shield, while Juliana stood with the new descendants, sword in hand.

Sam waved at Fionn with the Patton axe, and Fionn noticed the silver glint of his flute sticking out of his waistband. 'Just in case we need a victory song.' Sam winked as he patted it. 'Go on, then. Give us the big speech.'

Fionn glared at his friend. 'I'm not doing a speech.'

'Oh, is Fionn doing a battle speech?' said Una. 'Wait. Let me film it.'

'Please don't,' said Fionn.

'How indulgent,' muttered Elizabeth.

'I've come a long way to be here, so let the boy say his piece, Betty,' snapped an old woman. She looked uncannily like Elizabeth, only her silver hair was short and curly and her eyes were milky grey.

'You came from Cork, Marian. It was hardly a pilgrimage.'

'Says the woman who journeyed all the way from her kitchen.'

'I don't have anything to say,' said Fionn, but the

bickering Beasleys weren't listening any more.

'How about a little focus, ladies?' suggested a new Boyle arrival called Artie, in a thick Scottish accent. 'Some of us are actually looking to survive this battle.'

'And I *love* speeches,' said Juliana helpfully.

'Feel free to make one then,' grumbled Fionn.

'Ah, go on, lad,' said Sean, bringing his hands together in a rousing clap. 'We're all ears.'

The rest of the islanders joined in, and Fionn realised that he had little choice in the matter. He closed his eyes and imagined his grandfather standing beside him, a hand braced on his shoulder.

Go on, lad. Give them something to fight for.

He snapped his eyes open and cleared his throat. 'I want to start off by saying thank you. To those who chose to stay and fight when Morrigan broke out of her tomb, and to those who have come home to fight with us. I want you to know that no matter what happens from here, your bravery will never be forgotten on these shores,' he began, surprised at the conviction in his voice. 'I know we face impossible odds. I know we're all scared. Our weapons are heavy. Our hearts may be heavy too.' Fionn rolled his shoulders back, his grandfather's words springing from his mouth, as though they were his own. 'But the truth is, we don't know what we're truly made of until the world tests us. Today is that day. When we take the first step, there will be no turning back. Morrigan and her brothers will bring the full force of their army down on us.'

The islanders were nodding, their eyes were grim.

Fionn continued. 'So remember: never leave your back unguarded, keep watch over your fellow clansmen and, no matter what happens, keep fighting. As long as there's light in my eyes and breath in my lungs, I'll fight with you. I'll fight *for* you.'

Sam whistled under his breath, then made the OK sign with his fingers, as if to say *Well done, mate, that's over.*

But Fionn suddenly found he wasn't quite done. He raised his staff to the sky. 'I'll brew a storm so mighty they'll be able to see it from the mainland, and when magic rains down from the clouds, Morrigan will look up at us and cower. See, we have something she could *never* dream of. We have each other.' He looked around at faces old and new, all the long-lost sons and daughters of Arranmore, who had given up their far-flung lives to be here. 'We're bound by loyalty to this ancient place, and to our ancestors who faced this same challenge over a thousand years ago.' His gaze fell on Rose. 'Today, we will honour their bravery by showing it still runs in our veins.'

Perhaps it was Fionn's imagination but the crowd seemed to stand a little taller. They were raising their chins to the sky, squaring their shoulders to the ocean, and Fionn saw it properly for the first time:

There had been an army here all along.

'Victory is beyond the horizon. It is for us to reach out and take it.' Fionn pointed his staff out to sea, where the ravens were swarming. 'Those who fight for Arranmore will find their power on its shore.'

And I'll be the one to give it to them, Fionn told himself, and for the first time in his life, he truly, deeply believed it.

Then the islanders erupted in applause and Fionn found himself grinning as the crowd dispersed, each clan taking up their places along the cliffs.

Sam broke away from the Pattons and jogged to meet Fionn. '*Great* speech. Did you get it from a movie?'

Fionn shrugged. 'It just sort of spilled out?'

Sam palmed his axe. 'Let's do this then. For Shelby, yeah?'

'For Shelby.' Fionn's smile was tight. 'Good luck, Sam.'

'You too, mate.'

And then he was off, sprinting to join his family.

Fionn made his way across the headland, past the Boyles and McCauleys, until he reached the end of Eagle's Point.

There he stood alone in a shaft of morning sunlight, waiting for war.

It found him almost immediately.

Chapter Twenty-Six

MARCH OF THE
TIDE SUMMONER

The tide drew back, as though the horizon was taking a breath. Then the air changed. A layer of smog rolled over the headland, bringing darkness with it. It tasted like smoke and despair. Amidst the endless haze of Morrigan's magic, Fionn held Solas aloft like a beacon.

The islanders stood to attention.

An ear-splitting screech rang out and the island shuddered as Black Point Rock spat a cloud of ash up into the sky. It fell around them like a swarm of dead moths, turning the grass black.

'Show-off,' muttered Fionn.

Far below them, the first Soulstalker slipped

through a crevice in the mountain and stepped on to the pearly seabed. She took a stumbling step, then raised her head.

On the other side of the cliffs, where the Beasleys were stationed, an anguished cry rang out.

Fionn sucked a breath through his teeth. Even though he had prepared himself to expect this moment, he couldn't help the sudden twisting in his stomach. Shelby's clothes were in tatters, but the shell around her neck was polished and gleaming. Her face was vacant; a pale canvas in which two soulless eyes now pooled. On her feet, she wore a single, glittery shoe.

The islanders watched in muted horror as she drifted across the seabed, towards them.

'Remember, it's a trap.' Rose appeared at Fionn's side, her approach silent as the wind. 'Don't let it rattle you.'

'I won't,' said Fionn. 'I know what I have to do.'

His chest grew warm, the well of his power rippling as if someone had dropped a coin in it. Without fanfare, he set about brewing their power-storm. The first cloud broke off and floated into the sky. He sent another one after it, tendrils of violet and grey slowly pushing back against Morrigan's smog.

The islanders raised their weapons. One by one, sticks and poles turned to glimmering spears, until they looked like a string of Christmas lights stretched across the cliffs, all the way from Eagle's Point to the broken cusp of Hughie Rua's Cove.

Nobody moved to strike.

Tara appeared at Fionn's other side. 'I should go now, while she's still by herself.'

'It's too soon.' Fionn watched his best friend stumble across the damp sand, watched the Merrows watching her. They were smirking. 'They have a plan.'

'So do we,' said Tara, flexing the bullwhip. 'And ours is better.'

Fionn exhaled through his teeth. 'Please be –'

'Quick. Smart. I always am.' She winked at him. 'Do your job, Fionny, and I'll do mine.'

She took off in a sprint, her ponytail whipping out behind her.

'If you're going to make Clan Leaders, you need to trust them, Fionn,' said Rose, with gentle sternness.

'I know. But she's my sister.'

'She's a warrior,' said Rose, watching Tara run. 'Let her fight.'

Fionn kept one eye on the storm and one eye on his sister as she reached the cliffs. She wrapped the whip around her wrist, then slid over the edge, making quick work of the crumbling steps.

All the while, Shelby walked alone, step by step, towards her.

All the while, the power-storm grew bigger in the sky.

'Come on, Tara,' muttered Fionn. 'You can do it.'

The islanders reached up to the power-storm and began to brew a rising wind. They weaved their gusts together, quickly and carefully, as Tara landed on the seabed. She smoothed the stray wisps of hair from her face and marched towards Shelby.

The Black Mountain loomed over her, silent and still.

The Merrows crawled through the waning tide on their bellies. Lír gnashed her teeth, the bones of her crown gleaming through the smog. *Clink! Clink! Clink!*

The power-storm flickered.

'Concentrate,' hissed Rose.

Fionn reminded himself to breathe. His palms were sweating and his throat was dry. His sister and his best friend were closing in on each other, Shelby wandering listlessly, Tara marching like a soldier.

They were halfway between the mountain and the cliff when Morrigan made her move.

The Black Mountain released a keening groan. From the crack in the rock came a swarm of rabid Soulstalkers. They crowded in the narrow opening, in a tangle of snapping jaws and grasping limbs. They were crawling over each other, faces scraping on the jagged spire as they scrambled to get through.

These ones were long bereft of their humanity. Some were missing ears and fingers, clumps of hair and most of their teeth. They were all covered with bands of swirling tattoos – Morrigan's handprint glowing for all to see. Instead of drifting listlessly like Shelby, they skittered across the strand, like spiders.

Tara didn't even flinch. She reached into her pocket and stuck a candle between her teeth.

'READY THE WIND,' shouted Fionn. The storm was violet and grey now, the clouds hovering almost low enough to touch. The islanders raised their weapons, and with them, the wall of wind. It rallied about them in a fierce hurricane, casting their hair skyward and rippling through their cheeks.

The Soulstalkers screeched as they thundered towards Tara. But Shelby was within reach now, and Tara was quick. She flicked her lighter, and with the other hand unfurled the bullwhip. It curled around Shelby's waist, yanking the oblivious Tide Summoner towards her. The nearest Soulstalkers leapt at Tara, just as she raised the lighter to the wick and disappeared.

There was a sharp gust of wind, the seabed rippled, and then there was nothing. Just a cluster of confused

Soulstalkers, grasping at the spot where Fionn's sister had been.

Tara was gone. And she'd taken Shelby with her.

Fionn was seized by a rush of relief. 'She did it.'

'Give her time,' said Rose. 'She's not safe yet.'

'PUSH!' yelled Fionn.

The islanders rolled their tornado across the seabed. It took chunks off the cliffs, gathered up sea-slimed boulders and dead fish, clumps of seaweed and fossils older than the island itself. The Soulstalkers were blasted backwards, screeching at the top of their lungs. They crashed into the Black Mountain, bones cracking as they slid down the onyx face. Others were spun all the way into the sea, where they languished among the infuriated merrows.

Fionn scoured the headland, searching for a familiar puffy coat and long brown ponytail. Along the cliff-tops, the Beasleys were doing the same thing. 'Come on, Tara. Come back to us.'

'Give her a minute,' said Rose, straining just as hard.

Fionn glanced at the Black Mountain. The ravens were swarming. Morrigan's smog was seeping out again. Fionn could practically taste her anger in the air. 'We don't have a minute.'

A rogue gust blew across the cliffs. The air in front of

the steps flickered for the briefest second, and Tara's voice rang out. 'Help us!'

She was crouched halfway up the steps, lugging Shelby with her. They were both soaking wet. Wherever they had gone, they had landed in the sea. Tara had managed to swim them to shore and drag them on to the steps, but her shoulders were flagging and Fionn could tell she was out of breath. Shelby was struggling against the binds of her bull-whip. Bartley and Douglas swung over the cliff-edge and hurried down to help, while the other Beasleys leaned over, with grasping hands.

Shelby was hauled up first. The shell around her neck went with her, and far back, behind the mountain in the sea, the Merrows screeched. Tara scrambled up after Shelby, coughing and spluttering. The Beasleys crowded the girls, moving as a swarm towards the lighthouse, where Shelby was dragged, kicking and screaming, into isolation. Tara went with her, her captor and keeper.

Fionn blew out a breath.

'She's still not herself,' cautioned Rose.

'She will be once I rip Morrigan's cape off,' said Fionn.

To this, Rose said nothing.

Fionn sent up another burst of cloud. Without his anxiety running alongside his magic, the power-storm grew bigger more quickly, its underbelly soon crackling with lightning. With Shelby safely stowed away, the Beasleys hurried back to their perch along the cliffs.

They still had a sorceress to face.

And the seabed was beginning to tremble.

Chapter Twenty-Seven

BREDON THE BRUTAL

From the gash in the rock there now emerged a towering beast. Thick-necked and red-eyed, he moved from the mountain like a shadow.

'So, she's chosen Bredon,' said Rose darkly.

Fionn could see why. The brute was an army all on his own. Even the sight of him, standing all the way across the seabed, made the islanders stiffen. But Fionn had been expecting Morrigan's brothers, just as surely as he was expecting to face her.

They had a plan for Bredon.

Whether it was going to work was another matter entirely.

Bredon cast his ruby eye along the cliff-edge.

Fionn's stomach clenched when it landed on him. The power-storm flickered.

Focus.

The islanders were weaving another tapestry of wind.

Bredon smiled, savage and slow, as though he could see it.

Then he strolled towards them, without a care in the world.

Fionn bristled at his arrogance. 'PUSH!'

The wind shot out from the cliffs like a high-speed train, barrelling full-force into Morrigan's brother. He stalled for a moment, his slimy black hair thrown skyward, then he pivoted sideways and pushed against the raging wind, like a hell-born superhero.

'Rose,' whispered Fionn. 'It's not holding him.'

The wind battered Bredon, but all it did was slow him down.

'I think we need to try something stronger.'

'Don't *think*,' said Rose. 'Do.'

Fionn swallowed. 'Lightning, then.'

'Just keep that storm up.' Rose palmed her spear and marched to the other side of Eagle's Point. Her clan followed, their weapons raised to the heaving sky. If they were afraid, they hid it well.

'STRIKE!' yelled Fionn.

Fifty lightning bolts erupted from the Cannon side of the cliff and streaked across the seabed, like comets. They skewered the sand around Bredon, slashing at his arms and legs. One even struck him on the cheek, leaving a jagged black mark under his ruby eye.

He shrugged it off, and kept marching.

'WIND!' yelled Fionn, and another gust swept out from the cliffs. It stalled Bredon, but not for long.

'STRIKE!'

Fifty more lightning bolts sizzled in the air, seven took a bite out of Bredon. He was limping now. Another swarm of Soulstalkers crawled out of Black Point Rock. These ones were bigger and smarter than the first group. They moved sideways in an arc, pressing their backs against the wind.

Fionn piped another storm cloud into the sky, gritting through the pull in his chest. Sweat dripped down his forehead as another battalion squeezed through the rocks. They crouched low, using the first group as a shield as they crawled towards the island.

Fionn's breath was coming harder and faster, his fingers white-knuckled around the staff. He glanced across the cove, to where Sam stood with the Patton Clan. 'Rocks, Sam! Pick them off.'

Sam waved the axe back and forth in answer. 'ON IT!'

Within seconds, the Pattons were tearing chunks from the cliffs and flinging them across the seabed. They cracked jaws and kneecaps, bowled Soulstalkers back into the sea, but still more enemies kept climbing out of the rock. They were an infestation, with an inhuman stamina for pain.

Bredon was at the bottom of the cliffs now. He knocked the falling boulders away as easily as if they were shuttlecocks, and had stopped dodging the lightning bolts entirely. He let them land on his skin, watching it sizzle with bemusement.

He skewered the rock with his fingernails and began to drag himself up the vertical face.

'No no no no no.' Fionn's storm was in tatters in the sky. Fear had climbed up his throat. He tried to knit the clouds back together, to replenish what had been taken, but he couldn't shake the sight of Bredon dragging himself towards Sam.

'Fix the storm, Boyle!' yelled Bartley. 'We need more magic!'

'Give us something, lad,' called Niall frantically. 'Quickly!'

'Hold your nerve.' Rose slung another lightning bolt like an arrow and fired it across the cliffs. 'Remember the plan.'

The first batch of Soulstalkers made it to the cliffs. They divided around Bredon and began climbing the rock-face like cockroaches.

'Do something!' screamed Elizabeth Beasley. 'They're almost up!'

Fionn could feel the terror taking root inside him, dousing the fire of his magic. The islanders were panicking. The plan was already failing.

Then, from across the cliffs, Juliana yelled, 'I'VE GOT AN IDEA!'

She rounded the headland and barrelled through a slew of retreating Beasleys. She swung herself over the edge of the cliff, and down along the crumbling steps, the rubied sword of Rian Boyle shining in her hand.

With a look of fierce determination, Juliana crouched low and drove the silver blade into the underside of the cliff. There was a flash of bright light and then an almighty *crack!* as the steps beneath her crumbled. A Beasley hand shot down to stop her falling. Then a McCauley's and a Patton's and a Cannon's, all of them holding tight to Juliana's collar, before Tom Rowan skewered the hood of her coat with his pitchfork.

For a moment, Juliana hung limply in the air, while everything underneath her fell away, releasing a landslide. It crashed into the climbing Soulstalkers, flattening most of them on impact, while others were knocked from their perches and pinned to the seabed.

Bredon the Brutal looked up just in time to see the landslide come to claim him. He opened his mouth to scream, but the islanders never heard it. He was scraped off the cliff face and sent plunging to the seabed, where he splattered like a starfish, arms and legs splayed out beneath the rocks. His leg twitched once, twice, before going still. When Fionn peered over the edge, he could see nothing but that single ruby eye staring unseeing at the sky.

The remaining Soulstalkers froze.

Safe on the headland once more, Juliana raised her sword to the sky, a war cry bursting from her like the roar of a lion. The islanders roared with her. Fionn felt the mood shift around him, their collective confidence taking root again.

Bredon the Brutal was dead.

Chapter Twenty-Eight

A PLAGUE OF RAVENS

For a blessed moment, all was still. Then a blood-curdling shriek ripped through the sky and a new crack climbed up the face of Black Point Rock. It was the fissure of Morrigan's grief.

In revenge, she cast a plague of birds upon them. The ravens dropped from the sky in a tornado of black feathers. Fionn did his best to replenish the power-storm, but the birds came for him first, pecking at his cheeks and his hands and his eyes, shrieking in his ears, until he lost his concentration.

He stumbled backwards, beating at them with his staff. 'Get off! Get lost!'

For every raven he walloped, ten more came back

screeching, until Fionn couldn't see beyond the wall of feathers. They were in his hair and in his mouth, the collar of his coat and his sleeves too. In the distance, he could hear the cries of listless Soulstalkers as they dragged themselves up from the seabed.

'Help!' he called out, shielding his eyes from the onslaught of talons. 'I can't see! I need to see!'

The Boyles arrived first, thwacking and jabbing and slapping and cursing, as they beat the birds back. Fionn's uncles were hot on their heels, grabbing ravens right out of the sky with their bare hands and swinging them around by their talons.

And still the birds kept coming.

The storm was falling from the sky.

Sam appeared through the mass of black feathers, laying waste to twenty ravens in as many seconds. 'I'm really getting the hang of this whole giant shiny axe thing, you know!'

'Yeah, I can see that,' panted Fionn, as he punched a bird square in the beak. '*Ouch*.'

'Turns out heroism really suits me,' said Sam, knocking another one out of the sky, like a baseball.

'Your dad will definitely get a poem or two out of today,' said Fionn, side-stepping a jabbing beak. 'You'll be famous.'

'Do you think?' asked Sam, as he headbutted a raven.

'Definitely,' said Fionn, jamming his elbow into another.

After what felt like hours, the last of the birds retreated with a final battle-worn cry.

'Worse than rats,' said Fionn, watching them go. 'I *hate* ravens.'

'Uh, Fionn,' said Sam, turning on his heel. 'I think we've got a bigger problem now.'

The surviving Soulstalkers had made it up the broken cliff face and were dragging themselves on to the headland.

The power-storm had all but fallen and, without magic to fight back, the islanders were being reduced to their rudimentary sticks, pitchforks and curtain poles. Even so, the Clan Leaders made a line of defence, hoisting the weapons of their ancestors before them.

Fionn didn't hesitate. He poured his magic back up into the sky, until the air grew thick and hazy, and the power-storm spread out like a bruise. It was almost low enough to touch and yet no one was taking from it. Fionn spun around in panic. 'What's going on?'

The islanders were surrounded. Sam and his sister were fighting off three Soulstalkers at once. The Cannons were immersed in hand-to-hand combat, Niall crunching one Soulstalker in a headlock while his sister Alva roundhouse-kicked another. Fionn's mum and her brothers were fighting back to back, while most of the Beasleys, including a fire-eyed Marian, had closed ranks around a shrieking Elizabeth. Rose was springing and dodging, knocking Soulstalkers off the cliff, like bowling pins, but for each one that tumbled to the seabed, three more took their place.

The islanders could barely see the power-storm, let alone reach up for it.

Fionn left his perch at Eagle's Point and turned his magic on the enemy, sending out bolt after bolt of lightning. The air flashed silver and gold as they went up in sizzle and smoke. Islanders leapt away from them, snatching just enough time to get to their feet and grab their weapons from where they had fallen.

It was time for their next trick.

'FIRE INCOMING!' yelled Fionn. He pointed the staff at the headland, squinted with one eye and drew an invisible line between the lighthouse and cliffs. The Clan Leaders raced for the cliff-edge. The Soulstalkers, in their panic and confusion, charged after them. Fionn's magic sparked, and a wall of flames shot up. The fire was two metres high and blazing hot, snaking all the way across the headland in a rush of amber and gold. It sealed the

Soulstalkers along the cliff-edge, alongside the islanders who had led them there.

'CANDLES!' shouted Fionn.

They were already reaching into their pockets. They jabbed their candles into the wall of flames, and before the Soulstalkers could make sense of what was happening, the Clan Leaders disappeared in a *pop!* of air.

The wind rustled across the headland, burying them in different layers.

Fionn twisted his wrist and the flames surged, now a perfect burning crescent trapping the Soulstalkers at the very edge of the island. More Soulstalkers were still clambering up the cliffs, but there was nowhere to go, and no one to fight. Only an inferno. Or each other.

The rest of islanders peeled back across the headland. They gathered at the lighthouse to catch their breath and tend to the injured, who they carried inland to the safety of the pine forest.

Fionn returned his magic to the power-storm, counting the seconds in his head.

Three minutes. That's what they had agreed on.

Each one seemed to last an eternity – but finally, mercifully, the air began to shimmer. The wind rushed across the headland, and out of it walked the Clan Leaders, grinning from ear to ear. Rose had snow in her hair. Sam's cheeks were rosy, while Bartley was sopping wet from head to toe. Juliana had a clump of wild flowers in her hand. She waved them back and forth at Fionn.

They had made it to the other side of the flames. To safety.

'Finish it!' yelled Fionn.

They reached up to the storm, wreathing themselves in fresh magic. They raised a howling wind and turned Fionn's wall of flames into a mighty wave of fire. It leapt over the Soulstalkers in a rush of amber, turning every single one to ash and smoke.

A heartbeat later, the fire went out, leaving behind nothing but a swathe of burnt grass and charred rock.

The world fell eerily silent.

Gingerly the islanders drifted towards the cliffs.

Below them, nothing stirred. The Black Mountain was quiet. The sky was clearing. The Merrows had returned to the depths of the sea. Even the last of the ravens had retreated.

The islanders sank to their knees, exhausted. Others stowed their weapons and hugged each other tight.

Fionn stood alone on Eagle's Point, unease squirming inside him.

It was too quiet. Too still.

That's when he spotted Aldric the Silent.

Chapter Twenty-Nine

ALDRIC THE SILENT

Beyond the lighthouse and across the barren northern plains of Arranmore, Aldric the Silent came marching. He had breached the island somewhere in the south and cut a pathway through its heart. Now he moved like a shadow towards them, soundless and swift. At his back, like a grey smudge against the pine forest, was a new battalion of Soulstalkers.

These ones wore the waterproof jackets of fishermen, ripped wellingtons up to their knees. Others had donned knitted cardigans and cracked reading glasses, tracksuits and hoodies, jeans and trainers. One had a camera swinging from her neck, another wore a captain's hat. These were recent victims – dragged into the sea and brought to the mountain some time in the last two weeks. Chosen purposefully because Morrigan knew they would be harder to fight.

After all, they looked just like the islanders.

They looked just like Shelby.

Fionn screamed but it was already too late. Aldric had seized the element of surprise and his Soulstalkers were charging. In the blink of an eye, the balance had tipped out of their favour. Across the headland, weary islanders staggered to their feet as their enemy bore down on them, gritty and awful and unforgiving.

The next hours passed in a haze, Fionn's head thumping so hard he could barely see straight. He stood as far from the others as he could, sending his magic up, up, up, into the sky. The power-storm broke apart quicker than he could replenish it, wisps of grey and silver dissolving as soon as they were made. Aldric's Soulstalkers might have looked like Fionn but they fought like Morrigan. Ruthlessly, and without end. The islanders' strength was lagging. Many retreated on their hands and knees, while others curled on their sides, too exhausted to run.

Fionn's attention flitted between the tattered power-storm and his mother fighting along the cliff-edge. Every misstep, every blow. The lighthouse door was missing its Beasley guards. They were lying unmoving on the grass.

All around Fionn, people were falling. They had lost the cliffs and now the headland. The candles were gone.

He couldn't see Sam anywhere.

He didn't know if Tara was still safe inside the lighthouse, or if the Soulstalkers had overpowered her and recaptured Shelby.

He didn't know how much longer he could stand with trembling arms and shaking knees, while the island crumpled in on itself. Fear doused the fire in his chest, and the last of the power-storm came down in silver droplets.

'Fionn! The storm!' Rose hobbled to his side. Her hair was matted with blood and there was an ugly purple bruise blooming along her cheekbone. 'You need to give us something to fight with.'

'I want to fight too. My family –'

'Are only Storm Keepers with *your* help.' Rose's eyes flashed. 'We all know the cost. Brew your storm.'

Fionn craned his neck to see over her shoulder. There was so much shouting and screaming. Bodies falling. Others crawling helplessly towards him. 'I c-can't concentrate.'

'Then don't look. Don't *feel*.' Rose was close enough for Fionn to see his own fear reflected in her eyes. 'If you go down, we all go down.'

Fionn swallowed thickly. 'I thought Morrigan would be here by now. I just want it to *end*.'

'Once we take Aldric out, his Soulstalkers will panic. Morrigan will come out to avenge her brothers and there'll be nothing between you and her.' Rose glanced at the sky. 'Not even birds.'

'Just the cape,' said Fionn, seized by a bolt of determination.

Rose hardened her jaw. 'Just the cape. Focus on the cape.'

She turned and limped back across the battlefield. Fionn tipped his head back. The afternoon had quickly come and gone, and now the sun was sinking. He forced himself to look away from the islanders, to unhear their screams and unthink the worst.

Focus.

He pictured Morrigan's cape of souls in his mind, and with the anger it brought he cast a new cloud in the sky. This one was bigger and darker than all before it.

Don't think.

Don't feel.

There was a noise somewhere over his shoulder, footsteps crunching on the frosted grass. Fionn ignored it.

Don't think.

Don't look.

Another cloud broke off and floated into the sky. Somewhere beyond the lighthouse, the islanders pulled it down, wisp by wisp. Fionn hoped his mum was one of them. Still standing, still fighting. He hoped they were gaining ground.

Don't think.

Don't look.

Behind him, the grass crunched again. The sound was closer now.

Fionn's cheeks began to prickle.

A hand fell heavy on his shoulder and an awful shudder passed through him.

He spun around to find himself face to face with a living nightmare.

'*You,*' he breathed.

Until today, Fionn had never seen Aldric in the flesh. Of the three brothers, he was the slightest; a fine-boned creature, who could slip easily through the shadows of the world, and yet he filled Fionn with three times the dread of Ivan on his cruellest day, or Bredon at his most brutal.

In the chaos of the fight, he must have slipped free of the islanders and rounded the lighthouse to sneak up on him.

Fionn tried to run, but Aldric grabbed him by the collar of his jacket. He ripped the staff from his hands, flinging it far out of reach. Fionn squirmed as he was yanked nose to nose with Aldric. He made no sound, but the rancid stench of his breath seeped out through the gaps in the twine that bound his mouth, making Fionn's eyes water. He could feel the grief and anger rolling off Aldric. He had come to avenge his brothers.

Fionn tried to wriggle free. '*Get off me.*'

Aldric was stronger than he looked. He dragged Fionn towards the end of Eagle's Point. Fionn jammed his heels into the grass and shouted for help, but Aldric slammed a hand over his mouth, silencing him.

Fionn spied a flash of green out of the corner of his eye. Solas had landed near the cliff-edge. He made himself go limp. As he slid to the ground, Aldric momentarily lost his grip and Fionn managed to scrabble away.

They both lunged for the staff, but Aldric was faster. He grabbed it with a determined hiss and slammed it over his knee. There was a sudden, soul-crushing *craaaack!* as Solas broke clean in two.

'NO!' Fionn threw himself at Aldric. They fell to the ground, kicking and punching. Aldric threw the top half of the staff aside, the emerald rolling away and out of reach. Fionn whipped his head around to follow it and Aldric seized his distraction, pinning him to the grass and pointing the jagged end of the staff at Fionn's throat.

Fionn froze.

Aldric's smile was a gruesome thing. It grew wider

and wider, the twine around his mouth stretching as he leaned on the stake.

A scream built in Fionn's throat as his airway narrowed, and then –

Aldric jerked as a silver lighter whizzed out of nowhere and ricocheted off his head. The stake slipped. 'Get off him, you freak!' Bartley was thundering across Eagle's Point, the shield of Orla Beasley shining like a sun against his chest.

Fionn lunged forward and headbutted Aldric in the chin. Bartley charged him with his shield, slamming into his shoulder and knocking him off Fionn.

'Thanks!' Fionn panted, leaping to his feet.

'Yeah, yeah.' Bartley stood shoulder to shoulder with Fionn, the shield held high between them. 'Just hurry up and *do* something.'

'I can't,' said Fionn, as Aldric charged them. 'He broke the staff.'

'What do you mean he –' *Thunk!* They were thrown backwards, on to the grass. Bartley lifted the shield, just in time to stave off another strike.

Thunk!

'So, what now?' he hissed, from under the shield.

'We need to kill him!' Fionn hissed back.

'Well, obviously.'

Bartley jerked the shield, blocking another attack.

Thunk!

'Everyone's a bit *busy* right now!' said Bartley. 'And you've gone and lost your bloody staff!'

'We need a new plan, then.' Fionn peeked out from behind the shield just as Aldric ripped it away, nearly taking Bartley's hand with it. He sent it soaring across the grass like a frisbee, leaving both boys utterly defenceless.

'Or, we improvise!' said Bartley.

'That works!'

This time, when Aldric raised the stake, Fionn caught him by the wrist. Bartley grabbed the other one before he could strike back. They were both lifted off their feet, legs flying as they were yanked back and forth. Aldric released Bartley first, sending him pinwheeling towards the edge of the cliff, where he rolled over three times before slipping over it. He clawed at the grass, catching himself at the last minute. His face turned red as he clung on for dear life.

Fionn was thrown in the other direction, his scream following him as he tumbled across the grass. When he looked up, Aldric was above him again, his lips stretched into that disgusting smile. He had retrieved the jagged piece of wood. This time, he raised it right above Fionn's heart.

Fionn threw his hands up as a shield. 'No!'

The stake stalled in mid-air. Suddenly Aldric wasn't leering any more. He was grimacing. Then moaning, as black blood bubbled out between the gaps in his twine-mouth. He dropped the stake and fell to his knees, gurgling.

That's when Fionn noticed the spear sticking out of his back.

Rose was standing behind Aldric. She yanked the spear out, and cleaned it on the end of her cloak. 'I've waited a thousand years to do that.'

Aldric looked up at Rose.

She bared her teeth at him. 'Remember me?'

The Soulstalker blinked slowly, horror peeling across his face as he recognised her.

'I thought you might.' Rose slammed the blunt end of her spear into his cheek.

Aldric groaned as he slumped to one side.

Rose stepped over him. 'Your sister isn't the only one who knows soul magic, you sneaky, snivelling rat.'

'Nice,' said Fionn breathlessly.

Rose helped him to his feet. 'Are you all right?'

'Yeah, thanks. That was close.'

'Much too close.' Rose looked him up and down. 'Where's your staff?'

'Aldric broke –' Fionn stiffened, thinking too late of the emerald. He snapped his head around to find him crawling across the grass towards it. 'NO!'

Fionn ran but Aldric was closer. With the last of his waning strength, Morrigan's brother grabbed the emerald and smashed it against the earth.

There was an almighty *crrrraaaack!*

The island inhaled.

A sudden shiver of wind passed over the headland. It rippled up Fionn's spine, as he stared in horror at the broken gemstone. A fine silver mist was seeping out of it. It curled up, up, *up*. Aldric tipped his face back to watch it go, smirking through the pain.

When Fionn turned back to Rose, she was already an old woman. Her dark hair was wiry and grey, her green eyes dulling in the crevices of her face. She shuffled towards him, still holding tight to her spear.

Fionn's heart sank. 'Your soul. It's –'

'Here,' she said, closing her eyes. 'I can feel it.'

Fionn noticed the silver mist wreathing her body.

After all these years, her soul was returning to her.

It was *ageing* her.

'I'm going now, Fionn,' said Rose calmly.

'But I *need* you,' said Fionn, with rising desperation. 'I don't have the staff any more. I can't make the power-storm. I can't do *anything*. Please don't leave me, Rose. I'm begging –'

'The magic lives in the soul, not the stick, Fionn.' Rose

prodded his chest with the tip of her finger, her voice so feeble now, Fionn could barely hear it over the wind. 'Solas may have directed your magic, but it is not the source of it. It never was. You *know* that.' The silver mist was all but gone. There were only a few tendrils left, curling around her heart. 'Haven't I taught you anything?'

'But I don't know how to –'

'Yes, you do.' Her gaze shifted over his shoulder. 'The power flows in *you*. Use it. Be your own light.' She dropped her spear at his feet, then brushed past him. 'Now, if you'll excuse me, I have one last thing to do.'

When Fionn turned around, Aldric was on his feet, staggering towards them. His eyes were wired in red, his neck and stomach stained with his own blood.

With the last of her strength, Rose threw her arms wide open and barrelled right into him. She drove him backwards, and before Fionn could understand what was happening, they both tipped over the edge of the cliff.

'ROSE!' Fionn rushed after her, wincing at the sound of bones thudding and cracking off the rocks.

All the way down, Aldric the Silent didn't make a single sound.

Róisín, First and Fearless, never fell.

The last wisp of her soul returned to her as she leapt over the edge, her body finally catching up to her true age.

She smiled as she turned to dust, the last of her earthly form rising like a thousand butterflies in flight. A gust of wind passed over the headland, and carried them off, into the setting sun.

And then she was gone.

Chapter Thirty

THE CALM BETWEEN STORMS

Fionn fell to his knees, his hands coming around his middle to hold himself together. Time slowed, grief wrapping him in its cold embrace. It felt clawing and familiar.

Dimly he became aware of a gentle hand on his shoulder. A voice in his ear. 'Fionn? Can you hear me?'

Fionn gasped a breath; the world rushing back with it. '*Mam.*'

'I'm here, Fionn. I need you to get up now.'

Fionn scrunched his eyes shut, grief and pain shuddering through him in matching currents. 'I don't think I can do it any more.'

'Come on. I've got you.' Steady hands underneath

his armpits, a huff of exertion as his mother helped him stand. 'Lean on me. That's it. You're all right now. You're all right.'

And then Fionn was standing, and the earth was still turning. The Soulstalkers were retreating, falling over each other as they clambered down the cliffs, racing for the mountain in the sea.

Fionn watched them flee, with mounting confusion. 'Morrigan's calling them back to her.' The sun had melted along the horizon, and night was rising in a swell of cold. A strange hush had fallen over the headland. It raised the hairs on Fionn's arms. 'What is she up to?'

'I don't know,' said his mother quietly. She was covered in scrapes and bruises. 'Come on.' She pulled him away from the cliffs. 'We have our own people to think about.'

A quick glance at the headland revealed a host of new casualties. Tom Rowan, flat on his back, his pitchfork protruding from his ribs. Sam's mother, flinching through the pain of a dislocated shoulder. Bartley had hauled himself back on to the cliff and was now vomiting over the edge. Donal, crumpled and unmoving at the edge of the battlefield. Others were missing entirely. Far below them, the seabed was littered with new bodies, and Fionn couldn't tell which ones belonged to them and which ones to Morrigan – he knew only that the losses on both sides were many.

'We should rest while we can,' said his mother, as they drifted across the headland. 'Who knows what tomorrow will bring?'

Fionn glanced uneasily at the Black Mountain, as the last rays of sun melted into darkness.

* * *

By the time the moon came out, it was eerily quiet on the northern shores of Arranmore. The Black Mountain was still, the last of Morrigan's ravens perched around its summit, keeping watch. The Merrows were hiding, the tide lapping silently in the distance, as though it was trying to listen in.

After returning to the cottage on the headland for a shower and a quick change of clothes, Fionn hurried back to the lighthouse, armed with the spear of Róisín, First and Fearless, and a schoolbag full of snacks. He tossed a ham-and-cheese sandwich to Bartley, who was sitting in the tattered green armchair, watching the door. The Tide Summoner was on his lap, its pearly shell faded to a dull grey.

'Make sure to eat,' Fionn reminded him. 'Even if you don't feel hungry.'

'Did you get all the bodies?' asked Bartley.

Fionn shook his head. 'We won't be able to do a

proper count until the sun comes up.'

Bartley unwrapped his sandwich. There was a jagged red gash on his cheek.

Fionn hesitated by the stairs. 'That looks nasty. Did your mum look at it?'

'She was busy helping the others.'

'I think you need stitches.'

Bartley snorted. 'I'll get my stitches when you get my sister's soul back.'

'How is she?'

'Still the same.'

Fionn paused halfway up the spiral staircase. 'You should try to sleep. We don't know how long we have until Morrigan comes out.'

'*You* should be the one sleeping,' said Bartley, mid-chew. 'You're the one who has to kill her.'

On the top floor of the lighthouse, Tara and Sam were keeping watch over Shelby. Well, one of them was keeping watch, and it wasn't Sam. He was fast asleep by the lens, his back propped up against the glass. The axe of Sorcha Patton lay in his lap.

'I swear he could sleep through a hurricane,' muttered Fionn.

'Lucky him,' said Tara, who was wide awake on the window ledge. Fionn stepped over Sam's legs to get to her, casting an eye over Shelby who was sitting on the bed. She hadn't moved in hours.

Fionn tossed his sister a sandwich.

Tara caught it in mid-air, then noted the spear in his hand. 'Is that – ?'

'Yeah,' said Fionn, laying it on the floor.

Tara nodded. 'Mam said she went bravely.'

'She rammed Aldric off the cliff. Like a bull.'

'Fearless to the last second,' said Tara admiringly.

'I wish she was still here.'

'You still have me,' Tara reminded him. 'And I'm really brave too.'

Fionn snorted, but he didn't disagree. 'Just don't go leaping off any cliffs. Please.'

'I'll do my best.' Tara took a bite of her sandwich, chewing thoughtfully. 'I thought Aonbharr would come back today to help us.' She frowned. 'I mean, you did *make* him. It's a bit ungrateful of him to just fly off and leave you.'

Fionn shrugged. 'I think we're on our own now, Tara.'

'Well, at least Morrigan is on her own too.'

Fionn sank on to the bed beside Shelby. She was staring blankly at her lap.

He waved to get her attention. 'Hey.'

'She doesn't know you, Fionny. She's practically a zombie.'

Fionn ignored his sister. 'Are you hungry, Shelby? I've got your favourite crisps. And some ginger nuts.'

Shelby didn't twitch.

Tara rolled her eyes. 'We've tried talking to her. You're wasting your time.' She laid her forehead against the glass, her gaze turning to the Black Mountain. Sam's snores cast a gentle lull about the place. 'Get some sleep while you still can, Fionny. I'll keep watch.'

'I'm not even tired,' said Fionn, before dissolving into a traitorous yawn. He kicked his legs over the edge of the bed and leaned back against the wall. 'Maybe I'll just have a quick nap …'

When he closed his eyes he nodded off almost immediately, blackness closing around him like the mouth of a hungry fish.

Morrigan was waiting in the silence of his mind.

There will be no rest for you here, sorcerer. Not after what you took from me today.

She lurched from the darkness, like a ghost. Her eyes were wide and bloodshot, and her teeth were bared.

I *will haunt you as you sleep*, she hissed. She was fizzing with rage. It had a power all of its own. *You will lose your mind before your soul.*

Her dark magic moved like tentacles, worming further into Fionn's mind and reaching for his worst memories. First, his grandfather disappearing underneath the Northern Lights, then his father drowning in his lifeboat. The Whispering Tree crumbling to ash, taking Dagda with it, then Shelby losing her soul as she screamed desperately for his help. Fionn watched Rose ageing in the heart of Eagle's Point, her body withering as her soul seeped out of the emerald, then he watched her falling over the edge, again and again, and again, with his own scream ringing in his ears.

Fionn tried desperately to find a memory that could banish Morrigan's creeping darkness, but her shadows were everywhere.

Your mind is a graveyard, sorcerer. There is no hope here.

Fionn jerked away from her voice. He began to thrash wildly, his arms and legs flailing as he tried to free himself from the nightmare.

'FIONN! WAKE UP!'

Fionn snapped his eyes open. Someone was shaking him by the shoulders. Across the room, Tara had fallen asleep on the window ledge. The room was almost pitch black, the moon outside casting the barest sliver of light. It was enough to make out Shelby's face barely six inches from his own.

Her eyes were wide. 'It's OK,' she whispered. 'You were having a nightmare.'

'Yeah,' said Fionn, half breathless. 'Morrigan was in my head.'

'Are you all right now?'

Fionn nodded, then blinked. 'Wait. Are *you* all right?'

Shelby's smile curled. 'I'll be even better when you're dead.'

She struck lightning fast, tightening her hands around Fionn's neck and choking his scream from him. He tried to push her off, but she rallied, throwing them both off the bed and on to the floor. They landed with a hard thud, Fionn's eyes bulging as he struggled for breath.

'You pathetic fool!' Shelby bore down on him with her full weight, pinning him to the floor. She flung her free arm out, scrabbling for the spear.

'Get off me!' Fionn kicked out, catching Sam in the ankle. He jerked awake. When he saw what was happening, he launched himself at Shelby, knocking her off Fionn. They crashed into the lens, sending a giant crack spider-webbing up the glass.

Tara jolted upright at the sudden commotion. 'What the – oh my God.'

She rushed to help.

By the time Fionn was on his feet, Bartley had reached the top of the stairs. 'What the hell is going on?'

Sam and Tara were restraining Shelby, but she was bucking against them.

Bartley stared at his sister in horror. 'Sh-Shelby?'

'No,' said Fionn, rounding on her. 'It's Morrigan.'

Shelby spat at him.

'Told you we should have tied her up,' panted Sam.

'Get the bullwhip!' barked Tara. 'Before she hurts one of us.'

Bartley fetched it from the window sill and bound his sister's hands.

Shelby growled at Fionn. 'If you want rid of me, you'll have to kill the girl, little sorcerer.' Now that Fionn was wide awake, he could plainly hear the difference in his friend's voice. The tone was harsh and leering, and her smile was much too wide. 'I can get to you any time I want.'

'Then come as yourself,' said Fionn angrily. 'Stop hiding.'

Shelby's sneer made her almost unrecognisable. 'I will come to you in whatever form I please. I will take *everyone* you care about and string them to my cape, until you are all alone.'

'You mean the way you're all alone now?' said Fionn.

Shelby's nostrils flared.

A*h*.

'You don't like that, do you?' he needled. 'You *hate* that you're all by yourself now.'

Shelby's eyes flashed.

Fionn edged closer to her. 'Are you afraid of me now, Morrigan? Is that why you're still hiding?'

'Don't get too close,' warned Tara.

Fionn ignored her. 'That's it, isn't it? You've been threatening me for *months* now. But when your brothers were dying for you today, *you* were cowering inside your mountain.' He pounced, grabbing Shelby by the shoulders. She squirmed, but Fionn moved his hands to her cheeks to keep her head still. His gaze bored into hers. He was not looking for his friend now, he was looking for the monster behind her eyes. 'You're always hiding, Morrigan. Just like you're hiding now.'

'What are you doing?' said Sam frantically.

'If she can get to me through Shelby, then maybe I can get to her.' Fionn pressed his forehead against Shelby's and imagined himself barrelling past the barriers in her mind, into the shadowy wasteland, where Morrigan was skulking. Suddenly he could see her sitting on her throne of bones, surrounded by the last of her Soulstalkers. She looked smaller, somehow, and shocked. He had caught her off guard.

Fionn felt himself smile.

When he spoke, his voice echoed all around them, filling the caverns of the Black Mountain.

Come out of the darkness and face me, Morrigan.

Morrigan hissed through her teeth.

You won't, will you? said Fionn, pushing further into the damp squalor.

Because you're afraid.

There's no one else between us now.

Only your mountain.

Morrigan's cape of souls billowed between them. Fionn could feel it brushing against his cheeks. *If you want my cape, little sorcerer, you will have to come and take it.*

Maybe I will, said Fionn, reaching out to snatch it.

But Morrigan was already slipping from Shelby's mind. Like an icy wind giving way to a rush of warmth, she disappeared. There was only blackness, then. Fionn let himself fall out of it. He released Shelby and reeled backwards, blinking himself back to the present. 'Whoa!'

Shelby went limp between Sam and Tara, the bullwhip still tied around her wrists. Morrigan was gone.

'Well?' said Bartley.

Fionn blew out a breath. 'She knows I want the cape.'

Tara drifted towards the window. 'You can't go into that mountain, Fionny. No matter what.'

'It's the last thing standing between us,' said Fionn.

'Which means we have to destroy it.'

'How?' chorused Sam and Bartley.

Fionn traced the crack in the brass-rimmed lens, Rose's words stirring in his mind.

The power flows in you. Use it. Be your own light.

They were all staring at him now.

'Fionn,' said Tara urgently. 'There's something moving out there.'

They hurried to the window. The moonlight had been all but extinguished, but not by clouds. On closer inspection, Fionn could see the sky was filling up with smoke and ash. It made it almost impossible to spot the shadows scrabbling across the seabed.

Almost.

'Soulstalkers,' breathed Sam. 'Looks like you rattled her.'

Tara whirled around, wild-eyed. 'Quick! Turn on that lens!'

'No!' Fionn leapt in front of Bartley to stop him. 'Let her think she has the element of surprise.' He grabbed Rose's spear from the floor and sprinted for the stairs. 'Send word to the islanders. We have to fight one last time. I have a plan.'

'Is it a good one?' Sam called after him.

Fionn paused mid-way down the staircase. 'We're about to find out.'

Chapter Thirty-One

THE LONG-AGO LIGHTHOUSE

By the time Morrigan's Soulstalkers reached the cliffs, a group of islanders were already waiting for them on the headland. They crouched in the darkness with their weapons while Fionn pointed Rose's spear at the sky and sent up a cloud of crackling lightning.

Soon it became a power-storm.

The islanders fought, but they were fewer in number now, and weary after too little sleep. By contrast, the last of Morrigan's Soulstalkers were hungrier and angrier than before. They moved with Morrigan's rage, fighting not to kill the islanders, but to get past them as quickly as possible. They were looking for Fionn. They tracked him with grasping hands and gnashing teeth, bringing the battle out on to Eagle's Point. It wasn't long before he had to surrender the power-storm to defend himself.

The islanders rushed to help him.

'No sign of Morrigan!' shouted Sam as he fought his way through. 'We can't hold them much longer!'

'She doesn't even have the decency to try and kill me herself!' huffed Fionn.

Sam had to fend off three Soulstalkers before he could respond. 'They're. Not. Going. To. Stop. Until. You're. Dead,' he heaved. 'Whatever you're planning, you need to do it fast.'

Fionn looked around frantically. There was no way back from Eagle's Point. Every pair of blank eyes was trained on him. Every body was turned in his direction. The headland might as well have been a world away. 'Can you distract them, Sam? I only need a few seconds.'

Sam swung his axe at an advancing Soulstalker, knocking him to his knees. 'Here's three!'

'That'll do!' Fionn tucked the spear under his arm and took out the candle he had been saving. It was the last of the lot, small and slim and yellow – a *just in case*. He flicked his lighter and brought the flame to the wick.

It lit up in a silent *whoosh!*

A nearby Soulstalker lunged for him, but Fionn was already disappearing.

With a fierce and howling gust, the wind came and carried him away.

Fionn sank like a stone through the layers of Arranmore. The tide crept back towards the cliffs, the waves growing full and frothy as they crested the shore. The island rebuilt itself in shale and rock, while the Black Mountain was cleaved back into three separate shards. The grass grew wild and green at Fionn's feet, dotted with daisies and buttercups, and half-blown dandelions.

An afternoon sun hung like a coin in the sky and Fionn found himself aching for a time before last summer, when none of these things had ever mattered to him. Now that he might never see this kind of world again, it mattered more than anything.

It was a paradise lost.

The wind died away, casting the final layer over him. It was filled with children. Their laughter lingered in the air as they raced each other across the headland, flying kites. There was a gaggle of them, dressed in stripy shorts and T-shirts, summer dresses, and socks that climbed towards their knees.

Fionn hurried across Eagle's Point, hoping they wouldn't glance his way. When he reached the lighthouse, he pushed the door open. It swung on its hinges, and he slipped inside. He slammed it shut behind him and pressed his back against it.

Rose was standing across the room, staring at him. She was *here*. And she was old again, her green eyes flickering with curiosity. 'And you are?'

Fionn's heart clenched painfully in his chest. 'Just passing through.'

Rose noted the candle melting over his hand, her spear limp in the other. Her face paled. 'How long?' she croaked.

'Not for a while,' said Fionn gently.

She pressed her lips together. 'Was it fast?'

'And brave,' said Fionn. 'Really, *really* brave.'

Her smile was small, satisfied. 'Good.'

Fionn smiled back. 'See you again, Róisín.'

He raised the stub of the candle and blew it out. The room blinked and Rose disappeared, the layers ruffling back over him in a sudden flurry of wind. Fionn kept his back pressed against the door to anchor himself. When he caught up with the world, it was night time again. He could hear the clash and clamour of battle raging just beyond the door, the ragged anger of Soulstalkers trying to figure out where he had just disappeared to.

'You're back!' Tara was pacing in the space where Rose had just been. She was wearing the Tide Summoner around her neck. Shelby was sitting in the tattered armchair, her hands still bound by the bullwhip. Her head was lolling as though she was asleep, but Fionn could see her eyes were open. They flicked to him, her brows drawing together as though she was trying to remember him, then her face went blank again. 'How's it going out there?'

'Not great.' Fionn tossed the spear to Tara. 'Watch the door.'

Fionn made for the spiral staircase, wishing he could stall a minute to hug his sister and tell her the things she deserved to hear to make up for all the petty squabbles they used to waste their breath over. There wasn't time now. So instead he leaned over the railings and said, 'Cover me, please.'

'Of course,' said Tara, without a beat of hesitation.

'Thanks, Tara,' said Fionn, earnestly. 'You're a good sister. Always have been.'

She waved him away. 'Don't get soppy. Then you'll really start to worry me.'

Fionn smiled as he hurried up the staircase.

Chapter Thirty-Two

THE MAGICAL BEAM

O n the top floor of the lighthouse, the glass lens rippled like a giant bubble. Fionn cranked the gears at the bottom and turned it to face the sea. Then he got down on his hands and knees and crawled underneath it.

A single bulb sat on the plinth before him. Fionn cupped his hands around it.

The magic lives in the soul, not the stick, Fionn.

He closed his eyes and felt the well of his power rippling. There was no staff now, no spear or other conduit to rely on. Only his soul. His hands. His will.

Be your own light.

He made a tunnel in his mind, his thoughts and his magic directed towards one single point. His chest warmed, and then his hands. The lightbulb began to glow, softly at first and then a bright, burning silver, until it looked like Fionn was holding a star in his hands. It felt a little like that too.

He loosed a steadying breath.

Obliterate.

Power coursed through him like an electric current. The lightbulb flashed, sending a bolt of pure magic out into the world. The night lit up in a blaze of silver.

The lens shook as it passed through it. The room shuddered and the lighthouse windows shattered into a million pieces. A chorus of screams rang out across the headland. Fionn ducked as shards rained down like knives.

But somehow, the bubble of glass around him had held; now it was both magnifier and shield. He cupped the lightbulb again, pouring his magic through it. The lens turned it into a beam of pure destruction. It cut a silver line across the seabed, burning everything in its path. Dead fish went up in smoke, crabs cooked and seaweed sizzled, while rocks exploded into smithereens.

Down below, the chaos quietened.

The Soulstalkers were watching.

The islanders too.

Fionn grinned.

It was *working*.

The last flock of Morrigan's ravens shot out of Black Point Rock in a panic. The silver beam made shadows of them, flying fast towards the island, where they made a feathered tornado around the lighthouse. Their shrieks reverberated against the lens, their wings beating furiously as they tried in vain to stop Fionn. They toppled Rose's furniture, slashed their talons through her bedclothes and scattered her books across the wooden floor.

But it was too late.

The beam was almost at the Black Mountain.

Morrigan was trapped.

Fionn thought fleetingly of Dagda. Of Rose and his dad and his grandfather too. All of them – and thousands more – had given their lives for this moment and, for the first time in a long time, Fionn didn't feel like a disappointment.

He felt like a sorcerer.

This war might have begun long, long ago, but he was going to finish it. For Arranmore, and all of its people, both living and dead.

Obliterate.

The beam licked the bottom of Black Point Rock. The foundations exploded, like dynamite. Another surge of magic and the spear of light climbed higher. Debris shot out in every direction, bringing smoke and shale with it. The mountain roared as it crumbled in on itself.

The Merrows darted to the surface to watch, their sharp teeth glinting in the waves. Down on the headland, the Soulstalkers howled.

Obliterate.

Fionn fired blast after blast, the beam methodically shattering every square inch of rock until Morrigan's lair was little more than a collapsed ruin.

When there was nothing left to destroy, Fionn released the lightbulb. The beam flickered, and then went out. Darkness fell, but it was turning indigo, the deepest part of the night now behind them. Fionn's magic receded into his bones, leaving the barest thrumming in his bloodstream.

The tide rushed back towards the shore in a swell of froth and seaweed. Lír rode on the first wave, searching the seabed for Morrigan. Her army swam with her, the ocean leaping over masses of fallen Soulstalkers and folding them back into the deep.

Fionn knew there would be fallen islanders too – swept away by an impartial tide.

He pressed his forehead against the glass.

He needed a minute.

He needed a *year*.

The last of Morrigan's ravens flocked in through the open window and beat their wings against the glass, but he paid them no mind. He had spent all of his terror already. A few angry birds were nothing to contend with now.

When his heartbeat settled, Fionn opened his eyes.

'We did it,' he whispered. 'She's *finally* dead.'

His voice echoed back at him, too loud in his ears.

A manic laugh leapt out of him, something between a laugh and a sob. It hiccoughed in his chest, until he had to stop to take a breath.

Somewhere over his shoulder, the laughing went on.

And on, and on, and on.

Fionn stiffened.

Then came an awful, familiar voice. 'I'm afraid you are mistaken, little sorcerer. I am very much alive.'

Fionn spun around.

Morrigan was standing in the place where her ravens had landed. She looked like a ghost in the darkness, her cape of souls billowing around her.

'You have got your wish, Fionn Boyle. I have come out of my mountain to face you.' Her pale lips curled. 'Now the real fun begins.'

Chapter Thirty-Three

THE WARRIOR'S SACRIFICE

'Y-*you*,' said Fionn, half numb with shock. He had destroyed every *inch* of Black Point Rock and yet, somehow, Morrigan had escaped and crept up on him on the wings of her birds. One sat on her shoulder now, mimicking the tilt of her head.

'Did you expect me to cower in my mountain? To wait for the likes of *you* to come and kill me?' She clucked her tongue. 'The *arrogance*.'

Fionn's mind whirred. He had thought about this moment a thousand times, but he had never imagined it like this. His magic was unfurling again, the heat spreading across his chest, ready to strike. But he had to be smart now, and quicker than her.

'Took you long enough,' he said, studying the mechanics of her cape. How it attached itself to her collarbone, where he could rip it free. It fluttered in a non-existent breeze, upturning thousands of contorted faces. 'Seems cowardly to me.'

'Says the boy who stole his power from another.' Morrigan's teeth shone like fangs in the dimness. 'A child who could not face even the weakest of my brothers by himself.'

'At least I stand up with the people who fight for me,' said Fionn. 'I don't just let them die.'

Morrigan's laugh was ghoulish. Tendrils of her cape caressed the glass around Fionn. 'You are so brave in your bubble.'

'And *you* are still hiding,' said Fionn. 'Let's see how brave you are without your cape.'

'You will have to prise it from my dead body, boy.'

'Maybe I will.' Fionn pressed his palm against the glass. The lens exploded. It nicked his cheeks and cut his bottom lip open, embedding shards in his coat and his jeans as he jumped out of the frame. He lunged for Morrigan but her ravens came at him in a shrieking cloud of feathers. They pecked at his arms and beat their wings against his face as he tried to bat them away.

Morrigan shot her magic at him like a bullet. Fionn

was knocked backwards, his head slamming against the brass frame. 'N*ngh*.'

Before he could raise his head, Morrigan stuck her hand through the feathers and grabbed him by the throat. She poured her shadows down his gullet and doused the fire of his magic.

'You are no vessel for Dagda's magic,' she hissed. 'You are a ship sinking under the weight of his power. Unworthy to lead your people. Unworthy to stand here and face me.' Another cruel laugh.

Fionn gasped as a terrible coldness trickled through him. He tried to fight back but his blood had turned to ice in his veins and his chest was opening like a chasm.

'I will remake this sorry world, and I will fill it with Soulstalkers who wear your faces. Your mother's. Your sister's. Your friends',' Morrigan sneered. 'I will start with yours. For all that you have taken from me.'

Fionn felt the cleaving of his soul as it was unknitted from his body and pulled, like a thread from his mouth. His scream was soundless. Morrigan's cape closed around him and, in the patchwork, Fionn saw Shelby's screaming face.

He saw something else too, moving just behind the haunted veil. A figure creeping up the spiral staircase.

There was a flash of silver, and then Morrigan

shrieked. She stumbled backwards, her shadows recoiling from him like a snake. Tara was standing on the top step, holding the end of Róisín's spear. She had stuck the blade into Morrigan's side and was holding it in place.

She stared at Fionn with wide, terrified eyes. 'Run.'

Fionn vaulted across the room, to join her on the stairs. His body moved slower now, his magic was like a block of ice in his chest. 'M-my p-power's frozen,' he said, trying to pull Tara away. 'C-come on. Quick.'

Tara shook him off, tightening her grip on the spear. 'I said *run*! Save whoever you can!'

'Tara –'

'You *stupid* child.' Morrigan was already lumbering to her feet. 'I will *devour* you.'

'Come back for me,' said Tara, stepping in front of Fionn, making a shield of her own body. 'For all of us.'

'You can't do this for me, Tara!'

Tara squared her jaw as Morrigan's shadows lashed out. There was no fear in her eyes now, only determination. 'I'm your sister, Fionn. It's my job to protect you.'

Morrigan scoffed. 'You are no warrior.'

Tara twisted the spear. '*Yes. I. Am.*'

Morrigan howled as she smothered Fionn's sister. Tara and her spear disappeared beneath the billowing cape, leaving only her right foot. She used it to kick Fionn down the stairs. He flew backwards, tumbling down the spiral staircase in ten painful *thunks*.

On the bottom floor, Shelby was still sitting in the armchair. For a fleeting moment, Fionn thought about carrying her out with him. Then he heard the voices outside the lighthouse, islanders calling out for him, for each other. The ones he might still save with this precious head start.

With his heart cracking in his chest, he flung the door open and stalked outside, leaving half his world behind him.

Chapter Thirty-Four

THE LAST-MINUTE BLIZZARD

Outside the lighthouse, Fionn found Sam lying on the ground, groaning.

'Get up, Sam! I need help!' said Fionn, pulling his friend to his feet. 'We need to run! Now!'

Sam stumbled after Fionn, lugging his axe with him. His left ankle was badly injured, but somehow his flute had survived unscathed. It was still sticking out of his waistband. 'What's happened? Is it over?'

'Yes,' said Fionn tightly. 'We've lost.'

All across the headland, everyone was standing eerily still. Islanders and Soulstalkers had fallen out of their battles to stare up at the shattered lighthouse. It was belching. A thick, acrid smoke filtered up into the sky. In it, Fionn saw the imprint of his sister's soul.

She wasn't screaming.

She was steel-eyed.

And somehow, that made it worse.

'We're retreating! NOW! Anyone who can, *move*! Anyone left behind will be turned into a Soulstalker,' shouted Fionn, though the islanders had already rushed to that same conclusion. There were less than half of them on their feet now, and most were hobbling or limping.

They hurried away from the lighthouse, shouldering those who could no longer walk, slinging people over their shoulders or carrying one between two. Bartley jogged to meet Fionn and Sam. 'The worst injured are back in the trees,' he said, pointing inward. 'My gran is there with her sister.'

'We'll pick them up on the way.' Fionn tried not to wonder who had been thrown over the cliffs or washed away with the tide. Others had already fallen to the Soulstalkers on the headland. Juliana's mum was among them. The Aguero sisters pressed their heads together as they joined the retreat, sobbing quietly into their coat-sleeves.

Bartley flicked his gaze to the smoking sky. 'What about our sisters?'

'We'll come back for them,' said Fionn quickly.

Sam surveyed their grim surroundings. 'We have to get away first. Can you do something?'

Fionn clenched his fists and tried to pump some heat through his veins. Nothing. 'Not yet.'

His mother found him in the moving crowd. 'I'm going back for her, Fionn.'

'You can't,' said Fionn, grabbing her wrist.

'She's my little *girl*.'

'If you go back now, Morrigan will turn you as well. Please, Mam,' said Fionn. 'I can't face you like that too. I *can't*.'

She choked on a sob. 'Fionn –'

'Help me get the others to safety,' he begged. 'I need you and Sean and Enda to help as many people as you can. Or what happened to Tara will happen to them too.'

His mum's shoulders slumped. 'OK,' she said, quietly gathering herself. 'I'll do what I can.'

The world moved about them in a blur. Grief had stolen their senses, and there was nothing now but the machinations of an island in retreat, Fionn trying to keep his wits about him as he herded them inland.

His magic was slowly thawing in his chest, the heat of his emotions warming his power. 'Come on,' he muttered. 'Come back to me.'

By the time Morrigan emerged from the lighthouse,

with Tara and Shelby in tow, Fionn and the islanders had reached the pine forest. The injured were camped behind the treeline, where Bartley's mum was attending to them by torchlight. The islanders did their best to gather them up, but the burden of new invalids slowed them down.

Morrigan pursued them with a vengeance. She fanned her cape, and sent it after them like a vicious mist.

'Fionn! She's going to catch us!' Sam's limp was getting worse. He was dragging his foot behind him now, and flinching with every step. 'You need to do something!'

Fionn was rubbing circles along his chest. 'I'm trying!'

'Try harder!' cried someone else.

'It's right behind us!'

'I can't carry my mum any quicker!'

'Help us!'

Come on, Fionn begged his magic. *Come back to me.*

Please.

Please.

Please.

'Fionn, *please!*' cried Bartley. He had fallen behind. Elizabeth Beasley was wailing in his arms, and her sister Marian was refusing to go on without her. Douglas, red-faced and heaving, had stopped to steady himself against a tree.

'Come on, Dougie!' Enda sprinted back to help them,

278

shouldering the beefy Beasley. 'One foot in front of the other. That's it. Get a move on.'

It was already too late. The cape was nipping at their heels. A warning gust rippled through the forest. The trees bent backwards as the shadows rose up in a wave. When they came back down again, the Beasleys and Enda were gone.

'NO!' Fionn's rage ripped through him. His magic erupted in his chest and his vision tunnelled. The shadows reared up again, Morrigan gliding like a spectre behind it.

Fionn shot his hands out blindly.

The blizzard came as a surprise, even to him. It careened towards the shadows in whorls of ice and snow. The trees twisted and cracked. The grass froze at their feet, and across the island, a deluge of icy rain forced Morrigan to a grinding halt. Within seconds, the entire northern headland became as smooth and glistening as a diamond.

With his mum's hand on his shoulder to guide him, Fionn walked backwards, casting ice and snow over their tracks. Soon they could see nothing but howling swirls of white and silver behind them.

'We're at Cowan's Lake! Watch your feet!' Fionn's mum guided him around the water as he blanketed the mountains with frost, their humped backs glistening in the dying moonlight.

Beneath the ice, the rainbow trout watched him work. Where once Fionn felt nothing but indifference towards them, now he was sorry to leave them behind. He was sorry to turn his back on Cowan's Lake at all, this looking glass that held so many of the island's memories. Soon, it would belong to the Raven Queen.

With a lump in his throat, Fionn raised his palms to the swirling sky and pulled winter over the lake like a shroud.

Chapter Thirty-Five

THE MOSES PLOT

By the time Fionn and his mum reached the southern shore of Arranmore, the sky was turning bronze. Dawn was brewing somewhere behind the horizon. The pier alone remained untouched, and it was heaving with weary survivors.

Beyond them, in the crush of waves, Lír and her army lay in wait. They had come around the western shelf of Arranmore, and were patrolling the sea between the island and the mainland. Fionn's stomach roiled. Morrigan might have let the islanders run from her, but she would never let them leave. Even if she had to claw her way through a blizzard to get to them.

Lír hissed when she spotted him. Her Merrows

drifted closer, stealthy as sharks in the waves.

'There's no boat to take us across,' said Sam, hobbling to join them. 'Lír dragged the ferry out to sea.'

'They'd only capsize us anyway,' said Fionn. 'Then it would be Morrigan's jaws, or the Merrows'. Take your pick.'

'Huh. Neither?' said Sam.

With little else to consider, Fionn tracked to the end of the pier. The islanders, shivering from their teeth to their toes, parted to let him through.

Lír moved through the waves towards him. 'Sorcerer,' she said, baring her teeth. 'You have lost your Tide Summoner once more.'

'Only temporarily.'

Lír smirked. 'Power is no cure for foolishness.'

Her Merrows were circling protectively at her back.

'Are you interested in a truce?' asked Fionn.

Lír's laugh was a short bark.

Fionn cracked his knuckles, one by one. 'So, you're going to harm us, even though we're Dagda's people? Even though his magic flows in my veins?'

Lír watched his fingers move. 'We answer to the Tide Summoner. This you know.'

'The Tide Summoner is under the control of Morrigan. You're serving the Raven Queen,' said Fionn angrily. 'Are you happy with that?'

'Happiness has no bearing on our bindings.'

'Does *morality*?'

Lír smiled viciously. 'Obviously not.'

So much for words.

Fionn pointed his palms at her forehead, framing her between his fingers and thumbs.

The merrow didn't even flinch. 'Your blizzard cannot hurt us, sorcerer. We have long dwelled in arctic waters, in places even the sun can't reach.'

Fionn fired a bolt of lightning over her shoulder. It stabbed the sea in a flash of silver, and sent the Merrows scrabbling from its sizzling current. 'What happens to the Merrows when their queen dies?'

Lír stilled in the water. 'What happens to Dagda's heir when he turns on the very thing his magic created?' she countered. 'Does he become like Morrigan?'

Fionn cut his eyes at her.

'Will you take my soul too?' taunted Lír.

'You don't have one.'

'You are correct,' she said, pushing away from him. 'We have only one set of orders to follow. To your death or ours. That is the bond. Test it at your own risk.' She dipped under the water, her bone and coral crown disappearing in a silent ripple.

Fionn turned to find the rest of the islanders staring at him with varying degrees of horror.

'Well?' said Sam awkwardly. 'How did that go?'

Fionn frowned. 'She's very committed to killing us.'

'Then how about you kill her first?' said Una, who was staring menacingly at the sea.

'There are *hundreds* of Merrows,' said Fionn's mum. 'He'd never get them all.'

'We may as well die *fighting*,' said Juliana raggedly. 'Like Mama.'

'I think I have an idea,' announced Sam. There was frost in his hair, and his lips were turning blue, but his face was alight with a plan. 'Now, it's a bit off the wall and granted I am *highly* concussed, but are any of you familiar with a guy called Moses?'

Sam filled the dubious silence with the bones of his idea.

'Thanks for that,' said Fionn, once he had finished speaking. He looked around. 'Does anyone else have a better idea?' When no one answered – only stared at him in abject horror – Fionn shrugged and raised his palms to the sea. 'All right. The Moses plot it is.'

The request, when Fionn made it, was a simple one: *safe passage.*

His magic thrummed, his blood warming as it passed through his fingers and out into the world.

The sea trembled. Then it folded, the waves rising to frothy peaks as they galloped away from each other. Slowly, fluidly, the ocean split in two, the repelled tides parting it with the precision of a comb.

And in that parting, slim and softly glowing, the seabed emerged.

Lír screeched as she was thrown up with the waves, where she floated atop a giant wall of water. Her Merrows crowded on either side of the narrow passageway, peering over the islanders. They hurried on to the ocean floor in ones and twos, their arms tightly folded, as the sea sloshed menacingly on either side.

When the last of the islanders had been safely ferreted into the mouth of the sea, Fionn stepped off the island of Arranmore.

Safe passage.

The command throbbed like a second heartbeat in his chest.

Over his shoulder, the island was quickly lost in a swirling white cloud.

'This magic is too big for you, sorcerer,' came Lír's voice from above. 'The mainland is too far. The sea will swallow you whole, and my Merrows will rip your skin from your bones.'

'Go find something better to do with your time,' Sam

called back, as he limped alongside Fionn. 'Braid some seaweed. Flirt with a shark. I don't care. Just get lost.'

Fionn smiled at his friend. 'Concussion suits you.'

'I will stalk you until your passage collapses.' Lír's threat was amplified ten-fold by the ocean's tunnel. It echoed after them as they walked, and any islanders who dared to look up quivered at the sight of her. 'I will wait until the sea drowns –'

'He said *shut up*,' snapped Juliana.

Lír hissed.

Juliana hissed back.

'Your orders are false,' she went on angrily. 'They don't come from Shelby. They come from Morrigan. If you're too stupid or cowardly to see that, then you all deserve to get eaten by whales.'

Lír's laugh was as haunting as a siren's call. 'Let's see how brave you are when –'

'Oh, be quiet, you horrible creature!' shouted Fionn's mum.

'Can't you see we're too exhausted to cower?' added his Uncle Sean.

Una tipped her head back. 'You can't scare us. We're at capacity.'

'If you're going to eat us, then eat us,' added Sam's mum. 'Talk is cheap.'

One by one, the islanders piped up, and with each response, Lír withered on her wave. Every time she opened her mouth to hiss or threaten them, a survivor found their voice.

Eventually she slipped back into the waves, taking her Merrows with her.

After what seemed like an eternity, the mainland glimmered through a break in the waves. The sky here was brighter, the first whispers of dawn kissing the Donegal hills. There was a collective sigh of relief. Sam nudged Fionn with his elbow. 'You did it, mate. The light at the end of the tunnel.'

And then Ireland was before them, the earth rugged as it sloped down to the open sea. Gathering the last dregs of their energy, the islanders charged towards it, scrabbling on to the pebbled shore and stumbling across the beach, until the sand turned to rock and the rock to grass, and the grass to surety. To safety.

Fionn watched them go.

His mum helped the injured islanders up the slope, while the Aguero sisters herded the last of the stragglers across the sand. From there, they would make a course for Lackbeg, a sleepy fishing village nestled just beyond the beach. It was home to islanders who, over the months and years and decades, had made the short pilgrimage east from Arranmore.

It would be a refuge not too far from the storm.

A tucked-away trench in a battlefield that now stretched across the Atlantic Ocean.

Sam lingered on the shoreline, waiting for Fionn. 'You've got a strange look in your eye,' he said suspiciously.

'What kind of look?'

'The kind that makes me think you're about to do something reckless.'

'Define "reckless".'

'That's not funny ...' said Sam anxiously.

'Go on now, Sam.' Fionn stepped back into the ocean's tunnel. 'Your mum will be looking for you.'

Sam's face crumpled. 'Please don't go.'

'I'll be back.' Fionn tried to smile but his chin was wobbling. He was sick of goodbyes, sick of hope running like sand through his fingers. 'Will you look out for my mam? You know, just in case?'

Sam looked at his mangled foot. He nodded, glumly. 'Yeah, all right.'

'Thanks, Sam. You're a good friend.' Fionn turned and stalked back into the belly of the Atlantic Ocean. The water quivered around him, like a giant block of jelly, but he flung his hands out and held it in place. He could see the Merrows flitting about in his periphery. They didn't bother him any more; they just watched the lonely sorcerer tread a pathway home to Arranmore.

When Fionn was far enough away from the mainland, he began to draw the ocean back together behind him, like a curtain.

The narrow passage disappeared in a tidal rush of froth, and a frightened yelp rang out. 'Fionn! Stop!'

Fionn spun around to find Sam floundering in the waves. He was promptly flung out in a mass of writhing seaweed, where he face-planted on the seabed, right at Fionn's feet.

He raised his head and spat out a clump of wet sand. 'Ugh, *gross.*'

Fionn hoisted him to his feet.

'What do you think you're doing?' they both demanded.

'Following you!' said Sam.

'Making sure no one follows me,' said Fionn at the same time.

Fionn blinked, then frowned. 'I told you to look after Mam.'

'Yeah, yeah, noble stuff,' said Sam sarcastically. 'But then who looks after *you*?'

'This is my fight, Sam. I have to face Morrigan.'

'Yeah, well, I have to make sure *you* don't get killed.'

'Says who?'

Sam folded his arms, wobbling a little. '*Me*.'

Fionn gestured to his mangled foot. It was already dragging a dark line through the sand. Not to mention he had lost his axe. 'And how exactly do you plan on doing that?'

'Haven't quite figured that part out, to be honest. I'm sort of thinking on the go here.' Sam limped past him, beckoning for him to follow. 'But we'd better get a move on. And please. Try not to drown me again.'

With a world-weary sigh, Fionn threaded an arm through the crook of Sam's elbow and shouldered his weight. 'Come on, then.'

The ocean watched over them, glugging companionably as they inched their way back to Arranmore Island, together.

Chapter Thirty-Six

THE FOREST GOODBYE

When Fionn and Sam returned to the shores of Arranmore, the island was glittering. The snow from Fionn's blizzard had settled, but a chill lingered in the air. The wind was quiet, as though it, too, had fled from Morrigan.

'Creepy,' whispered Sam. 'It's like a graveyard.'

Fionn helped his friend over the beach wall. 'Just keep your wits about you.'

'I'm one hundred per cent wit at all times.'

The sky was still smoky, but dawn was fighting its way through. Morrigan's dark magic was seeping across the island, filling the air with the stench of rotten eggs.

Sam gagged into his sleeve. 'Ugh. It's like the island *farted*.'

'It's only going to get worse,' said Fionn as they tracked the scent inland.

It led them north, past the pier and through the heartland of Arranmore, where snow-speckled animals looked on from abandoned farms. Death had crawled over the island like a shroud, and the closer they drew to the northern cliffs, the more of it they saw. The trees loomed over them like an army of skeletons as they reached the forest.

Sam squinted up through the needle-less canopies. 'Still no sign of Aonbharr. Honestly, what is the *point* of him if he's just going to let us all rot? Maybe you could send up a signal or –'

'No,' whispered Fionn. 'We can't afford to attract any attention to ourselves.'

They slipped quietly through the trees. The rotting stench was so strong, Fionn had to breathe through his mouth. Beside him, Sam's leg was getting worse. He had to stop every couple of steps to catch his breath now, his face twisting in agony. 'It's just the smell,' he kept saying, over and over, but Fionn could see the sweat on his brow, the pain shuddering through him.

When they reached the other side of the forest, they stalled between the trees and watched. Across the withering headland, Morrigan was standing in the heart of

Eagle's Point. Her cape was spread out in full behind her. It was a terrible, sprawling thing – much larger than even he had realised.

'It's the size of a soccer pitch,' breathed Sam.

Fionn could only stare at it in horror. To rip away an ancient garment forged by the darkest magic imaginable was one undertaking, but to wrestle with one *this* size …

He swallowed thickly. 'I didn't think there'd be so many souls.'

Shelby was standing on Morrigan's right-hand side, the shell hanging from her neck once more. Fionn could hear the waves crashing against the cliffs. The tide had come in and so had the Merrows.

The rest of the Soulstalkers were arranged in a semi-circle around Morrigan, the newest ones at the front, awaiting their orders. Even though they were facing away from Fionn, he could make out the swoop of Tara's pony-tail and her bright pink scrunchie.

He turned to Sam, who was leaning heavily against a tree. 'I'm going out there. And I need you to stay behind.'

Sam's eyes darted, panicked. 'I can't just let you –'

'I need you to stay hidden,' said Fionn quickly. 'If I fail, you'll have to warn the mainland. The world.'

'But I could –'

'And if things go right, which I think they will,' lied

Fionn, 'someone will need to write it down. Or sing about it.' He smiled, and though he was frightened, it came easily. 'And who better than you, Sam?'

'But I want to help.'

'Stories are important too,' said Fionn. 'They're living memories. Just like Arranmore.'

Sam shifted his weight, then winced again.

'Please,' said Fionn.

Sam's lips twisted. 'Well, I am extremely creatively gifted,' he said quietly.

Fionn gestured to the flute sticking out of his waist-band, bemused to find it had survived the battle. 'That's why you're the Fantastic Flautist of Arranmore.'

Sam snorted. Then his gaze flickered over Fionn's shoulder, to Morrigan. 'What are you going to do?'

Fionn's fingers were already sparking. 'I think I'll start by getting rid of all this darkness. What do you reckon?'

Sam nodded, but his eyes were wide and his chin was trembling. 'I'll be able to see you, then.'

Fionn squeezed his shoulder. 'Just make me sound like a hero, yeah? Even if I crash and burn.'

'You are a hero, mate.'

'Not yet.'

Sam grabbed Fionn's shoulder too. 'You *are* a hero.'

'Well, if I'm a hero, then so are you.'

Sam's grin pressed a dimple into his cheek. 'Yeah, *obviously*.'

Fionn chuckled as he turned away. He crept across the headland under the waning sky and, when the light-house stood before him and he could hear the shrill echo of Morrigan's voice on the wind, he raised his palms and sent a towering inferno right into the heart of Eagle's Point.

Chapter Thirty-Seven

A LESSON IN LOYALTY

The darkness shattered. The sky turned amber and gold. The Soulstalkers scattered as Fionn blasted a trail of fire towards Morrigan. She moved like a beetle, whipping her cape behind her and firing back with her shadows. She matched him in strength and speed, dark against light, cold against heat, both of them pushing and pushing and *pushing*.

Sweat poured down Fionn's face.

Morrigan grimaced.

She inched to the right, Fionn to the left.

The column of flames grew higher. The shadows climbed up after it.

'You can't touch me!' Morrigan shouted, but Fionn could hear the strain in her voice. A chink in her armour.

'Not yet!' he called back, his eyes on her trailing cape. 'But I'll stand here until morning if I have to.'

Another flare of fire; another surge of shadow. The clouds were turning crimson, the sky blushing just behind them. Dawn had come.

They circled each other, Morrigan leading, step by step. Soon Fionn stood with his back to the Atlantic Ocean, and she with hers to the island. She smiled, and the slow reveal of her incisors sent a trickle of dread down Fionn's spine.

He sensed he had made a mistake.

He wiped the fear from his face. 'If you think you can push me off these cliffs, you're wrong!'

But Morrigan was inching backwards now. 'Oh, I have no intention of pushing you off this island, Fionn,' she leered. 'Why would I sully my own hands?'

The darkness shifted, and through whips of shadow and flame, Fionn saw the Soulstalkers assemble in front of her. One by one by one, they formed an unbroken chain.

A shield of bodies.

Her shadows recoiled and Fionn's fire inched closer. The Soulstalkers' faces glowed beneath the flames. Among them, Fionn recognised new faces.

Bartley.

Elizabeth.

Douglas.

Enda.

Shelby.

Tara.

Fionn closed his fists.

The fire went out in a single *whoosh*.

Morrigan's cackle echoed across Eagle's Point.

'Tell me again what you said about loyalty,' she taunted. 'Are you willing to die for it? Are you willing to *kill* for it? Or are you still too *weak* to strike your own people when they come for you?'

This time, Fionn said nothing. The Atlantic Ocean crashed and foamed beneath him, Lír and her merrows waiting in its folds.

'You really don't get it, do you?' Fionn's fingers sparked, but he curled them until his palms ached. 'It's not weakness. It's *strength.*'

Morrigan chuckled. 'Let's find out, shall we?'

She flicked her wrist, and as one, the familiar-looking Soulstalkers marched towards Fionn.

Chapter Thirty-Eight

THE SONG AT THE END

Fionn had less than ninety seconds to make a decision. His life or theirs. Strategy or loyalty.

Clink! Clink! Clink! The Merrows were gnashing their teeth.

Crunch. Crunch. Crunch. The Soulstalkers were marching through the frozen grass.

Thud! Thud! Thud! Fionn's heartbeat was pounding in his ears.

Too much noise.

Too much chaos.

Sixty seconds.

He could see Tara's face too clearly, the wisps of dark hair framing her face. Her expression was blank.

The Whispering Tree's words echoed in his head.

Your loyalty will be tested when you find yourself alone,

Choose light or darkness when you stand against your own.

Fionn opened his palms and sent out a gust. The Soulstalkers halted, but only for a moment. Morrigan batted the wind away.

Forty-five seconds.

This time, Fionn chose ice. To freeze, but not to kill. Morrigan crushed his blizzard with her shadows, before it even crossed the headland.

Thirty seconds.

Fionn drew a protective line of fire. Morrigan doused it with a flick of her wrist.

Clink! Clink! Clink!

Less than twenty seconds now.

Crunch. Crunch. Crunch.

Fionn couldn't push them back; he could only strike to kill. That was the point; that was the test. Either way, he was going to fail. Desperation took hold, and with it came his own voice ringing in his ears.

'Please! Stop!' he shouted. 'Tara! Shelby! It's me, Fionn! I don't want to hurt you!'

Morrigan howled with laughter. '*Please! Stop!*' she mimicked. 'How pathetic you look. Backed into a corner, like a quivering rat.'

Crunch. Crunch. Crunch.

Ten seconds.

Fionn was standing on the knife-edge of the cliff. Rock and shale broke off and tumbled down to the sea. He could taste seaweed in the air, the tang of salt on the back of his tongue. The ocean was waiting for him.

'*Please*,' he rasped, one last time.

It was a final plea, sent not to Morrigan, but to his sister. To his best friend.

There was a beat of silence – of hesitation – and then an unexpected sound filled the air.

No, not a sound – a song.

The first stirrings of *The Eagle's Call* fell around them like raindrops.

The island exhaled.

Tara stopped walking.

And so, too, did the others.

Chapter Thirty-Nine

THE SEVERED S✸ULS

Fionn whipped his head around. Sam was hobbling across the headland, playing his flute. His fingers moved expertly along the keys, the melody unfaltering even as he limped.

White-tailed eagles cried as they dropped from the sky and circled the headland. The Arranmore wind came back in a sudden, fierce rush. It rippled up Fionn's back and ruffled his hair. From the corner of his eye, he swore he saw a shape in the breeze. The edge of a familiar bulbous nose, the sheen of horn-rimmed spectacles glinting from another layer. When he looked straight at it, it shimmered like dust, too faint to make out.

He felt a weight on his shoulder.

Grandad.

On his other side, another hand.

The air was shimmering here too. A whisper of curls, narrow shoulders and ears that stuck out just a little.

Dad.

All across Eagle's Point, dust was curling in a warm breeze, bright and golden as the dawn. The eagles were singing. Fionn might have been standing on the edge of a cliff, but he wasn't alone.

He had never been alone.

The Soulstalkers stood frozen on the headland. They tipped their heads back to watch the birds.

Tara kept her gaze on Fionn.

She was straining, as though she recognised him.

Almost.

'What are you waiting for, you *imbeciles!*' shrieked Morrigan. '*Move!*'

Some of the older Soulstalkers at the back tried to push through, but the newer ones didn't budge.

'What *is* this?' hissed Morrigan, whirling around. She seemed to be the last one to notice the music. 'You all answer to *me.*'

Now it was Fionn's turn to smile. He flicked his gaze to Sam, who was leaning against the door of the lighthouse, still playing his flute.

'This is loyalty.' Fionn stalked towards Morrigan, and the wind moved with him. 'I have an army too. Can't you see them?'

Morrigan cut her eyes at him. 'Lies.'

'Arranmore is *built* on loyalty. It's got a magic of its own that can't be broken or stolen.' Fionn's power crackled in his fingers, whips of lightning glowing white-hot in his palms. His eyes were on the Raven Queen's cape. 'This island has a *soul*. One you can *never* turn.'

Another rush of wind, dust floating like fireflies around him. In it, faces flickered. Men and women, teenagers and children. Fionn's ancestors. His grandmother, Winnie. Róisín. They were all here. He could sense them.

The Soulstalkers fell back from Fionn.

Morrigan fell back too. Fear flitted like a shadow across her face. She searched the air around him, her chin jutting, like she could finally sense the same things he could. A magic all of its own. The kind of loyalty that transcends death. An island that lives and breathes with the spirits of its people.

'Kill him!' Morrigan hurled a Soulstalker across the headland, flung another into the lighthouse until all his bones crunched. 'Kill him now or you will all pay dearly!'

Fionn halved the distance between them. The wind was like an invisible shield around him, the eagles still circling overhead. No one could touch him, not even the oldest, most rabid Soulstalkers. 'I told you, but you didn't listen. There's power in loyalty. There's power in standing for something more than just yourself. That's the kind of magic you will never have,' he shouted. 'This is *our* island. And you are not welcome here!'

Morrigan's nostrils flared.

She turned sharply and made a beeline for Sam.

'SAM! RUN!' Fionn broke into a sprint.

The notes of The Eagle's Call turned screechy, then stopped entirely when Sam saw her coming. He tried to run, dragging his foot behind him as he limped away from her. 'Help me, Fionn! She's going to take my soul!'

Morrigan flitted towards Sam like a bat.

Sam flung his flute at her.

She caught it easily and broke it in two. '*Fool!*'

'Fio—*oof!*' Sam stumbled on to his hands and knees. He started dragging himself through the grass. 'Help!'

It was like watching an injured antelope try to outrun a lion. Fionn knew the ending before it happened. With a resounding cry, he leapt. The wind rallied at his back and catapulted him through the air. He flung his arms out, grasping at the end of Morrigan's cape. His fingers found purchase. He dug his nails in. The souls flitted about beneath his hands, icy and slick. They filled Fionn with a sickening dread, but he didn't dare let go. He dug his feet into the earth, using his body as an anchor to slow her down.

Morrigan stiffened, her head jerking backwards.

Fionn clawed his way up her cape, sinking his fingernails into the shifting shadows, setting a course for the milk-bottle column of her neck.

Sam kept crawling.

Fionn was shuddering right down to his bones. He tried to ignore the contorted faces but the sight of their screams rippled over his skin in goose-bumps.

Still he climbed.

Morrigan screeched. In rage or pain, Fionn couldn't tell. She whipped her cape, and sent it soaring into the air. Fionn rose with it, holding on for dear life. It felt, suddenly, as though he was trapped on the dome of a parachute.

The Soulstalkers peered up at him with glazed eyes.

Sam was halfway to the trees now, but he kept looking back over his shoulder.

The cape twisted on itself. Fionn was flung left to right and back again, the whole world spinning around him in shadow and dawn-light. The eagles shrieked as he slid down the cape, his fingers aching as he tried to save himself.

'You truly think you can take my shroud from me?'

Morrigan sneered. 'More than a hundred lifetimes of unmatchable power?'

'I'm not giving up,' yelled Fionn, as another gust sent him skyward. He was closer to the cliffs than he'd realised. He could hear the Merrows shrieking in the waves below. He looked down on Morrigan. 'Not until every soul is free!'

Morrigan's eyes glittered darkly. 'Well. Perhaps I can spare a few.'

She pounced. Fionn jerked backwards, but Morrigan wasn't going for him. With a blood-curdling shriek, she brought her fingernails down and sheered a jagged line through the end of her cape. It tore away with a frightening *rrrrrrrip!*

Fionn cried out as the freed souls splintered around him. They dissolved like mist, until there was nothing and no one to anchor him. He was sent freewheeling through the air, right over the edge of Eagle's Point. The wind rallied around him, but this time it wasn't enough. The last thing he saw as he tumbled over the cliffs was the wicked gleam of Morrigan's smile.

Then there was nothing but the roar of the Atlantic Ocean, and the *clink-clink* of gnashing teeth.

Chapter Forty

FLIGHT OF THE SORCERER

Fionn braced himself for the crush of icy waves. Instead, he landed with a hard thud. His body flattened like a starfish as his breath whooshed out of him in a painful wheeze.

He raised his head.

He wasn't falling any more.

He wasn't drowning, either.

He was *flying*.

On either side of him, majestic white wings stirred the air. Fionn's fingers were curled in a fine, silver mane, the rest of his body sprawled out on a soft white coat. A gentle whinny roused Fionn from the dregs of his confusion.

'Aonbharr.' Fionn scooted towards the horse's broad

shoulders and threw his arms around his neck. 'You *came.*'

Aonbharr tossed his mighty head. Fionn's cheek brushed against his mane. It was warm and silky soft, his tears melting into it as relief trickled through him.

He was *alive.*

He was with Aonbharr.

They were gliding fast and low over the ocean, hugging the cliffs along the northern shelf of Arranmore, so as not to be seen from above. Slowly Fionn sat up. The world whipped past him in a blur, the taste of seaweed and brine hitchhiking on the wind. Dawn's golden fingers were reaching over the horizon.

Towards the boy and his flying horse.

When they were a safe distance from Morrigan, Aonbharr climbed up into the sky. Fionn squeezed his legs and wound his fingers tightly in the horse's mane as the island melted away below them.

The morning clouds swallowed them up. The mist was cool against Fionn's face, unfallen rain turning to droplets in his hair. Aonbharr tossed his head back, drinking it in, and Fionn, seized by a sudden fit of exhilaration, began to laugh.

'We're flying!' he said, between hiccoughing gasps. 'We're really *flying*! And Morrigan thinks I'm *dead*!'

By the time they left the clouds behind them again, they were turning orange around the edges. Aonbharr tucked in his wings and dived towards the sea. Fionn yelped all the way down, his grip so tight his fingers went numb.

They levelled out again, the dawn wind rippling through Fionn's cheeks and stealing his laughter.

Like a plane preparing to touch down on a runway, Aonbharr fanned his wings wide and began to circle above a familiar slip of sea. Somewhere to their right, the little village of Lackbeg stood watch over the shores of Ireland.

To their left, Arranmore still languished in darkness.

All was silent, still.

Aonbharr turned his head, one clear brown eye watching Fionn.

'Oh.' Fionn understood why they were hovering between two places. Between two choices. Aonbharr was waiting for his answer.

'Home,' said Fionn, without a beat of hesitation. 'I'm afraid we still have unfinished business, Aonbharr.'

Aonbharr brayed in approval. He lifted his mighty wings, and a fresh gust of wind stirred about them. They rode it all the way back to Arranmore.

When they reached the shore, they dropped from the

sky and flew swift and low along the pier. Fionn rose to his haunches like a jockey, charting the fields as they turned inland. Soon the land grew spiky with trees.

Sam had made it to the forest. Fionn could see him hobbling through the skeletal trunks, heard his whimpering on the wind. Aonbharr descended, his wings rustling the topmost branches until Sam tipped his head back.

He gasped. 'Fionn!'

Fionn grinned as he waved, then pressed a finger to his lips.

They left Sam behind them, Aonbharr dropping from the sky and drawing level with the northern headland, until his hooves skimmed the grass. Fionn flattened his body and began to draw on his power. He called his magic up from the depths of his soul, until it crackled on his tongue and sparked between his fingers.

Up ahead, Morrigan had gathered her Soulstalkers along the cliff, and was exacting their punishment, by marching them over the edge one by one. Her back was turned to Fionn, her tattered cape languishing along the grass. The wind quietened as they drew near, gliding through the grass and past the lighthouse, until the only sound was the rattle of Fionn's breath and the soft *whoosh* of Aonbharr's wings.

Morning had broken, and with it, light had come.

A *new dawn begins when the winged stallion flies.*

Fionn had only seconds now – one last chance to put an end to Morrigan for good. His heart thundered in his chest as they soared across Eagle's Point. In the middle of it, Morrigan stood, tall and ancient as a statue.

She turned her head sharply, and sniffed the air.

Fionn swung his leg over Aonbharr's back and crouched behind his wing. 'A little closer.' He flexed his fingers. 'A bit lower.'

One by one, the Soulstalkers looked up.

Shelby gasped.

Morrigan whirled around just in time to see Fionn leap from the winged horse and come down on her with all the power of an ancient thunderstorm.

Chapter Forty-One

THE FALLING TOWER

Fionn landed on Morrigan's back. Before she could shake him off, he dug his knees into her sides and closed his hands around her neck. She shrieked as he released the full might of his magic, sending a lightning bolt crackling through her from head to toe.

Her skin flashed as Fionn ripped his way through her magic, turning it from dark to light. For a long time, the world was silver and white, everything around Fionn blinding and burning. Morrigan bucked and screeched but he only held on tighter, gritting through the ebb and flow of his power.

Finally the binds of her cape went up in smoke.

Morrigan howled as it snapped away from her. Fionn cried out too, as his magic finally bottomed out.

The cape was swept away in a rush of cool air, its souls taking flight like a flock of starlings in spring. Most of them soared up, up, up, into the sky, where they shone amber in the rising sun. The rest drifted across the headland to where Morrigan's army stood with grasping hands and gasping mouths, reaching desperately for their humanity.

Fionn's grip on Morrigan loosened. His head drooped as he slid on to the grass. Morrigan fell to her knees and dragged herself towards him. Without her cape, she looked like a broken doll.

'Now it's a fair fight,' heaved Fionn. 'Just you and me.'

Morrigan bared her teeth.

'It's over, Morrigan. You lost.' Fionn peddled feebly at the grass. 'Give up.'

She kept coming. 'If I must meet oblivion like this, then I will drag *you* down with me.'

She flung her hand out, summoning the last spark of her magic.

A shadow whipped past Fionn's ear.

He flopped back against the grass, chuckling weakly. 'Missed me.'

There was an almighty *crrrraaaack!*

Then a slow, rumbling creak.

Then Morrigan was chuckling too. 'Did I?'

Dimly Fionn was aware of shapes moving in the

distance. The wind was tugging at his sleeves but he was too tired to move. The sky above was golden. The clouds were breaking, the departing souls flittering through them like butterflies.

Peace had come.

Peace, at last.

Closer to home, the creaking was getting louder. Bodies were scrambling along the headland, and there were voices now. Familiar voices. Fionn couldn't hear what they were saying. He could only hear the slow thud of his heartbeat in his ears.

Fionn thought of Dagda the Good, lying on the shores of Arranmore over a thousand years ago. Ready to sleep. Ready to die. His eyes glazed over, and for a passing moment he thought he caught the sorcerer's shape, shimmering in the morning breeze. He swore he heard his whisper on the wind.

Get up, Fionn.

Run.

Morrigan was clawing at Fionn's ankles, pulling herself towards him with deep, sucking breaths.

Then there were other voices. 'Fionn! Run!'

Shelby.

'It's coming down, Fionn! It's going to crush you!'

Fionn rolled his head around. His lids were heavy but

he could see it now. The white column looming over his shoulder, the final cleaving of stone around its base. The lighthouse was teetering towards them.

Morrigan collapsed on his chest, crushing his lungs as she anchored him to her. To this fate.

Fionn had no energy left to push her off. He had given the island everything he had – the fullness of his magic and all of his strength too. Darkness rose up to claim him, the world getting fainter and fainter as the white tower fell.

Then there were hands on his shoulders.

Real hands.

Fionn was yanked out from under Morrigan's body, and whipped away from the moment of impact with less than a second to spare.

The last thing he remembered was the earth-shattering thud of the lighthouse as it flattened the mortal remains of the Raven Queen. And within the chaos and commotion, the sound of his sister's voice, close to his ear. 'Fionn? Can you hear me?'

Then the rising sun on his face as her strong arms dragged him to safety.

'I'm right here, Fionny. I'm right here.'

Chapter Forty-Two

THE AWAKENING

When Fionn opened his eyes, it was morning. The grass was soft beneath him, the sun warm on his cheeks. His head had stopped spinning and the weight on his chest had shifted. He drew in a breath and felt an ember of magic flickering in his chest.

He smiled.

'Hello, stranger!' Shelby leaned over him, the ends of her hair tickling his chin. 'Long time no see.' Her lips twisted. 'Well, actually, I saw you a lot. I was just trapped in a dark soulless prison where everything was bleak and nothing made any –'

'OK, my turn.' Sam jostled her out of the way. 'So, that was *insane*. I saw the whole thing from the trees. Right down to the lighthouse toppling over and *squishing* Morrigan.' He grinned. 'Very *Wizard of* Oz.'

Fionn rose to his elbows. 'Not really what I was going for,' he croaked.

'*Ding-dong, the witch is dead*,' crooned Shelby. She hugged the Tide Summoner to her chest. 'You did it, Fionn. You freed our souls. You freed the island.'

'Ahem, I think you mean *we* did it,' came a voice from above. Tara's shadow blocked out the sun. 'Now move aside, please. I need to check on my brother.'

Sam and Shelby scrabbled away to give her room. Tara's brows hunched together as she studied Fionn. 'How do you feel?'

'Alive,' said Fionn. 'Thanks to you.'

Tara smirked. 'I told you I'd look after you.'

She helped him to his feet. The headland was emptier than Fionn expected. The islanders and mainlanders who had been returned from Soulstalkers were milling about, trying to make sense of it all.

'Lír's dragging the ferry back in so we can get the mainlanders home,' said Tara. 'Their families will be worried sick.'

'We should tell the others at Lackbeg what happened too.' Fionn pictured their mother, standing alone on the shore, staring out to sea.

'I think those two might have found a quicker way to

do that.' Tara grinned as she pointed over his shoulder. 'I think they're waiting for you.'

When Fionn turned around, Sam and Shelby were standing beside Aonbharr. The winged horse had come to rest along the headland. '*Please* can we have a go!' begged Shelby. 'I know we're not technically about to die any more, but this is literally my life's dream! And he's *right* here.' She pressed her cheek against his mane. 'He's so soft, Fionn. He feels like a cloud.'

'And how else will I get to a hospital?' said Sam, tapping his twisted leg, then flinching. 'If I wait for the ferry I could end up getting gangrene or frostbite or … or … or trench foot.'

Fionn arched a brow. '*Trench foot?*'

'It's my birthday!' Shelby burst out.

'Your birthday's in May,' said Fionn.

'PLEASE!' they chorused impatiently.

Fionn stalked towards them, chuckling. 'Do you mind?' he said to Aonbharr. 'I know it's not exactly life or death …'

Aonbharr blinked his big brown eyes, a breath ruffling through his nose. Then he dipped his head, and bent his front legs, to lower himself to the earth. He pulled his mighty wings back. Shelby squealed with delight as she clambered on. Fionn gave Sam a careful boost, Shelby pulling him up by his arms until he was sitting on top of Aonbharr too.

Then it was Fionn's turn.

Tara came to wave them off. Bartley was with her, clear-eyed and short-haired. The circles under his eyes were already fading and though his clothes had seen better days, he was smiling. It was an unusual sight.

'I'll be back soon,' Fionn told his sister. 'Then maybe you can have a go.'

'He's not a carousel,' said Tara as she waved them off. 'And anyways, I think I'd prefer to stay here with my feet on the ground and the sun on my face.' She smiled. 'To tell you the truth, I never thought I'd get to enjoy it again.'

Aonbharr took off in a rousing gust, climbing skyward with remarkable speed. Shelby and Sam laughed in giddy delight as they zoomed through the clouds, catching droplets on their tongues. The horse turned south then, carrying them over the Arranmore strand and the abandoned pier, the wind racing alongside them as it tried to keep up.

Beyond the beach, the sea had turned quiet and gentle. The horse dived down to meet it, braying contentedly as his wings skimmed the waves.

Shelby caught a mouthful of froth on her tongue. 'Tastes like magic!'

'Feels like fish pee,' joked Sam, catching some in his hands. 'Usually I hate turbulence but I've never been so happy to be in the air.'

They glided across the ocean, the mainland soon filtering into view. Along the shoreline, anxious islanders were watching the waves. Fionn's mother was among them, her arms pulled tight around her. When she saw them soaring overhead, she let out a cry of relief, waving her hands over her head as she ran into the shallows. The others rushed down to join her, the weary warriors of Arranmore whooping and hollering until it sounded like the sea itself was singing.

Chapter Forty-Three

FIONN THE BRAVE

Fionn Boyle sat on the shores of Arranmore Island, with his knees tucked into his chest, and watched the waves lap against the sand. It was mid-morning on a sunny Saturday, and the tide was coming in. The sky was blue, and the birds were chirping, the first week of March gently warming the air.

Shelby sighed. 'Is it weird that I'm starting to miss the Merrows?'

'Definitely,' said Sam, who was reclining on the sand beside her. His crutches were propped nearby, a plaster cast reaching all the way up to his right knee. Una had painted it to cheer him up, and now it looked like a shark was devouring his leg. 'Lír gave me nightmares.'

'Even when she was on our side?'

'Especially then.'

Shelby harrumphed. Now that Morrigan was gone and the tide was their own, she no longer wore the shell around her neck. It was at home, tucked safely away at the back of her wardrobe. 'Everything just seems so *boring* now.'

'I'll take boring any day,' said Fionn. 'I prefer it to constant mortal danger.'

'It's just a pity we had to go back to school,' grumbled Sam. 'I can't say I have the same appetite for maths any more.'

Shelby tapped Sam's cast. 'At least you get this ugly thing off soon. I didn't want to say anything before, but it doesn't go with *any* of your outfits.'

'Thanks, Shelby,' said Sam drolly. 'I'm glad you survived the end of the world too.'

'I'm glad you both made it,' said Fionn, who was thinking, as he often did, of the islanders who hadn't survived to see the spring. Those who would never again know the raging howl of a winter storm or the baking heat of a midsummer sun. In the end, Fionn and his friends had been luckier than most. That their victory at the eleventh hour had come with great sacrifice was not something he would soon forget.

Sam lifted his coat and pulled his flute from his waist-band. He stroked it lovingly, some distant thought glazing in his eyes. 'And I'm glad for this too.'

Shelby gasped. 'Is that Maggie's flute? I thought it broke.'

'Dad got it fixed up on the mainland yesterday,' said Sam. 'You never know when the Fantastic Flautist of Arranmore might need to save the day again.'

Shelby shook her head. 'I can't believe that nickname stuck.'

They were interrupted by the clip-clop of approaching footsteps. Bartley and Tara peered at them over the beach wall, their half-eaten ice creams glistening in their hands.

'What's up, losers?' said Bartley. Apart from a thin scar along his right cheek, he looked thoroughly like himself again. He was dressed in a navy cashmere sweater, dark jeans and his signature deck shoes.

'Your hair's grown back even longer than before,' said Fionn with surprise. 'Did you water it or something?'

Bartley smirked. 'Good genes, Boyle. Not that you'd know anything about – *Ouch!*'

Tara punched him in the arm. 'Hey! Shut up about our genes. We're *perfect*.' She pulled three chocolate Magnums from her hoodie and dropped them in Fionn's lap. 'Here you go, Fionny. Don't say I never do anything nice for you.'

'Thanks, Tara.' Fionn passed an ice cream to each of his friends, before tearing into his own.

'Don't spoil your dinner, yeah?' Bartley warned Shelby. 'We're having a barbecue later. Aunt Marian's making her famous potato salad, and Douglas said I could do the grill.'

'Mmm, food poisoning,' said Sam. 'Are we all invited, then?'

Bartley snorted as he walked away. 'Glad to see you haven't lost your sense of humour, Patton.'

Fionn and his friends quietened as they set to work on their ice creams.

'Do you think that's it, then?' asked Sam after a while. 'No more Storm Keepers on Arranmore?'

'I don't know,' said Fionn truthfully. 'I suppose there's no one left to protect it from.'

'*You* still have your power though,' Sam pointed out. 'What do you think you'll do with it?'

'If you wanted to make another flying horse, I wouldn't complain,' said Shelby hopefully. 'He could live in my garden.'

'Or how about a flying sheep?' suggested Sam. 'Just to change things up a bit.'

'I suppose I'll have to think about it,' said Fionn mildly. He turned his hands over. His fingertips were crackling, but he was used to it now. The war against Morrigan was over, but he was still a sorcerer, and sooner or later, he would have to figure out what to do with all the magic still fizzing inside him. For now, though, he curled his fingers into fists and pushed thoughts of the future to one side. 'Maybe I'll find a way to finally beat you two at Mario Kart?'

Sam threw his head back and laughed. 'Oh, mate. There isn't enough magic in the universe to help you there!'

Fionn chuckled as he rolled to his feet. 'Well, I'll keep trying. Come on, then.'

'Fionn the Try-Hard,' teased Sam, taking his hand. 'That's what they'll call you.'

'No, they won't.' Shelby leapt to her feet. 'They'll call him Fionn the Brave.'

Fionn blew out a breath. 'I don't know about that.'

'Like your dad,' said Shelby, with conviction. 'And your grandad.'

'And the island,' said Fionn.

'Well, of course,' said Shelby, as they helped Sam over the beach wall. She flashed her braces at Fionn. 'Where do you think *they* got it from?'

Up on the strand, Sam brandished a crutch in the direction of the Arranmore hills. 'What do you two say to a quick detour on the way to my house?'

Shelby and Fionn exchanged a knowing glance. 'Go on, then.'

The rainbow trout were swimming along the surface of Cowan's Lake when Fionn and his friends reached it, a family of bluebirds chirping merrily from a nearby tree. The ice had thawed weeks ago, and now the water shimmered softly in the sunlight. Fionn stood on the edge of the lake with his hands in his pockets, and cast a silent wish.

Sam reclined against his favourite boulder. He closed his eyes and began to play *The Eagle's Call*, grinning to himself when the birds joined in.

Shelby sat cross-legged in the long grass, swaying back and forth. 'Do you think we'll ever get tired of coming up here?'

'No,' said Fionn, watching the water ripple. 'I don't think we will.'

After all this time, a new face was rising to meet them.

Fionn came to his knees. '*Grandad.*'

Malachy Boyle was wearing his fullest smile, his eyes as blue as the sea on a summer's day. As blue as a sky without clouds. Reason told Fionn it was an illusion, but he swore – in that precious, fleeting moment – that his grandfather was looking back at him.

'I really miss you, Grandad,' whispered Fionn.

The lake shimmered, casting a twinkle in his grandfather's eye.

'I think I always will.' Fionn was not as sad now as he was before. He was getting used to the ache in his chest. It was like a footprint on his heart – a testament to how much he had loved his grandfather – how he loved him still. 'And I think maybe that's OK.'

The lake began to ripple again. His grandfather threw his head back, and opened his mouth until Fionn could see all of his teeth – the greying and the white – and laughed as he disappeared. He laughed and laughed and laughed, and even though Fionn couldn't hear the music of it, he imagined it was sweeping around him in a tornado, the winds of it playing his heart like a fiddle.

And in its sweet and silent melody, he heard his grandfather's voice.

I'm still with you, lad.

Every step of the way.

When the lake was still and the birds were quiet, they set off again for Sam's house. Spring bloomed alongside them, bringing new life to Arranmore. The island was flourishing once more, and every beautiful flower and cheeping bird was a reminder of all those who had died to save it. They were on the other side of the wind now, in a place where neither time nor death could touch them.

As the weeks wore on, and the days grew warmer, Fionn found he could feel that wind more keenly. Sometimes, if he didn't look too hard or for too long, he would catch a shape moving in the breeze. The contour of a bulbous nose or the edge of a horn-rimmed spectacle. The echo, perhaps, of a familiar laugh.

On Arranmore, through winters dark and summers bright, he knew he would never find himself alone again. In fact, he had never been alone here. And that, above all else, was the real magic of the island.

ACKNOWLEDGEMENTS

W riting the Storm Keeper trilogy has truly been an adventure of the heart. I am grateful to so many people for coming on this journey with me.

Thank you to Claire Wilson, my wonder-agent, who continues to be an absolute tour de force. Our creative adventures together may have begun in the gritty underworld of Chicago, but I am glad to see it meander to more magical pastures on the little island of Arranmore. You have been behind this trilogy, heart and soul, from day one, and your unwavering support, insight, humour and kindness has meant the world to me.

A huge thank you to Ellen Holgate, who received this story in its infancy and immediately understood (perhaps even better than I did) what I wanted to do with it. You have an uncanny ability to look at the bones of a story and see the beating heart beneath, and I appreciate, now more than ever, how you guided me towards that heart with remarkable care and patience. I could not have written (and rewritten) this story without you, and the reason I am so deeply proud of it today is because of you.

Thank you to Bea Cross, who is the most impressive, and perhaps only, dolphin-publicist in the world. Every event we did together felt like an adventure, including the time we nearly blew away from the top of a lighthouse. Thank you for being an incredible publicist and a one-in-a-million friend. Not many people in my life would catch a giant daddy-long-legs in their bare hands, while I stand, shrieking, in the middle of a crowded restaurant. For that, and everything else, thank you.

I am hugely grateful to the rest of the Bloomsbury team, who welcomed me (and Fionn) with open arms and have made me feel at home. Thank you, in particular, to Cal Kenny, Emma Bradshaw, Charlotte Armstrong, Jade Westwood, Emily Marples, Grace Ball, Mattea Barnes, Fliss Stevens, Tram-Anh Doan, Sarah Baldwin, Nova Hekne, Flavia Esteves, Alice Grigg, Josephine Blaquière and Rebecca McNally. Thank you to my brilliant copy-editor Nick de Somogyi for whipping each book into shape.

Thank you to Patrick Moy, narrator of the Storm Keeper audiobooks. You have told this story with such skill and care (not to mention an impressive array of regional accents) that it has been elevated to another level entirely.

Thank you to Bill Bragg for providing three beautifully illustrated covers that perfectly encapsulate the tone and vision of each book.

I'm immensely grateful to all the bookshops that have supported the Storm Keeper series and given it precious space on their shelves. Thanks in particular to Florentyna for your kindness, support and enthusiasm, which has made all the difference in the world. I'll never forget it. Thanks to Eason's bookshop, and Dave O'Callaghan, in particular, who is a tireless champion of Irish books, and the most fantastic friend. Dave, I am proud to know you, and even prouder to have beaten you at Mario Kart.

Thank you to all the amazing booksellers, librarians and bloggers who have gotten behind the Storm Keeper trilogy. It has been such a pleasure getting to meet some of you on my travels around the UK and Ireland.

Thank you to all the teachers who have introduced their students to Fionn Boyle. Thanks in particular to Mr Scott Evans and Mr Ashley Booth for your enthusiasm, hard work and tireless commitment to promoting reading among your students and many others!

I am eternally grateful for the support and kindness of my friends (many of whom just so happen to be authors I hugely admire). Thank you to Anna James, Katie Webber, Dave Rudden, Sarah Davis-Goff, Kevin Tsang, Ross

Montgomery, Kiran Millwood Hargrave, Kate Rundell, Deirdre Sullivan, Abi Elphinstone, Lauren James, Miriam Prendergast, Samantha Eves, Sinead Lydon, James McGee, Katie Harte, Bríd O' Connor, Becky Ryan, Susan Leonard, Sheila Spokes, Steph Gibbons and Katie O' Boyle. Jess, thank you for insisting on celebrating every milestone and making every book feel truly special, and for being the best lifelong sister-friend I could ever ask for. Thank you to Louise O'Neill for your stalwart support (personally and professionally) throughout the years and to Richard Chambers (the nation's sweetheart) for your friendship towards me and also Ireland.

Thank you to all my amazing aunts and uncles and cousins, who come to every book launch – rain, hail or shine – and buy multiple copies of my books, somehow managing to retain the same sense of enthusiasm and unconditional support for each and every one. You are all incredible people and I'm so grateful to have you in my life.

Thank you to the Webbers – Virginia, Jane, Rob and Nora – my up-and-coming family. To Katie for introducing me to her brother Jack, and to Kevin for helping to mastermind an ambitious trans-Atlantic love story that will soon culminate in a wedding. And thank you to Virginia and Rob, who, when they heard their son was seeing a random Irish girl from halfway across the world, took it in their stride and welcomed me with open arms. Who saw this coming, eh? Thanks to Jane for being the most charming, witty and empathetic little sister I could ask for.

And thank you to my littlest friend and most adorable niece, Evie, purveyor of cats and rice cakes. I can't wait to watch you grow up.

Thank you to Jack – for keeping me alive while I was in the editing trenches and adding a new layer of whimsy and laughter to my life. I'm so glad I imported you from the United States, and I can't wait to marry you, thus completing my lifelong goal of becoming Katherine Webber II.

Thanks, as always, to my parents, Grace and Ciaran. Mom, that trip we took to Arranmore five years ago changed the course of my life forever. I'm so glad we got to experience it together. Dad, thanks for being a great listener, and for giving me all your best ideas. Long may our business lunches continue!

Thank you to my brothers Colm and Conor. *The Storm Keepers' Battle* is, among other things, a testament to the enduring bond between brother and sister, and a reminder that no matter how cranky or sarcastic or *annoying* your sibling might be (especially when they're a teenager) they will always end up in your corner, fighting harder for you than anyone else. Even though I'll never, *ever* say it to your faces, you are two of my favourite people in the entire world and I would gladly stick a magical spear into the side of an all-powerful, evil sorceress for you. Probably. And to Ali Murray, my soon-to-be sister-in-law, I'm so glad that Colm has found someone as witty and smart and kind as you, to keep him from some (if not all) of his future hare-brained schemes. Welcome to the family!

Endless heartfelt thanks to Caroline McCauley, Joe Boyle, Angela McCauley, Phillip McCauley and Mary McCauley for sharing your incredible stories with me, and for graciously showing me around the island. I'm so proud to call you all family.

Lastly, I would like to thank my grandparents, Captain Charles Boyle and Mamie McCauley of Arranmore Island, for inspiring this trilogy, and for always inspiring me. Growing up as your granddaughter has been the greatest pleasure of my life.

Buíochas ó chroí le muintir Oileán Árainn Mhór for always welcoming me home.

ABOUT THE AUTHOR

Catherine Doyle grew up beside the Atlantic Ocean in the west of Ireland. Her love of reading began with the great Irish myths and legends, and fostered in her an ambition to write her own one day. She holds a BA in Psychology and an MA in Publishing from the National University of Ireland, Galway. *The Storm Keepers' Battle* is the final instalment in the trilogy which began with *The Storm Keeper's Island* and its sequel *The Lost Tide Warriors*, and was inspired by her real-life ancestral home of Arranmore Island, where her grandparents grew up, and the adventures of her many seafaring ancestors. Catherine is based in Galway but spends a lot of her time in London and the US.

Read the whole magical, spellbinding trilogy

AVAILABLE NOW